IMPERFECT ILLUSIONS
DEVASTATING MAGIC
BOOK ONE

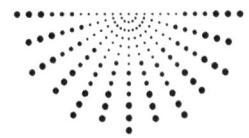

VANORA LAWLESS

Copyright © 2022 by Andrea Lawless

All rights reserved.

No part of this book may be reproduced in any form or by any electronic or mechanical means, including information storage and retrieval systems, without written permission from the author, except for the use of brief quotations in a book review.

This is a work of fiction. Names, characters, places, and events are either a product of the author's imagination or are used fictitiously.

Cover art by Klayr_de_Gall.

❀ Created with Vellum

CONTENT WARNINGS

Potential spoilers to follow. Feel free to skip if you don't need warnings.

On page:
    Violence
    Graphic Sexual Content
    Homophobia
    Smoking
    Drinking
    Being forcibly restrained
    Death of a friend

Discussion of:
    Suicide

CHAPTER ONE

May 3, 1917
Chicago

IT WAS NOT ELLIOT'S finest moment. Looking up from where he'd slipped face first into wet snow, he met the laughing faces of five gleeful children. Five devious children, more like.

"Uncle Elliot said a bad word!" Alice shouted to a chorus of faux gasps.

"Snow angel!" Thomas, the youngest, cried as he flopped beside Elliot and wildly flapped his arms and legs, revealing muddy grass beneath the scant inch of snow next to the sidewalk.

"Take them for a walk, Elliot. It's magical to have snow this late in the year, Elliot," he mumbled to himself as he wallowed in the damp. "It'll be fun. I won't skin you when they come back covered in dirt and sopping wet, Elliot."

"Mama didn't say the last one," Eleanor informed him right before Joseph shoved her and sent her tumbling into a bush.

Chaos. This was chaos. How on earth did his sister ever get a thing done? They hadn't been outside ten minutes, and it was all gone to shambles. Precisely as it always had whenever May and her tiny entourage visited.

"She's right," Joseph said. The oldest, at ten, one would hope he'd be the voice of reason. One would be *acutely* wrong. He grinned at Elliot, a toothy little evil expression. "You're going to get in so much trouble."

Scooping up a handful of snow, Elliot launched it at him. Joseph cackled, dove to the side, and the battle was on. Swiftly rolling out of the way, Elliot got to his feet with two snowballs. "You're extremely lucky I care enough about you to take the blame. Now you better run before the big, bad, snow ogre gets you!"

Shrieks of joy rang out and the children scampered around as Elliot chased them down the sidewalk, all the way to the gate in front of Palmer's Mansion. Towering gray stone turrets vaguely reminiscent of an old castle rose far overhead, and in Elliot's opinion it seemed part fortress, part ostentatious monstrosity.

The tuckered-out children stared up in wonder. They were used to the high life, but even by their standards, this was extravagant. Something out of fairytale daydreams.

Once when they were young, May had asked Elliot to recreate the mansion in a dream so she could explore inside. He'd always had a wild imagination, so he'd made it absolutely absurd. He could almost hear May's girlish giggling as she raced along ornate golden hallways and climbed twisting fairy-floss stairs.

Alice sighed wistfully. "I want to live in a castle someday."

Joseph wrinkled his freckled nose. "Not me. I can't imagine it's very warm in the winter."

"Castles never are," Elliot agreed, thinking of those he'd visited on his travels. "Too many rooms and too much cold stone." Too many politely rude, ignorant people, he didn't add.

Alice shrugged. "That's what coats and gloves are for. And warm blankets. I could live anywhere with warm blankets."

Chuckling, Elliot shepherded his subdued hoard back along North Lake Shore Drive. Lucky most people were inside and warm, not out and staring at the spectacle of Elliot with this parade of messy children. Not that he'd care who was watching, but his sister might. She was always more concerned about what these people thought of her than Elliot.

Put him in an artist's colony or a writer's retreat, and that's when Elliot's insecurity kicked in. The upper-crust bores he'd grown up with hardly rated. Wealth gave him leeway to appear eccentric, and he banked on it more often than his father and brothers approved of. But what else use was it? He couldn't buy more talent or a personality that kept anyone around as long as he'd like.

Back at the mansion he'd inherited from his late uncle, everyone tromped inside, the promise of warm food and drinks luring them. Elliot was momentarily spared his sister's inevitable wrath at the state of her offspring by his flustered housekeeper, Mrs. Roberts.

"There's a military man waiting for you in the parlor," she said, voice too-quick, her normally happy round face pinched with concern. "Wouldn't say what he was here for, just that he urgently needed to speak to you and that he'd wait until you got back even though I said I'd no idea when you would be—"

"It's all right. I'm sure it's…" He was sure it was what? He had no idea, but he didn't want her to worry. "I promised the children treats, do you think you can keep my promise for me?"

She dimpled, her soft spot for the little ones winning over her concern. "Of course, Mr. Stone. Been preparing all morning, I have."

After Elliot thanked her, she rushed off for the kitchen, and he detoured to the parlor.

There was indeed an old, weathered man in full military regalia waiting in the pale mint green room among the worn furniture. Elliot never had gotten around to leaving his mark on the place. He'd never intended to stay so long. At least he loved that deep blue settee near the fireplace.

Elliot approached the man and offered his hand to shake. "Hello, sir. I hear you've been waiting for me. Not too long, I hope?"

The man's grip was firm, his dark gaze devoid of warmth. "You're Mr. Elliot Stone?"

Faint derision in his tone put Elliot on the defensive. He struggled to keep his arms relaxed at his sides instead of crossing them, intensely aware of his wet and dirty clothing. "I am. I didn't catch your name I'm afraid."

"Major Alfred Allen. I'll get right to it, Mr. Stone." Allen's posture was ramrod straight, his expression serious. Elliot instantly disliked him. "We're in a state of war, and I've been sent to recruit you. As an officer, naturally, your family being who they are. Not to mention that degree. Have to maintain appearances, you know. You'll start as a cadet while you train, but by the time you go over, you could make Captain."

He...wait. He couldn't be serious?

"Captain? I'm sorry. Perhaps there's another Elliot Stone? Some hardened man who spent his youth playing soldiers, unlike myself. I can't imagine the military requires a poet of extremely limited success to lead anyone."

The flash of teeth Major Allen gave him wasn't kind. "No, I wouldn't think so. But you're more than that façade, aren't you?"

Prickles of unease tingled along Elliot's spine. "Pardon?"

"You're a man of many talents. One might even say skilled."

He couldn't know. Hardly anyone knew about magic. Fewer still would use that word to describe it, an instinctual distancing from persecution. "I wouldn't call myself that, no."

Allen's eyes narrowed. "How does magical sound, then?"

Christ.

"Absurd." It came out infused with the sort of contempt that typically made men want to curl up and disappear from his presence, even as Elliot's thoughts raced and his stomach hardened into a knot of fear.

"We know all about you, Mr. Stone. All about your kind. What you can inflict with a touch, to start. You've probably got some tricks left up your sleeve, I'll give you that, but we know much more than you think."

How did he know? Their family worked hard to keep the magic that flowed through their bloodline a secret. Much as other families did. Protecting themselves, protecting everyone skilled. History had shown time and again that when their secret slipped, lives were lost. If Allen was telling the truth, the government knew and the secret was out. Elliot's breathing faltered. What would they do with the knowledge? What did they want?

Body reacting to the threat before his mind decided a course of action, Elliot started to move closer. Allen didn't let him get more than a step in. "Ah! Keep those hands where I can see them, Mr. Stone. It's all documented. And there's nothing to gain by attempting to manipulate me. Got a lot to lose, though, haven't you?" He peered around the parlor, dispassionate gaze lingering on

Elliot's favorite uncle's belongings. Martin had spent his life traveling to every corner of the globe, collecting knickknacks from magical communities that he'd proudly displayed in this room. More than once he'd taken Elliot on whirlwind adventures during school breaks and was largely responsible for Elliot's own appreciation of travel, good poetry, and healthy disregard for social convention.

It had been five years since Martin's death, and the loss still stung. Allen's judgmental perusal of Martin's legacy only heightened the tension coiling in Elliot's body, his shoulders stiffening, his fists clenching at his sides.

"You come from a wealthy family," Allen continued when Elliot didn't respond. "Very close to your sisters and their children. Would be a shame if information to jeopardize those relationships came to light."

Weighing his options, Elliot remained motionless and kept his face blank. *Don't give him anything to use against you.* When he was a child, it was a lesson repeatedly reinforced at school. "You can't blackmail me with magic. My family knows all about it. Who would believe you if you tried to make it public?"

More people than would be good for Elliot's continued health and wellbeing, he feared, but maybe there was an advantage to making it sound ludicrous.

"No," Allen said, drawing the word out. "No, we can't blackmail you with magic. Not without fully exposing its existence. Think of the uproar that would cause. Another witch hunting panic like Salem. Imagine all the poor individuals who haven't used magic a day in their lives who'll get caught up in the crossfire."

"I don't have to imagine," Elliot snapped. "I can simply read history books. The witch hunts are common enough knowledge."

"Exactly. How many of them were innocent, do you think?"

Fighting a losing battle with anger, Elliot muttered, "All of them."

"I suppose I should've specified; how many weren't even playing with magic?"

Stubborn, Elliot kept his mouth shut this time. His temper, fed by fear, was far too close to the surface. He needed to think. If they weren't going to blackmail him for magic, then there must be something else. But what was it? Internally, he groaned. What wasn't it, would be the easier question to answer. He didn't have much regard for certain backwards laws in this country. And he'd been much less careful since he'd returned from Paris than he should have been.

"No guesses? I'd wager a lot of them. You fellows are rare enough, I just can't wrap my mind around there being all that many of you. But they tell me there are a fair few and that it runs in families. Maybe we ought to be taking a closer look at yours after all."

Allen paused as though he was letting his words sink in. Elliot waited for Allen to get to the point, his impassivity a cover for the anger and fear amalgamating and crawling beneath his skin. Not everyone in his family was skilled, but enough were. May was.

"If I'm honest, we'd rather not blackmail you to begin with. What do you say we skip it? We're willing to overlook your deficiencies in favor of the skills you'll provide."

"My skills wouldn't be useful in war. They're hardly useful in everyday life." What use would dreams be? Or the power at his fingertips? When Elliot thought of the war, he certainly didn't want to be close enough to the enemy for touch.

"Only because you fail to utilize it. Or you've never had the opportunity to really see what you can do. A training camp is being constructed for skilled recruits. Specialized education, physical fitness, and magic development programs have been crafted. All we need now are the recruits. And that's where you come in, Mr. Stone. Where's your patriotism? Hasn't this country done a lot for you?" Allen pointedly glanced around at furnishings that only appeared rich if you didn't know most of them were older than his uncle had been and you weren't examining them closely.

What was he supposed to say? 'No, I'm not patriotic. This country hates me for who I choose to love. What exactly has it done for me?' Further to the point, he wasn't a fighter and not fit to be an officer. Not someone as selfish and self-indulgent as he was. Soldiers deserved someone responsible issuing orders, someone who believed in what they were doing. Not him. No, nothing about the prospect appealed.

"I'm not sure what you think you know," Elliot said, coldly. "But if any of that was meant to entice me, you're nowhere close."

Allen's features hardened, and he crossed his arms. "Hmm. Notice I said we'd *prefer* not to blackmail you, not that we can't. Some might even say it's our duty to bring your illicit activities to light. Does your family find it suspicious? How much time you spend with friends? Gentleman friends, that is? Are all the ladies you've been spotted around town with for show?"

Teeth grinding, Elliot's body flushed with an angry heat. He jerked his chin up, refusing to be shamed. "No. Not *only* for show." He didn't need to explain his preferences to this bastard son of a piss. His fists curled tighter, and he dug in his nails to stop from saying something he'd regret. He curved his lips in a smile that felt grim as grave dirt. "It's starting to seem like you're not very reluctant to blackmail me at all."

"Not going to bother denying what you get up to?"

It was a taunt. A dare. Christ, Elliot hated this man. He

clenched his jaw so tight it hurt. "How long do I have to consider your offer?" Loathing coated the last word, impossible to hold in.

Triumph briefly glittered in Allen's flinty eyes, and Elliot hated that too. "You'll receive a letter next week with your train ticket. Be on the train, Mr. Stone. Or don't and see what happens. I guarantee it won't be pleasant."

He left. Elliot stood in the parlor, unmoving, body blazing rage that made his muscles quake with the necessity of restraint.

How had his entire life unraveled in the span of one conversation? What was he supposed to do?

The unfairness of it burned in his chest, made him want to shout and knock things over. Nothing he'd ever done had hurt a soul. Not the men he spent the night with, not the women either. He was always attentive with his lovers. They left satisfied, and it was no one's business but theirs.

Except small-minded people would always be waiting to judge, to ostracize him. Even if he believed at least some of his family might stand by him—May would—could he subject them to that?

And the threat about examining the rest of his family, the idea of them knowing May was skilled, the thought she could be ripped from her children and forced into a war she had no business being anywhere near, made Elliot's blood run cold.

His choices were to stand his ground and live to see twenty-six or give in to blackmail, keep his family intact, and likely die on foreign soil before his next birthday.

The uncomfortable sogginess of his clothes eventually pulled him to action. Elliot forced himself upstairs to change, physical imperative overriding his mental crisis. Buttons were something he could handle; the looming prospect of his participation in a war he'd already lost so many overseas friends to wasn't.

Bile rose in his throat, and he swallowed hard.

Love of Christ, he hadn't been in so much as a fight since he was five and the bigger kids had picked on him. His charm and good looks kept him from needing to. Now they expected him to what? Shoot at people? Kill people? Enemies or not, how could he?

But if he didn't. If they took May instead...

Hell. He had to go.

CHAPTER TWO

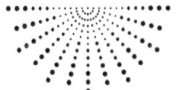

MAY 13, 1917
Chicago

SULLY CREPT DOWN THE hall in his socked feet, sensible shoes in his hands. It was shortly after nine. His cousin, Anne, should've left for her lessons already, and Edie, his boss, would've already gone out to work. He focused on sifting through the emotional background noise from the surrounding apartments just in case one of them was sneaky enough to stay behind and try to catch him making a break for the office on his last day home.

"I thought Edie told you to take time off," Anne said, crossing her arms as she appeared in Sully's way, blocking the door out of his boss's apartment, where they were staying. Sully startled even though he'd been half-expecting it. 'Least he only jumped a might.

They'd spent the last two nights at Edie's place, where Anne would stay while he was away. It wasn't like she could've stayed in their apartment on her own. She was only sixteen. And he couldn't afford to pay for a place no one would be living in, so he'd moved all their possessions into storage.

"She tells me lots of things, means about half of 'em. Don't you have art classes to get to?" Sully asked as his heart rate steadied again. He wished he could escort her like he used to, but he wouldn't be here to look after Anne like that anymore, not after today. Not when he was being shipped off for training. Better if she learned to rely on herself in case he didn't make it back. Sully swallowed thickly.

At least he could send money home. He'd told Anne he'd send back half, but what she didn't know was he planned to send a lot more than that. What was he gonna use it for anyway? He could do without. Anne deserved better.

"I can miss *one* day, Sully." He didn't need to be skilled at sensing emotion to know she was miserable and trying to act normal by being a thorn in his side. The churning anxiety and fear were right there in front of him, shifting around and raising the baby hairs at the base of his skull. He ignored the sensation.

"Not after I scraped up the money to pay for them, Annie. 'Sides, you love painting. You're not gonna want to miss out just to be bored out of your mind with me all day." She had better things to do than that. Even if part of him wanted to spend the day doing all of the childish things they'd done around the neighborhood growing up. What Anne needed was to establish a new routine, normalcy in her new setting. Not for him to make her sad, just by being around and dragging out the inevitable.

She wrinkled her nose. "You're not boring. Thick headed sometimes, but not boring." Her expression brightened. Excitement bubbled around her. "Oh! I could come with you. Edie said maybe while you're gone I can help her at the agency, this could be on-the-job learning."

It was Sully's turn to glower. "I'm gonna have to murder her. It's the only option."

"You can't. Then who'd stay with me until you come back?" Anne's voice was light and teasing, but her smile was wrong, and her hazel eyes got wet. The same sad feelings she'd been holding back for the last week and a half trickled out to wrap around him like a chilly mist.

She hated him leaving. Made two of them, but he had to go. After the government made it clear they knew all about his illusions and just as bad, who he fucked, he couldn't refuse. There'd been statements from men he'd had back-alley encounters with. How they'd gotten those confessions when Sully didn't even know most of their names, he had no clue. He certainly remembered the acts described. Witness statements corroborated he'd been seen with three of the men on key dates and close enough to the times that it would cast suspicion on him, whether or not it was provable in court.

But living in the kind of poor neighborhood they did, the fallout might not even be so bad. He'd helped out enough people, done enough favors, that his neighbors might look the other way. They weren't the types to be shocked by human nature, and everyone knew what rich people paid for was worse than anything Sully might've done. Two streets back that was exactly what happened in the shadows.

He didn't even have any friends to lose. Not really.

The problem was, he couldn't risk the scandal they'd threatened to unleash touching Anne and Edie. Edie would never fire him or let him quit, and the business she'd built from the ground up after her husband's death would suffer for it. And that... he couldn't let that happen. Couldn't keep himself home to take care of Anne at the expense of making their lives so much harder than they already were. For what? Anne had so much more to live for than him anyway. A whole life ahead of her.

'Sides, what if they figured out Anne was skilled too? Or Edie? What if they already knew? He had to keep them safe any way he could.

So he told them he'd enlisted because it was the right thing to do. Protecting them meant going to war in Europe. Just a fact of life. He'd learned early to adapt to change. That nothing was ever guaranteed to last. Real fear, stinking and sweaty and clammy, didn't sink in until much later. The one that reminded him he'd never even left the United States. He couldn't wrap his mind around crossing the vast, deep ocean, and setting foot on foreign land.

"Hey." Sully drew Anne into a hug, the warm nostalgia of wrapping her smaller body in his arms almost enough to drown out their mutual misery. She held on tight, burying her face against his chest as her shoulders heaved with her breaths. God, when did she get so big? It felt like yesterday he was cradling a toddler and now she was just half a foot shorter than him. "We'll get through this. You'll see, Buttercup. Promise."

Pulling back, Anne wiped away the wetness on her face, avoiding his eyes. He paid careful attention to the way she was feeling, made sure there wasn't anything darker, more frightening beneath the loneliness and fear. He didn't find any, but it didn't stop him worrying.

"Don't make promises you can't keep. You taught me that." Anne's voice waivered.

Sully tapped his temple with two fingers. "Exactly. That's how you know I'll keep it."

Anne managed a weak chuckle. "I'm not a kid anymore, Sully. I know a lie when I hear one. I can't lose you too."

"You won't. You know how stubborn I am. No way I'm not coming back. And Edie won't let anything happen while I'm gone. So don't worry so much." She'd been happy to take Anne in—always collecting lost people. Like when she'd given him a job he hadn't known he was wasting away without.

Sully wasn't entirely sure he trusted her to keep Anne out of trouble since she constantly managed to get him into it, but she was all they had. He'd just have to have a very pleading talk with her about keeping Anne out of any Detective Agency business. It was too dangerous.

Nodding, Anne pulled her shoulders back and smoothed her expression. On the surface she was calm and collected. Underneath was fear and loneliness that saturated her core. The unknown did that to people. Almost all her life he'd been there. Still remembered being eight and falling asleep on the thin rug beside her crib whenever she cried in the middle of the night. Her tiny fingers clutching his hand through the bars. Aunt Maggie used to say he was spoiling her, but her voice was warm, and he'd known she was more amused than exasperated.

"Since I can't come with you, and you're not planning to stay home, I better hurry and get to class on time," Anne said, rubbing a hand across her cheekbone like that might keep gathering tears from falling. "You'll be home for supper?"

"Wouldn't miss it, Buttercup."

An hour later he snuck into the offices of Edie Isle's Detective Agency, hoping the boss herself was already out for the morning. His desk had been cleared out, no room for wasted space. Someone had to be hired to replace him while he was gone. His active cases had already been turned over to Edie's younger cousin Lillian Isle—a brilliant young lady skilled at communing with the dead. She didn't typically deal with the same types of cases he did, but he knew she'd have no problem solving them. Wished her all the best, really.

There was just one he wanted to—

The creak of Edie's door opening made Sully glance up sharply from the empty desk he'd been creeping toward. Caught red-handed.

Edie tsked as she approached. Her blonde curls were mostly hidden beneath a fashionable hat, and her dress was fancier than she typically wore to work, a slinky number that had to have cost more than a reasonable sum. What was she up to? Could he convince her to let him tag along?

"Didn't we discuss taking a little time off?" she asked, archly. "Having a break before the army runs you through the grinder? I'd pretend I'm shocked, but we both know I'm not."

Squinting at her, Sully casually crossed his arms. "Funny. Where are you off to?"

Edie tilted her head to the side and mimicked his posture. "You're not going home no matter what I say, are you?"

Sully gave her his most unrepentant grin as he tucked his hands in his pockets. She knew him so well. "Nuh-unh."

Sighing, she leaned against Lillian's desk. A glimmer of something part amused, part gloating peeked past the steel trap Edie usually kept on her emotions. What was that about?

Most people couldn't help the way their emotions leaked into the air around them, certainly didn't expect someone to pick up on them. The same way Sully couldn't help being that someone. Feelings shouted at him or whispered or rippled, caressed, stabbed, often they were nothing but sensation without name. Strong ones close by almost always caught his notice. Especially when he knew the person.

Except for Edie. She was the only person he'd met who could

lock down her emotions at will without making his head throb in pain. So something getting past her defenses was suspicious.

"Fine. I'll make you a deal," she said.

Couldn't be too awful, right? Scratch that. He *hoped* it wasn't too awful. "Let's hear it."

Her smile turned predatory. That expression signaled trouble with a capital T, always had. "You can help me close out this case. But tonight, you're going out on the town. I'm locking you out after supper and you'll go have fun. You're not allowed to feel guilty or worry about tomorrow. Do whatever you want. Have one last big hurrah before you go."

Frowning, Sully considered it. He wanted in on the case, no doubt about that. And this wasn't half so bad as what else could've come out of her mouth. Things like 'You have to file the paperwork after', or 'You have to be the lookout'. But... "I can't afford to go spend the night somewhere."

She wasn't impressed by his weak protest. "You're an illusionist, Sully. It's not gonna hurt anyone, and you deserve it. Do something selfish. Everyone should be selfish at least once in their life. So go out and do it."

'While you still have a chance' was left unsaid, but they both knew it.

"I'm fine. But Anne—"

Edie held up a hand to stall him. "She came up with this scheme. I swear. Didn't I just say something about not feeling guilty? Or was that a fever dream?"

Sully didn't give her the satisfaction of a reply, but the smirk that turned up the corner of her ruby red lips said he didn't need to. She raised an eyebrow and asked, "So you want in on this case or not?"

He struggled with himself a moment more. Could he really do this for himself? Was it really as good an idea as it felt?

"I'm in."

Her eyes danced with victory. "Wonderful. Now, let's go catch a thief."

CHAPTER THREE

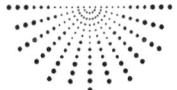

SULLY WAS A FRAUD. His best suit shabby compared to everyone else's, his shoes near worn out. Didn't matter, he wouldn't let them see anyway. Using his skill like this in public wasn't something he liked doing; there was always the slim chance someone skilled might see through it if he tired himself out too much. He'd only been caught twice, when he'd been so exhausted he could barely see straight and he was fine now, but it was still a risk.

Then again, so was fucking a man he met in a fancy lounge, but he intended to do that tonight too. Might be his last chance.

A haze of smoke wafted through the dim lighting. The scents of stale tobacco and spilled liquor curled warmly in his lungs after the chill of the cool night. Spring was supposed to have sprung, but you couldn't tell it from the weather. Only ten days ago they'd had a sudden inch of snow. And hadn't it been fun to chase down a blackmailer as they both slipped around in slush? Sully shivered remembering the icy water that had flooded his boots.

For a Sunday evening, The Green Lounge was crowded. Men stood in clusters or sat at dark wood tables while a cheerful band played. A brunette in a dress sang, her voice full of rich smokey enjoyment. Most of the crowd was paying attention to her dimpled smiles while Sully was paying attention to the crowd.

This wasn't the sort of place he ever went for a good time. Left to himself, he'd have spent tonight miserable and guilty and secretly afraid. But he promised Edie he'd go out and have some fun. Considering it was his last night of freedom, he deserved a bit of luxury too, didn't he?

Judging by the desperation on several faces in the crowd and the background hum of fear and excitement buzzing at the edges of Sully's senses, he wasn't the only one shipping out in the morning, headed for training. Not the only one after for a good time either. He shoved down his own instinctive response to the swirl of those emotions, the ones he'd been repressing all week.

Captivating eyes met Sully's once more from across the room. He couldn't tell what color they were from this distance and wanted to see. The second he'd walked into the lounge he'd spotted the blond man with the pretty face. And wanted.

Placing an order for his second drink, Sully studied him from the corner of his eye. The man was sedately surveying the room at large, not a participant in the tableau but a dispassionate observer. He sat alone at the farthest table from the door, drinking something amber, a sly smirk slowly twisting his mouth.

Everything about him was pale, from his hair and tailored gray suit to the matching fedora on the table in front of him. He seemed like he should be quietly haunting some English manor house, sitting around all elegant and bewitching.

His gaze swept to rest on Sully briefly for the third time. Bold. A spark of attraction simmered along Sully's awareness and he basked in it, letting it warm him from the inside out as he looked right back.

Reading emotions came in handy at times like this; made finding someone for the night less dangerous. Anything complex was difficult to interpret, but this was straightforward, nothing confusing about it. Blood-hot lust flared like a beacon every time their gazes met. An eager thrill settled in Sully's gut as he made his way to the table and took a seat in the vacant chair. He'd been after a distraction tonight, and there one was all right, so perfectly promising.

Those eyes he'd wondered about were the lightest shade of blue, like something from Anne's childhood watercolor paintings—endless summer skies and lakeshores. Beautiful and compelling.

"Have we met?" The man asked, delicate eyebrows lifting curiously.

"Not a chance, I'd remember a face like yours." Sully repressed a smile smug as that accent. The stranger was well-off, well-educated, and his words dripped refinement. "Eyes like those."

A frisson of excitement and playfulness the man attempted to conceal from his face fluttered in Sully's stomach. Told him he was on the right track. "Hmm."

The skillfully played trumpet and percussion echoing off walls, along with noise of chatter around them, lent the illusion of privacy and Sully pulled magic from the ether to enhance it.

"Got a name?" he asked.

The man's eyes sparkled, amusement in the sensual curve of his mouth. "Do you?"

"You can call me Warren." Not that anyone else did anymore, but it was better than giving up the one people knew him by. "Your turn, ain't it?"

"Elliot," he said after a moment's hesitation, first-rate manners probably kicking up a fuss about skipping to given names straight away. Politeness wasn't what either of them were after though.

Elliot, huh?

Sully turned that over in his mind. How would it taste on his lips later when they were twisted together, panting? His thoughts must've shown because faint pink dusted Elliot's fine cheeks, and he ducked his head to sip from his glass. "I was being kind, by the way, when I asked if we'd met. I'd remember you as well. After all, it's not every day I'm pursued so rapidly upon making acquaintance."

Bull. The way he looked, all tall and lean and prettier than any man Sully had ever spoken to, people must've been eating out of his palm the second they met him. "Handsome guy like you? That I find hard to believe."

A devious grin tugged at Elliot's mouth, quickly constrained into something more cultivated. "Not so often by the sort of person whose interest I'd like to return."

"Oh. And what sort's that?"

Elliot leaned forward. His voice dropped to keep his words from reaching unintended ears or to get a rise out of Sully. It worked on both counts. "I think you'll simply have to share a drink with me to find out."

"Suppose I gotta." There was a wicked, tantalizing edge to the checked desire Elliot unconsciously aimed his way. Sully couldn't help playing along, wanting to draw this out. *One night.* He had one night. If he could, he'd make it last forever.

"Are you always this confident of your reception?" Elliot chased a drop of condensation down the side of his glass with the tip of his index finger, and Sully tracked the movement, wetting his lips.

"Got a sense. You always this coy?"

"Never, but I'm finding I rather enjoy it." He scrunched up his nose, blue eyes bright with mischief. "I suspect you do too."

Sully crafted a subtle illusion concealing them completely from view. No sense drawing unwanted attention. He dipped his chin and lifted his lashes slowly, openly flirting now. "Bet I'd enjoy anything you do."

That earned him a genuine laugh, one that turned Elliot's graceful features boyish and delighted. "Cocksure, aren't you?"

"When it's worth the risk." Sully raked his gaze heatedly over Elliot, scraping his teeth across his bottom lip in appreciation. "And I bet you're *very* worth it."

Sharp eyes evaluated Sully, then glanced at patrons minding their own business, not paying them the slightest mind. Shit. What was Elliot thinking? Maybe Sully had taken it too far; they were in public after all, even if Sully knew no one could see them. He ought to know better than—

"You're skilled." The adorable pinch between Elliot's perfect brows smoothed as he faced Sully again.

Sully's stomach clenched hard. He kept his voice calm, pitching it low and hoping Elliot would take the bait. "At seduction?"

"Supernaturally," Elliot clarified. Then at whatever panic seeped into Sully's expression he went on, "It takes one to know one." The companionable grin Elliot offered eased some of the tension in Sully's shoulders.

This was an interesting turn of events. He could count on one hand the number of skilled people he knew well. Three of them were in his line of work. He met more on the job. No one he'd be interested in forming friendships with. Outside work he didn't get to know anyone enough to figure out if they were skilled.

So curiosity pricked at Sully, provoking him. "What's your skill?"

"A touch personal, wouldn't you say?" He paused thoughtfully, and Sully's cheeks heated. Then Elliot's mouth curved, and Sully had to admit he liked self-satisfaction on his face. "I'll show you mine if you show me yours."

Right. Yeah. He could do that. Pursing his lips, Sully debated how much he was willing to reveal. *An illusion?* Nothing strong, just a glimpse at what he was capable of. He didn't like people to know how he could sense emotions. It made them nervous around him. Their attempts—poor as they might be—to conceal how they felt brought his ability uncomfortably to the forefront of his awareness. And almost always resulted in a splitting headache.

"All right," he said, sitting up a little straighter. "Now you see me..." Sully fixed his gaze on Elliot's face and concentrated. Power flowed into him like warm water as he distorted Elliot's perception.

Surprise made Elliot's lips part and his eyebrows shoot up. "Now I don't. Where did you go?"

"Still here."

"That *is* impressive, Warren. Are you actually invisible?" He was looking at a spot slightly left of Sully, which made laughter bubble up in his chest. He squashed it, before it escaped, but it infused his voice anyway.

"It's only an illusion. If you reach out and touch me, your mind will overpower it." He didn't add that he was perfectly capable of convincing a person they weren't touching him at all if he put enough effort into it, and they were susceptible.

Elliot's hand slid slowly across the tabletop. Sully placed his palm down in its path. Soft fingers bumped into his, tickling faintly as they glided up and over, until Elliot's warm palm was flush with the back of Sully's hand. It took a moment, then Elliot's gaze shifted, sandy lashes flickering, and focused on him. An amazed smile gradually lit up his face.

God, he really is handsome.

"Quite the trick. And you've been surrounding us with something similar?" Elliot didn't move his hand from where it engulfed Sully's. Heat tingled up Sully's arm. He nodded. "How long?"

"On and off since you first spotted me. Just in case." Sully bit his lip and watched Elliot's eyes darken.

"Shall I show you mine?"

"I'm watching," Sully assured him, confident like his heart wasn't beating chugging-train fast in his chest at simple contact.

A quick blinding grin edged with hunger was the only warning before molten pleasure rushed through his veins, spreading to the tips of his toes and the ends of his hair. His mouth fell open on a gasp, face flooding with scorching heat, body flushing like he was lighting up all over, his trousers suddenly much, much too snug. Sully kept a grip on his magic by the barest thread. It was the one thing keeping this shameless display from getting them thrown in jail or worse.

As fast as it came on, it ended, and Sully gaped, ears ringing, blood pounding. Winded and wanting.

When he could finally speak, his voice came out scratchy and silken at the same time. "What the fuck was that?"

He blushed further at the sound of clear desire as it gave away exactly how affected he was.

"The kinder side of my favorite skill—euphoria. Its less pleasant counterpart is horror."

Sully shivered and sipped his drink, hardly noticed the burn of it. He hoped his voice was back to normal as he restlessly shifted in a vain attempt to relieve some pressure without being obvious. "Wouldn't wanna feel that one."

Elliot's face turned grim as he drew his hand back. "No, you wouldn't." Then he flashed his too bright smile and winked. *The bastard.* "Don't worry. I only use that skill in dire circumstances. You're safe from me."

One corner of Sully's mouth lifted. "Not too safe, I hope. That all you can do?"

With a wry look Elliot said, "No, but secrets make the world turn. Surely you've your own to keep."

Didn't they all?

"Right." Sully squirmed again in his seat. Did Elliot realize how worked up he'd gotten? Did everyone have that reaction? He tried for casual. "You been in Chicago long?" Elliot's brow raised. "Don't sound like you're from here's all."

"I was born here actually. But I was sent abroad for education at twelve. Then when I was old enough, I traveled extensively before my sisters begged me to return. I suppose that's what you hear. A little bit of everywhere or maybe nowhere at all."

Sully had the decency not to voice all of the questions that crossed his mind. He smiled at the fondness in Elliot's voice when he talked about his sisters, though. "Older or younger?"

"Both." He rolled his eyes heavenward, but his tone made it indulgent not dismissive. "And I've two older brothers."

"Big family."

"Very. You?"

"Only me and my cousin. She's like a little sister. We were raised together." He didn't want to think about Anne, about the fear and loneliness she'd tried to hide or the way her slim shoulders trembled with repressed sobs. The sadness she covered with a smile when they said goodbye.

"I don't know where you just went, but perhaps a diversion's in order. Lucky you, I'm extremely willing to provide one if you'd like?" Elliot asked. The one raised brow and crooked smile made his meaning obvious. Sully swallowed loudly.

He made himself stop and take a breath, his voice rougher when he continued. "Yeah. I really would."

Five minutes later Elliot had him shoved up against the scratchy brick of the back-alley wall, mouth hot on his, teeth catching at his lower lip. Sully's heart sprinted as a soft involuntary sigh escaped him.

This wasn't how he expected it to go, but the insistent press of Elliot's thigh against his stiff cock was as persuasive as Elliot's skilled tongue taking possession of his mouth. Arching into the contact, he pressed his hips forward helplessly. He'd intended to be the aggressor. Always was, but Elliot had upended the notion the moment they stepped into the shadows. He was slimmer and only an inch or so taller than Sully, but there was something commanding in the way he'd guided him backward, crowded in close, and watched Sully's face in the dark, holding his chin between forefinger and thumb, pinning him for the taking.

Sully gasped as Elliot tightly gripped his hips, dragging him closer. The hard, hot length of him pushing against Sully's groin. He was submerged in sensation, in the desire he sensed emanating from Elliot, in his own echoing need. He wanted so much more— skin and sweat and pulsing pleasure.

Fingertips grazed along the waistband of his trousers, a brazen thumb dipped inside. Paused in question, so close to where Sully desperately needed to feel him. Giving in would end this too soon. He could picture it now, fast and frantic and still better than any other time he'd ever done this. But…

Drawing a shaky breath, he closed his hand over Elliot's. "Not here," he said. "I got a room not far."

"Do you?" Elliot's perceptible skepticism was warranted. Sully didn't talk nearly as fancy as someone with a room in this neighborhood ought to. He was probably wondering what hole in the wall place Sully would drag him off to.

"I do." A private smile graced Sully's mouth. "Someplace nice. Trust me?"

The soft pad of a thumb stroked slow and sweet over Sully's wet lips, softest satin and gentlest pressure. He flicked his tongue against it, and Elliot's sharp inhale blazed like a bright ember of satisfaction in Sully's gut.

"How far?" Elliot's strained and heated voice made Sully reconsider the notion of self-control.

"Few blocks. I'll make it worth legging." Sully sweetened his plea with a graze of lips right below Elliot's ear, eliciting a shiver. "Promise."

Elliot swayed closer, fingers digging into Sully's biceps. The flicker of lust in the air spiked red hot, then he let out a sigh and pulled away to recline against the dry brick beside Sully. He pushed his hands through hair that had been perfectly styled, fetched the hat that had been knocked onto the cold dusty ground, and patted the dirt clear before placing it on his head. "I'll require a moment to...ah..." He gestured at his lower body. Sully kept his gaze up. He only had so much restraint.

They could hardly see one another in the shadows between the two buildings, but Sully tossed him a crooked grin. "If you wanna wait. Or we could go now, not waste time. Long as you hold my hand, no one'll look twice, like inside. I'll keep you safe."

"You can—well I'm rather more impressed. Holding hands...is that something you enjoy, or does it pertain to the skill?" The question was teasing, the sentiment below it sweet.

"Can't it be both? Touching makes it easier to include you in an illusion. You hold on to me, magic naturally extends to you. If not, I waste more energy."

"Ah. Wouldn't want you depleting yourself, would we? Not nearly yet, and for much more pleasurable reasons when you do." Elliot reached out a hand, and Sully clasped it. Their palms fit neatly, fingers twining seamlessly like they'd always done this when Sully *never* did this. Not like this. Sully's heartbeat pulsed faster in his fingertips. Could Elliot feel it racing?

"Come on." He tugged Elliot down the alley into the street. The sidewalks weren't flooded with people at this time of night. Nor were they deserted. Groups of men in suits, and nicely dressed ladies clutching their arms didn't so much as glance their way as they passed. He felt Elliot's heart speed and nerves ratchet every time someone got close enough to glimpse them holding hands, then slow as they strolled by without incident. It was intoxicating. The power of giving someone like Elliot a thing he couldn't get anywhere else.

Turning onto LaSalle Street, Sully smiled at Elliot's growing confusion. Felt that piercing incredulous gaze studying him. He slowed shy of the Hotel La Salle. The mammoth building offered some of the most luxurious accommodations in the city. Far, far beyond Sully's means.

"You have a room?" Elliot gazed at intricate cream stonework fading to red brick and back to cream, stretching high above them in splendor.

"Sure do. Established that earlier, I thought."

"Here?" Elliot's eyes flicked between him and the structure, cheeks flushing.

Sully fished a key out of his pocket with his free hand. The hotel name and room number were emblazoned on the brass fob reflecting in the streetlamp. "Here."

He wasn't about to admit he'd hoodwinked his way into possession of the room through magic, but it had to have been obvious. Sully expected a flash of contempt. Instead Elliot's lips quirked.

"Right. Should we put it to good use?"

His easy acceptance perversely pricked Sully's conscience. He didn't want Elliot walking around with the wrong idea, thinking he was a grifter. "I don't normally use it for this sort of thing. For myself. I got a good reason."

"I believe you."

That easily? Who was this guy? How could he mean it? Men like him didn't give men like Sully the benefit of the doubt. But sincerity practically glowed off him like a summer sunrise. Sully wanted to bathe in it. *He can't be for real. Can he?*

God, he is.

Suddenly much too desperate, Sully reached up to the back of Elliot's head and pulled him into an urgent kiss—right there in the street—mouths colliding. Elliot's lips parted in shock or invitation —it was impossible to be sure which—maybe both. Sully took advantage. Delved his tongue inside to flick and slide over Elliot's, tasting fancy liquor and the faintest trace of expensive cigar. Elliot smelled like indulgence and felt like luxury. His hands clutched at Sully, pulling him closer, kissing him with something like wonder-tinged desperation until the need for breath broke them apart.

Thinly banked desire pulsated in the air around them, through Sully's veins.

I've never wanted anyone so bad, he didn't say. *I'd let you do anything you wanted to me. Anything.*

Regaining a semblance of sense, Sully inclined his head toward the entrance. "This way."

He forced his gaze from the naked amazement and sweetness in Elliot's shocking baby blues and dragged him into the swanky lobby.

Even worked up as he was, the grandeur still hit him square in the chest. Made him feel small and unworthy. He cut straight through it. Tonight might be his only chance to see a place like this. Beautifully carved mahogany woodwork and brass accents gleamed. The cream marble floors were shiny and spotless beneath their feet.

Easing up on his magic a bit because Elliot fit right in here, Sully led him to the elevator. As they waited for the car he recovered his manners. "Ever stayed here before?"

"A time or two." Elliot glanced at him. Sully couldn't help but notice how flushed he was, and his newly vulnerable stance. Confused emotion hid beneath the surface, a shy nervousness Sully didn't understand. One that hadn't been there earlier.

A downright ludicrous idea occurred to him. But no. He had to be wrong. He drew on more power again so no one would overhear and asked anyway. "You've done this…haven't you? Been with a man?"

Of course he had. A man who looked like him, who kissed like that, who took charge the way he had. Sully had to be misreading the raw sensations. Didn't he?

"Yes, of course. Well, no, not entirely. I've fucked plenty of men, been fucked, but I've never kissed one on the sidewalk in the middle of the street with people around. I never dreamed I could, and you…as though it was easy. As if you didn't have the slightest fear of—"

Sully sent him a crooked smile. The ornately styled brass elevator doors opened. "Promised I'd keep you safe, didn't I?"

CHAPTER FOUR

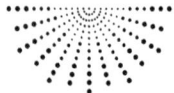

SULLY HELD HIS BREATH. The room was stunning with beautifully patterned cream wallpaper. Lavishly furnished, a huge, rounded mirror hung above a dark wooden mantle, polished to a high shine. On the mantle's ledge crystal vases caught in the light, overflowing with pink and white flowers that had to cost a fortune this time of year.

The main attraction was the sprawling four-poster bed. Far grander than the single he crammed into at the two-bedroom apartment he and Anne shared.

One of the first things he'd done earlier, after he explored the gleaming private bathroom and luxuriated in running hot water, was flop down on this bed. Emerald green satin sheets had slipped and slid under his naked skin. He shivered with remembered sensation, and Elliot pressed against his back gently guiding Sully forward. His damp, warm mouth grazed the side of Sully's neck, raising goosebumps.

"Let's get these off, shall we?" Elliot murmured, lips clinging, breath puffing against sensitive skin. Elliot's graceful fingers reached around Sully's chest to unbutton his coat, then went to work on his vest and shirt. Sully hummed appreciation and helped pull garments off. He rushed to open the buttons of his own pants and got the first one undone, then Elliot took over and finished the job. The haste with which they moved in pursuit of a single purpose was exhilarating. Heat pooled in Sully's groin, spread outward in a dizzying ripple as his cock sprang free.

Hissing in relief, he half-forgot his pants, pooled around his ankles and caught on his boots. Fingers cool from night air curled around his swelling shaft. Tipping his head back on a groan, Sully reached up behind himself, sliding his hand into the soft hair at the back of Elliot's head.

He could feel Elliot's excitement in the hard press of him against Sully's backside, yes, but deeper too, rising in shimmering sultry pitch as he rocked into Elliot's smooth, clever grip. Gentle friction tingled along his nerves, quickening his breaths and his pulse.

The disorienting intensity of Elliot's undivided focus on Sully's pleasure thrilled him. Most of his previous encounters with men had been rushed. No room for exploration and teasing touches. It was stolen in snatches and instantly forgotten. This…this would be addictive if he had the chance to sample it for more than a night. He wished, really wished, he could.

"How should we do this? What do you enjoy?" Elliot asked, kissing a distracting, tantalizing path to Sully's ear.

"Uh—I—*oh.*" His wicked tongue stole Sully's ability to form a coherent reply.

Elliot pet him with the lightest touches, open palm gliding silken up and down his cock, thumb sneaking out to send tingling sensation over the head, causing Sully to helplessly moan. An almost-whimper that made his face flush, his cheeks tight and burning.

"Cat got your tongue?" Elliot asked, low and amused.

"Fuck me." Sully's entire body went hot with the demand. "However you want, just make it last as long as you can. Need it to last."

Elliot's palm stroked a slow path up Sully's abdomen and chest, coming to rest at the hollow of his throat. "I rather enjoy the sound of that. It brings so many vivid fantasies to mind. I'm not sure how I'll choose. Except whatever we do, I swear I'll go very, very slowly. Until you're so painfully stiff you hardly recall your name let alone what's on that beautiful mind. And I'll keep you there, directly on the precipice, my name the only thing on your lips, my swollen cock driving into you over and over." Their breaths were ragged. "Until you can't hold back any longer."

Sully reached back, grasped a handful of Elliot's coat and pulled him closer. "I'm halfway there already."

As Elliot nipped Sully's ear sweet sensation fizzed around them like sparks in the dark of night. *Proud of himself.*

He ought to be.

"I want you on the bed," Elliot murmured in honeyed tones.

"Will you get undressed if I do?" Sully wanted to see what Elliot looked like under that neatly pressed bespoke suit. Would he be as confident when he was every bit as bare as Sully? Would Sully still feel so damn unbalanced?

None of this seemed real, not since the moment he'd met those knockout eyes across the room. It was too good. Like they were in a dream, and it was slipping through his fingers, unattainable no matter how hard he wanted to hold on.

"I will *absolutely* undress for you, if you get on that bed." There was a wicked lilt to his voice, and Sully rushed to comply.

Prying off one boot, then the other, he kicked his way out of his pants. Crawled up onto the bed and flipped over onto his back. One arm tucked under his head for support, wearing only his socks.

At the twist of mirth when Elliot noticed them, Sully rolled his eyes. "My feet get cold, sue me."

"I can think of better things to do to you." Elliot's darkening gaze heated Sully's skin. Squirming, he instinctively squeezed his own cock. Velvety skin slid warm beneath his fingers as he loosely stroked himself.

Sizzling elation shrouded him, stemming from Elliot. *Gratification. Elliot must like this.* Liked how Sully looked doing it. Maybe even liked that he was the reason for it.

Sully watched Elliot's nimble fingers slip buttons through holes and remove layers, revealing pale skin dotted with the occasional freckle. He was slim with narrow hips. His nearly hairless flat chest bore rosy pebbled nipples, and his build said he'd never done a hard day's work in his life. That shouldn't be near so arousing as it was.

Sully lowered his gaze to the faint dark blond dusting of hair that trailed below Elliot's navel to well-groomed curls above his jutting cock, and Elliot stood there a moment, letting him look, self-assured while Sully unabashedly stared.

He was Elliot's exact opposite in most every way. Broad chest and strong arms defined from daily exercise and the exertions of work, liberally covered in dark hair. The contrast piqued Sully's interest, and his heart flipped oddly in his chest.

God, look at him. He's beautiful. Could watch him for hours like this, flushed and hard for me. Wanting me.

At last, Elliot moved deliberately forward, climbed between his legs. Their lips met in an insistent kiss that slowed time and narrowed Sully's existence to soft mouths, sharp teeth, and gentle gasps.

The electrifying press of tongues, the graze of straining cocks, the glide of smooth skin, all drove his rising need for more. "Elliot," he whispered, tugging at his shiny blond hair. Sleek strands slid between his fingers.

"Mmm." Elliot was pressing open-mouthed kisses down Sully's neck, pausing whenever Sully couldn't hold back the gasps or whines crowding his throat. The upward twist of Elliot's lips against his skin each time fluttered a dizzying somersault in Sully's stomach, and pulsed heat straight to his cock.

He continued down Sully's chest and abdomen, teasing his tongue over tight nipples, scraping with his teeth until the only thing Sully could focus on was that soft wet mouth and those talented satin hands all over him.

And then Elliot was there, poised over Sully's engorged cock. His breath gusted over the damp head, sent a provocative shock of lust prickling over his flesh. Sully fisted his hands in the sheets because he wanted to cling to Elliot and couldn't bring himself to. He could *feel* how badly Elliot wanted to put his mouth on him, and it made everything hotter, strung him tighter.

Their eyes met, Elliot's searching, scorching. Sully nodded. Couldn't get words out, not with Elliot right there. Not with how badly he wanted this. The upward twitch of Elliot's lips was rapidly becoming familiar, cherished. He was lucky to be allowed this much. Cursed it couldn't be more.

Here, too, Elliot took his time. His lips skimmed, tongue darting out to smooth and curl—surrounding Sully with wet heat, moving so slowly his thighs trembled. His abdomen clenched with the effort to remain motionless as pleasure mounted, but he couldn't quiet the sounds escaping him. It was all he could do not to shove into the reverent mouth sliding up and down his cock in exquisite torture.

The appreciative noises Elliot made around him buzzed under Sully's skin. He couldn't think. Could hardly breathe. Skin too snug, body tensing. The real miracle was that he didn't spend within moments.

His toes curled, heart thudding. Blue, blue eyes watched him with such intensity his balls throbbed, and he was so close. So damn close. He wanted to look away but couldn't. *God.*

"Elliot," Sully gasped. "Elliot, I—shite—if you don't stop, I'm—"

Instantly, Elliot released him, temptation gone. Sully let out a choked breath, thwarted need buffeting him. He fought hard against the desperate urge to reach down and push himself to climax. That wasn't what he wanted. Not if he was honest.

Elliot's reddened lips grazed Sully's stomach, teeth nipping here and there as Elliot crawled back up and took possession of his mouth once more. The erotic and primal taste of his own arousal on Elliot's tongue filled Sully's senses, made him ache with need. Sully arched against him, moaning his pleasure. He sucked and savored the shuddering surge of desire he elicited.

"There's—mmph—petroleum jelly in the nightstand. I know—" Sully broke off with a groan as Elliot's hips pressed forward, rubbing them together. Squeezing his eyes shut for a second, Sully struggled to speak. "Know I said slow, and that was swell and all, but you're killing me, Elliot. *God.*"

Elliot's pleased expression was so bright it almost hurt to see. "Swell was it? I think we can do better than that. Can't we?" He rolled off Sully, stood in front of the nightstand, and dug out the small tin Sully had stashed there.

Sully drank in the sight of him. Long lean legs, sharp hipbones.

The cut of his groin drawing his attention to Elliot's thick cock, darker than the rest of his skin, curving slightly upward to a shiny pink tip. His perusal swept lower to the heavy rounded curve of Elliot's balls. Sully's mouth went dry, and he swallowed hard.

Why's he got to be so pretty all over?

"All right. Get a wiggle on, sweetheart," he managed, forcing his gaze up to meet those smiling eyes. Glossing over the pet name, he added, "Let's do better."

Elliot bit down on a wide smile. His face screwing up like he was trying not to laugh as he tossed the tin onto the bed. "Right then. Roll over for me?"

"Mmm, when you ask so nice." Sully got onto his hands and knees, skin prickling with the awareness of Elliot's gaze on him. A warm hand caressed his back, confidently skimming up between his shoulder blades and back down to squeeze his arse. Sully sighed and arched into it, felt Elliot's answering excitement. It was different, acting like this. Letting someone else take care of him for once. Sully was used to being responsible and relied upon. Had gotten in the habit of never letting loose. Not all the way. Not like this.

He'd been fucked before. Once for curiosity's sake, twice more because he liked it. Had always managed to keep himself emotionally detached. Now…There was something about Elliot. Or this night. Or what was coming tomorrow. It carved his chest into a scalding messy tangle that wanted to lash itself to Elliot and never let go. Every inch of Sully reeled, wishing for more than he had any right to.

The slippery slide of fingers pressing into him was everything he wanted when he set out tonight. Trembling sensation pulsed through him, the whisper of Elliot's desire burned fever bright over his skin, pleasure riding him roughshod as Elliot curled and stretched his fingers inside. No room for anything but feeling this—right here and now.

"God," he panted, pushing into Elliot's touch. "God, Elliot. Just like that."

"You're beautiful, Warren," Elliot murmured. Sully's heart flipped wildly in his chest hearing his first name from that mouth, breathless, and honest, and *hell*. No one ever said stuff like that to him and meant it. But Elliot did, it was blazing and bright and all around them. "You've no idea how amazing you feel, how sweet and yielding you are. I can't wait to be inside, feel you tight and clutching around my stiff prick."

Sully's stomach muscles clamped down, strangely exulted. He wasn't one for much talking during sex, but with Elliot stroking and rubbing, his husky words were oil on fire, and Sully shivered, a broken whimper wrenched from him.

"Oh fucking—ah. Please just—unh, fuck me already. I can't—I need—Elliot. *Damn it.*"

As Elliot withdrew his fingers, Sully tried to catch his breath, grasping the emerald satin blanket in white-knuckled fists. The slick sounds behind him, and the image they flashed across his mind snatched it away faster than he could pursue. Commanding hands clasped his hips, angled him, and Sully let himself be maneuvered, reveled in giving up control. Elliot's smooth, solid cockhead aligned with his entrance, pushed relentlessly inside, and tight pressure gave way. Nerves firing, muscles spasming, Sully's body accepted the intrusion.

A helpless sound escaped Sully's control. A low, desperate thing. Much louder than Elliot's pleased grunt. Sully's face scorched, but the responding pleasure emanating from Elliot eased the embarrassment. And Sully couldn't hold himself back anyhow, so he quit trying.

Deeper and deeper, Elliot steadily pushed inside until they were flush hips to arse. Gasping with it. Sully shivered in the still aftermath. Elliot closed his mouth on the nape of Sully's neck, teeth grazing, tongue soothing, and Sully bucked back against him. Need hammered in his chest.

"Come on," Sully growled. "I—fuck, just fuck."

"At your pleasure." Elliot's voice was tight with restraint. Even then, a hint of teasing shone through. *Does he ever stop?*

He shifted and complied, pulled back, shoved deep again. Solid hot flesh filled Sully, pushing the breath right out of him. Elliot's thrusts were experimental at first, testing out depths and angles, and Sully somehow knew he was searching for ways to make it better.

It was already perfect. Already amazing. They worked in tandem, fell into a rhythm. Slow and steady and hot and aching.

Sully collapsed forward onto one forearm, reached beneath himself to stroke his own cock. His grip light for fear of spending too fast.

He's so good at this. He's so good.

"You feel—" His breath hitched, and he squeezed his fingers tighter.

"Shit. Christ. Are you touching yourself?" Elliot demanded. Sully moaned his affirmation. Elliot echoed him. Gave several hard, deep thrusts, cursing, and then to Sully's disappointment withdrew entirely. "I need to see. Roll over for me, love."

Disappointment fizzled out in a wave of shaky, urgent lust. Sully hadn't ever—not on his back—not ever. It was too vulnerable. He hadn't thought he was missing out on anything, but the demand in Elliot's rich aroused voice made him want to try with a ferocity he couldn't explain away.

Turning, Sully let Elliot steer him half into his lap. He closed his eyes at Elliot's fevered gaze, too defenseless to hold it. Elliot pushed inside him, a slick, throbbing pressure he trembled with. Sully reached for his own cock again and sought some control. Elliot's hands massaged Sully's thighs, thumbs digging into the creases of his groin. The overwhelming pressure of Elliot's cock drove into him, his gentle hands caressing, tugging, his complete attention focused on Sully. Fierce desire rose and swelled and swirled around them, flooding Sully with emotion. Elliot brushed against that spot inside him over and over, the one that sent jolts of pleasurable sparks cascading up his spine and tightened his balls. Sully cried out, muscles clamping down on release desperately held at bay.

He wanted so badly he could taste it, but didn't want it to be over. Couldn't let it be over. Conflicting imperative impulses warred, and Sully squeezed his eyes shut tighter, tears stinging behind his closed eyelids. He choked them back. God, he hated them. Hated how weak they made him feel.

Suddenly, Elliot froze. He must've sensed something amiss. Sully's heart blocked his throat.

Then Elliot shifted forward, his thumbs swiping Sully's damp lashes. He carefully cradled Sully's face. "Am I hurting you?" Sully couldn't trust his voice, so he shook his head. "Tell me what's wrong."

Shame boiled in Sully's veins, made his closed eyes feel hot and his throat click when he swallowed.

I'm ruining this.

It was wonderful, and he was wrecking it by acting like a crybaby. What the hell was wrong with him? Couldn't he have saved it for later when Elliot would be gone?

"Nothing," Sully finally said, thickly. He bit his lip and forced the scratchy lump in his throat down. "Please, don't stop."

"If you want me to keep going, I need to know you're all right. If you're not...Warren, I can't."

Why does he got to be so sweet?

Sully shut his eyes against the heartfelt concern in those watercolor eyes. He couldn't shield himself as easily from the cool silky worry shrouding Elliot.

"Any other night," he whispered, raw words rushing out ahead of his good sense.

"Pardon?"

Sully opened his eyes and steeled himself. "I wish we'd met any other night. I wish we had longer. Tomorrow...I'm not ready for tonight to be over. I'm going..."

Understanding lit Elliot's face but did nothing to dim the concern. "You're headed for the war." He drew in an unsteady breath, dark blond lashes drifting closed. *Regret.* He pressed his forehead to Sully's, still buried within him. Sully shivered, heart squeezing. "So am I."

It's not fair.

"So am I," Elliot repeated, lashes lifting. Sully got lost in those impassioned eyes. Resolve sprang up and gripped him hard. "But tonight hasn't ended. It won't until the sun comes up. And I'm not going anywhere. Not yet."

Sully's heart soared straight to the stars, expanded and collapsed with the weight of the universe and everything he couldn't face. With everything he wanted and couldn't have. With the one thing he could. "Please."

Elliot's mouth closed over his, urgently kissing as Elliot thrust inside him again. This time Sully let himself cling, let himself hold on to Elliot as tightly as he'd been dying to this whole time. Elliot clung right back, fingers knotting in Sully's hair, grabbing his thigh, guiding him to wrap his legs around Elliot's waist. Fucking him with determination and making it feel so damn good.

They made it last as long as they could. Desperation and need growing between them until they lost themselves in one another. Until the only word Sully remembered was Elliot's name, exactly as promised. He whispered it fiercely, repeatedly. A plea, a prayer.

Sully's body tightened; orgasm close enough it grazed his awareness with every powerful thrust Elliot delivered. His breaths faltered as he strained toward release. His fingernails dug into the slick skin of Elliot's back and the nape of his neck. Their mouths met. Clumsy breaths against sensitive lips, not quite kisses.

Elliot slipped a hand between them, stroked Sully's cock with a firm, glorious grip. "I—God—you," Sully arched up, words melting into a drawn-out moan, pleasure cresting madly. It lashed through him, rushed out in pulsing shocks, shook him apart in euphoric agony.

Somewhere in the midst of it all, Elliot stiffened within him, panting, "Warren."

Sully flattened his palms against Elliot's back, held him close. He sucked in harsh breaths and tried to keep himself from thinking. For a few too-short blissful moments he succeeded.

CHAPTER FIVE

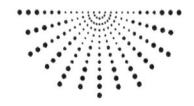

CHARMED. THAT WAS THE only word for it. Elliot was utterly charmed by the man whose firm chest rose and fell beneath his head. He closed his eyes and listened to the steady beating of a strong heart. He stroked his fingers through a tangle of dark chest hair, wisps of it tickling the side of his face and his nose. The masculine scents of cooling sweat and sex teased his nose and made him half-hard again already.

Warren's work-roughened fingers laced with his, stilling Elliot's hand. How had they gotten like that? What did he do for a living?

There were a thousand inane questions he wanted to ask of this man and none of them emerged from his mouth when he finally opened it.

"So you leave tomorrow?" Elliot asked. Like dabbing antiseptic on a wound, it would sting, and then it would heal. Why this should concern him so much was another matter altogether, but he found he did care, deeply, what would become of Warren. Perhaps he was displacing his own fears or perhaps they'd forged a deeper connection than either of them intended. The consequence was the same. Elliot was dreading the unknown with renewed vigor.

Warren hummed a yes. "You?"

Pursing his lips at his own dismay, Elliot's stomach wrung tight. "The same."

Silence. What was Warren thinking? Was he worrying too?

"S'pose you'll be in officer training?"

"Apparently, a college degree, a lucrative family, and a little magic proclaim me fit to lead," Elliot said wryly. He didn't feel fit to lead. A lifetime spent as a pleasure-seeker did not a quality leader make.

Warren's chuckle jostled him, and Elliot smiled in response. "What kind of degree?"

"English. I write terrible poetry I like to imagine is rather good. Do you think that makes much difference in war? I find myself unconvinced."

"Yeah, can't see how that's gonna help."

"Yet, here we are. And you?"

"No degree. I was a private detective of sorts, not that it matters now I'm enlisted. My skill's not flashy enough that I can't work it in front of other soldiers, so they told me I'm going to be at the front somewhere, working with regular troops. No family name to save me either."

Bloody unfair that something so out of someone's control determined how they served. No one chose who they were born to. No one chose how their skill manifested. If Elliot's skill—the one the government knew about—hadn't been short-range, and he'd been born to someone of lesser means, he'd be enlisted too and headed for the kind of carnage that made him want to weep for Warren. "It isn't fair."

"Never is. This time tomorrow I'll be at Camp Devens."

Oh. Now that was interesting. "As will I."

That hung awkward in the space where warm camaraderie had been only moments before.

"We won't be able to fraternize there." Warren sounded apologetic. "Even if we had time, which I doubt, they know about me. That I...have sex with men. So an officer I have no reason to communicate with? They'd assume the worst. They could make my life, and my cousin Anne's, pretty damn uncomfortable if they went public with what they know about me. And I just can't risk that."

He was right. Elliot knew he was right. And it shouldn't hurt so much hearing it. Had he seriously considered seeking Warren out?

It was an impulse. Only wanting a connection to someone in the frightening future. Nothing real. Nothing to worry about. "You're not wrong, unfortunately. They have me over the same barrel. I wasn't as discreet overseas as I am here. No. We can't."

So the only thing on offer was this one night. Elliot had to be satisfied with that, no matter how enchanted he was.

Stretching, Elliot arched his back and took notice of the warm skin he was resting against. He propped himself on one elbow, gaze lingering on Warren's kiss-bruised lips and muddy hazel eyes. What colors might he be able to pick out in the sunlight? His dark hair had dried with an irresistible curl to it. Was the dimness of the lamp concealing highlights? Elliot brushed errant strands from Warren's forehead and willed himself to remember every last eyelash and freckle. He wanted to be able to scribble them in words in the morning so he wouldn't forget.

Something he could carry in his pocket if he was mindful of how he wrote it.

"I suppose you'd like to sleep?" Elliot asked.

"Couldn't if I wanted to." Warren's eyes darted shyly away. Elliot was infatuated. "Maybe if I knew what to expect tomorrow." He reached up and tucked a lock of Elliot's hair behind his ear. Elliot's lashes fluttered shut with the sweetness of the gesture. His heart aching in a familiar way. This was how it always started. "Why? Do you want to sleep?"

"Not a chance. I'd much rather talk to you. I'll sleep when I'm dead." He winced at his own words. Warren blinked a couple of times before he appeared to recover.

"So poetry, huh? Can't say I've read much of it, but my ma used to read me some from a book Da gave her before I was born. Always liked those. She said they reminded her of stories her ma told her back in Ireland."

Elliot rather desperately wanted to know more. "By whom?"

A furrow creased Warren's brow as he thought. "Can't remember the fella's name, but I still remember some lines."

"Recite away, perhaps I can guess."

"I can't think of how it starts…um. Come away, O human child. To the waters and the wild. With a faery, hand in hand. For the world's more full of weeping than you can understand." Warren paused forehead wrinkling further in concentration, eyes distant. His head tilted slightly as if he was listening to his mother's words and repeating them. "Where the wave of moonlight glosses the dim gray sands with light, far off by furthest Rosses we foot it all the night…" He blinked rapidly, grimacing. "And then there's something about dancing and the hills above Glen-Car, but my memory's shite. I always wished I packed that book when…well anyway, that's all I can think of."

Elliot smiled triumphantly. "Yeats," he declared. "It was published in a book called *The Wanderings of—*"

"Oisin and Other Poems," Warren finished, grinning beautifully back at him. "That's right, I guess this was the one that Ma read the most from it, because I hardly remember bits of the others."

"It's a great story, visually evocative and nostalgic. Mysterious beings enticing and beguiling a child away with promises to shield him from the harshness of reality. It has a sort of sinister undertone if you think of the way old myths go." Elliot's face heated. He was rambling out an unasked-for analysis. Only bores did that. "I'm glad I recalled the author, perhaps you'll read it again someday."

Warren glanced up at Elliot from under long dark lashes, his impish eyes glittering. Gorgeous. And clearly more appreciative of the analysis—or of Elliot in general—than he'd thought. "I could listen to you talk like that all night if we had longer. It's fascinating, really. But I can think of a better way to spend the rest of the time we've got left."

"I'm sure you can," Elliot murmured, obliging when Warren tilted his chin up for a kiss.

Yes, charmed was absolutely the word. And if Elliot had any sense he'd climb out of the bed that instant and walk out the door before he lost every tender feeling brewing inside of him to soft lips, curious fingers, and a man destined for the front.

Then again, no one in their right mind suspected Elliot had sense to begin with. Why prove them incorrect now?

CHAPTER SIX

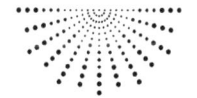

May 28, 1917
Camp Devens, Massachusetts

ELLIOT NARROWLY AVOIDED THE small fist on a collision course with his face. The moderate temperature and occasional brisk breeze did little to prevent sweat from sticking the olive wool of his uniform to his damp skin. It restricted his movements as he twisted to grab at Cadet Winifred Bell, Bellona as he'd dubbed her for a Roman goddess of war. She was the only woman in their program, and despite doubts, she'd proven time and again she belonged there. Precisely as she was doing once more.

Elliot's fingers grazed her arm. She sucked in a sharp breath as he focused on a small burst of horror. Flashing out of existence in front of him, she wasn't gone for long. A foot to the back of his knee knocked him off balance. He turned his stumble into a spin and came back up facing her. They panted and assessed one another for weakness. Bellona's raven hair was pulled into a tight bun. Her face shone with perspiration; determination etched in every feature.

"Oh come, Stone, is that all you've got? I think I could win this in my sleep." She flashed her teeth.

"I doubt that very much." Elliot winked at her, turning to keep her in his sight as she circled him.

One moment Bellona was laughing at his theatrics, the next she appeared directly in front of him, using his surprise to shove him to the ground. She landed on his waist and scrambled to pin down his wrists.

Grunting at the impact, he tried to buck her off. He managed to roll with her, any compunctions about fighting a woman lost over weeks of having his arse gleefully handed to him. Elliot got a hand on her neck, and she went limp beneath him, admitting defeat. Her eyes went watery like she might cry. Was he hurting her? He relaxed his grip infinitesimally and suddenly found himself pressed face down in the dirt. Her full weight on his back pinned him. Her hands crushed his wrists into the dirt. If it didn't hurt quite so much, he might have enjoyed the sensation of being helpless beneath a strong woman.

"All right," he grumbled. "You've won. I can't believe I fell for the sad eyes. Again."

She snickered. "And you were so close, too."

There was a hum of grudging approval from nearby. Colonel Cooper. He'd been one of Bellona's largest critics though he'd come to respect her abilities and grit, if not women in general. Elliot couldn't see how being a woman mattered a whit when she continued to prove herself capable, but he couldn't deny most men believed they had no place in battle. Most men simply didn't pay enough attention to who the women around them were, or they would notice plenty more they oughtn't underestimate.

"Excellent work, Cadet Bell. Cadet Stone, in the field, you finish the job. Let your guard down like that, you'll be dead. I expect more from you, young man."

Elliot held back his grimace; Cooper wasn't wrong. He couldn't afford to be sentimental when it came down to it. That didn't make it feel any better to accept the criticism. "Yes, sir."

"Go again." He moved away to observe another sparring match.

By the time they were all dismissed to lunch, Elliot had scraped in a win by the tips of his fingers. Every muscle in his body protested its use.

After he helped Bellona to her feet, they wandered their separate ways to wash up before eating. Cadet Swift, Ollie as he'd enthusiastically introduced himself at the first opportunity, joined Elliot on the walk, bumping his shoulder in a friendly gesture as they strolled. His golden hair was shorn short. Attractive seafoam eyes sparkled above his bright white grin, set in a delicate, nearly feminine, face. He was the first friend Elliot had made upon arrival, and one he was glad of. He'd have been bored to tears if he hadn't anyone to speak with.

"Better luck against her than me?" Swift asked, cocky with good reason.

"Tied. One win apiece. She's scrappier than you, but at least she's got a vulnerability."

"Hey, I have one too," Swift argued.

"Yes, but not when you've only yourself to worry about protecting."

Flashing him another bright smile, Swift dipped his head in acknowledgement. "True."

They'd sparred earlier. Elliot's skills only functioned properly if his opponent lacked defenses against him. He was forced into using horror more often than he liked. Today, he'd attempted it to ascertain if it functioned in the face of Swift's shielding since euphoria hadn't. The result was less than stellar. It left Elliot open to a well-timed knee in the groin that paved Swift's path to victory. Which was utterly humiliating since Elliot was not only a few inches taller than the boy, but Swift's build was even slimmer than his. Magic more than made up the difference between them.

Elliot vastly preferred when euphoria provided a sufficient distraction to gain the upper hand. None of the cadets had the reaction Warren had that night in the lounge, only the typical extreme burst of happiness or a lesser form of giddiness depending on their susceptibility.

Was it something particular about Warren that had caused such a response in him? Or was it that he—or more accurately they—had been thinking rather sordid thoughts from the moment their gazes first met? Elliot wasn't sure which notion he preferred. Self-preservation insisted he not dwell on either.

Walking on, Swift chatted idly about the rest of his morning. As they passed a company of soldiers resting in groups, Elliot's gaze met familiar hazel eyes, brownish-green more dazzling in the full sunlight. He almost tripped over his feet. Undefined mangled emotion rose in his chest. His heart tumbled. Surprise, followed rapidly by something warm crossed Warren's face, and Elliot wished he could walk over, simply say hello and discover how he was faring. He appeared healthy if not quite happy. Who would be in these conditions?

Under no circumstances could Elliot do so. It wasn't safe. It was bad enough they were staring at each other like this. Someone was bound to notice.

"Stone?" Swift's voice was slightly exasperated. Elliot realized he must have missed a question. He looked away from Warren with a pang of regret and apologized for his lack of attention.

Lunch consisted of bland fare that Elliot forced himself to eat. If he was to spend the entire afternoon in a classroom, listening to lectures on battle strategy and theories of warfare, he required sufficient fuel. Early on, he'd been informed he ought to get used to the quality. It was only likely to deteriorate overseas.

Listening idly to the voices surrounding him, he pulled a face at the texture of overcooked meat and limp vegetables. Christ, what he wouldn't give for a meal made by Mrs. Roberts. Her succulent roast duck was heavenly. If he imagined it strongly enough, might the memory block his sense of taste?

"Still too good for the food, huh?" Hoffman asked, voice husky from disuse. He was in his thirties, and broad shouldered. He was average in height and appearance with a slightly crooked nose—which Elliot had to assume had been broken when he'd been rude to the wrong person—and dark, intent eyes. Perhaps in another life Elliot would've found him alluring in a hateful-fucking sort of way. However, he was all but certain Hoffman wasn't interested in men, and secondly, in no form was he interested in Elliot. Nor was Elliot interested in him, the bore.

"The food's still rubbish. I happen to believe rodents are too good for it as well, if it makes a difference," Elliot said, deliberately haughty.

"At least you're actually eating it, even if you look like you'd rather die than take another bite."

Elliot pushed his lips out as if he were considering it, and Hoffman glanced at the ceiling, presumably searching for patience.

"Oh, leave him alone Hoffman," Bellona said, seated on Elliot's right. "Just because your tastebuds clearly died decades ago, doesn't mean Stone's wrong."

Cracking a grin, Elliot nodded at her. "As she said."

Hoffman's lips quirked at that. My god, was that actually a sense of humor peeking out?

Conversation from a nearby group of cadets filled the momentary silence at their table.

"Of course the German's have got skilled soldiers at the front, you dolt! My brother's over there fighting with the French and he said in a letter they're even using them out in the open sometimes."

"If that's true, how come all of Europe don't know about magic?"

"Reporters aren't allowed at the front much for one. For two, my brother says they come up with ways to spin what happened so the troops don't get all freaked out. Like, he said one time there was a necromancer and when she raised the freshly dead, everyone got told the Germans came up with a drug to delay death for a few minutes."

"And people believed that bull?"

The cadet shrugged. "People don't want to believe in magic, do they? They want to believe in the world as they know it."

Bellona drew Elliot's attention back to the table when she said, "My brother is over there too. He's a pilot for the French Army. He flew over a pyrokinetic once who almost caused him to crash."

Swift sucked in a breath through his teeth. "I'm glad he didn't. Is he—?"

"Perfectly fine, according to his last letter." There was concern in Bellona's voice. "If they're using those kinds of skills out in the open, imagine what they're doing where we can't see."

That grim thought silenced them all. Elliot grimaced at his food and sighed, appetite vanished.

Later that evening, he stretched out on his spring and straw mattress., the iron cot squealing as he tried to find a position that didn't hurt. His overstrained muscles vehemently protested the lack of softness to rest on. As he draped his arm over his eyes, he groaned dramatically.

A soft laugh issued from the bed beside his. "You keep scrunching your face up and rolling around like a dog trying to get comfortable," Swift pointed out as if it had escaped Elliot's notice.

"Yes well," Elliot muttered. How he mustered the energy to do even that much was a mystery. Two damned weeks of far more rigorous and prolonged activity than he'd endured his entire life was taking its toll, and there was no end in sight. Was this supposed to get easier? "My kingdom for a larger bed."

"Do you actually have one of those?"

Elliot peeked out from under his arm and caught sight of seafoam eyes watching him. "A larger bed or a kingdom?"

Swift's mouth curved with amusement. "A kingdom, you dolt."

Elliot laughed, moving his arm beneath his head to prop it up. "Would I be here if I did?"

"You do act like the ruler of a small nation sometimes. The way you push back against the colonel's orders, I shouldn't like to be in your position when you do."

Elliot winced at the reminder. His distaste for authority kept getting him into trouble. The first few days he hadn't wanted to use horror at all. Colonel Cooper had known he was holding back and imposed gruelling physical activity designed to cow Elliot. It wore him down but didn't stop him from pushing at boundaries.

The low voices of the others in the long room having their own conversations before lights out provided enough privacy that Elliot felt confident no one else was listening, and he admitted, "I've never been one to conform to rules. My mouth fires before I can think better of it. At least my father will be glad of the military's attempt to break me of the habit."

"Oh, I don't know, you don't seem so easily broken to me." That came with a cheeky grin. Elliot bit back his own in response, rolling his eyes instead. Swift was remarkably attractive, but Elliot's mind—and at least two other parts he could think of—were occupied with someone else entirely. It was unfair when he couldn't do a thing about it.

He needed to halt the lingering feelings he had for Warren. Even if he was prone to falling in love easily. Even if he was most of the way there by the time they parted in the skyscraper shadows of early morning. They never lasted, these passions he found himself absorbed in. If he put his mind to actively ending it, his willpower would prevail. Obsessing over Warren would only end in heartbreak. Hadn't he had enough of those?

Elliot shifted and flopped his arm back over his face, wriggling once more to get comfortable. "Yes, be that as it may, broken or not, I am rather in need of sleep. Not all of us are eighteen."

"Nineteen," Swift corrected firmly, with the rigid sense of injustice only the young retained when someone guessed their age too low.

"My deepest apologies, how could I possibly have failed to guess at that extra year? You're correct, it does show terribly. Just as the many, many years I have on you must."

Swift snorted and Elliot heard the squealing springs that signaled him moving about on his own bed. "I can't possibly be convinced that you're any older than twenty-five."

Elliot grinned lazily. "You've got me there. Exactly that and I feel every day of it and thirty more."

"All right, all right. Get some rest, Stone. I'll leave you be. I've got to write back to my little sister anyway. It's her birthday next week. She'll be twelve."

"Wish her a wonderful birthday for me, then," Elliot sleepily mumbled.

Swift's soft chuckle was the last thing Elliot heard as he nodded off.

∼

ALL-ENCOMPASSING BLACK STRETCHED out in every direction. Labored breaths heaved all around Elliot. There was a moment of confusion when he couldn't tell whose dream he was in. Then the shelling started. Explosions burst around him, lighting up the moonless night in white lightning flashes. Guns fired deafening shots. Bullets tore up the earth. Smoke drifted over moss and dirt and horrible rivers of gore and blood.

Amid the chaos, Warren knelt stock-still, staring with anguished eyes at a lifeless body on the ground before him.

Elliot had a policy—a well-established and essential policy—do not interfere with the dreams of those he hadn't received waking consent from. It was deeply unjust and overly intimate to appear in someone's mind uninvited. And if they remembered the next morning it could be terribly complicated. He had a *policy*, and yet...

The anguish transforming Warren's face was a hook and reel dragging Elliot forward. As he neared, Elliot recognized the crumpled bloodied form on the damp earth as his own. A lump lodged in his throat. Warren was cradling the corpse's head, murmuring indecipherable words that hurt to hear. Guilt propelled Elliot farther. He wasn't even certain *why* he felt miserable, he hadn't done anything to feel guilty about. This wasn't his dream. It wasn't his fault. The flushed, wounded sensation in his chest remained, and he was compelled to act.

Two more steps placed him directly in front of his own body. A shiver trembled down his spine. "Warren."

He made no response. Elliot cleared his throat and reached down, palm sliding over the curve of a perfectly shaven jaw, tilting Warren's face. Stubbornly, Warren refused to follow the physical directive and look up, his subconscious resisting. "Warren, it's Elliot. Look at me. I'm not dead. I'm right here. All you need to do is see."

Blinking hard, Warren's long lashes stuck wetly together. A single teardrop trickled from each wide eye, cascading over cold cheeks. One pooled against Elliot's thumb.

The noise around them ground suddenly to a halt. Elliot's heart froze. Then Warren's gaze fixated on him, and his heart took off a thousand times faster.

Brow furrowing, Warren blinked again. The night around them brightened as his gaze sharpened. Elliot forced his own attention to reshaping the dream. He whisked away the bodies and war-ravaged soil, then replaced them with unblemished grass, a clear summer night, a bright full moon and a swath of glittering stars shimmering above instead of artillery fire flashing. A warm breeze ruffled their hair.

"Elliot," Warren whispered, choked, disbelieving. "But you're dead." He looked down, as if expecting to find the body. His eyes widened with surprise when he didn't, and his bow-shaped lips pressed together. Trembled.

"I'm all right. As are you." Elliot stroked his thumb over the soft skin of Warren's cheek.

Warren's confused gaze lifted from Elliot's shiny black shoes and met his own once more. "I don't understand. I saw you shot. Saw them all shot."

A sharp pain lodged below Elliot's ribs. "I expect you did, but

I've the great pleasure of informing you none of it was real. You're dreaming, love."

Warren seemed to process that for a moment, wetting his lips. Memories darted to the forefront of Elliot's thoughts, an urgent yearning he stuffed down. He was already intruding here; he wouldn't do *that*.

"So...I'm dreaming you? You're not real?" Warren asked, attempting to solve a puzzle Elliot hadn't yet given him all of the pieces to.

"You're dreaming, and I *am* real. If you'll recall, I informed you I had secrets. This is one."

"But how are you here?"

Elliot lifted a shoulder and offered a nervous smile. He finally noticed he was looming over Warren and moved to sit beside him instead. Warren didn't match Elliot's relaxed pose with his legs stretched out before him and crossed at the ankles, instead he huddled with his arms wrapped around his knees, still visibly shaking off the effects of his terror. "I haven't the faintest how it happens. How does any of it, really? The magic? I go to sleep as anyone might. Then I open my eyes and find myself in a dream not my own. Quite honestly if it was my own, I'd likely die of shock."

"Why?"

"Oh. I've never experienced a dream of my own. I always appear in another's. Most often, people I—" Elliot cut himself off, face heating. Why couldn't he still his tongue? It kept getting him in trouble. Lord knew seeing Warren around camp in his too-snug uniform hadn't done Elliot any favors, but he was supposed to have been forgetting about Warren, not nursing a growing tenderness. Not getting so attached he invaded the man's dreams. What happened to willpower?

"People you what?"

"Uh...care for. People I'm close to. Generally speaking."

"Oh." Color spotted Warren's cheeks. His rigid hold on his knees loosened. "And now you're here."

Elliot's own face must be scarlet—it burned enough. He cleared his throat to buy time. "Now I'm here, yes."

Warren studied him, lips pushed out thoughtfully. "When you say c—"

"While we're on the subject of dreams and entering another person's," Elliot hastily cut off that line of questioning, embarrassed quite enough for one night. "I must apologize. I wouldn't usually interfere without permission, but you were..." He shook his head softly. "I couldn't walk away from you like that. Not when I could offer assistance."

Warren's smile was indulgent in a way Elliot wasn't sure he deserved. "I'm glad you didn't. What didja mean, walk away? Where would you go?"

"Hmm? Someone else's dream. I travel between them. I often visit my sisters, May and Hazel. I used to help with my mother's nightmares." Elliot stared up at the magnificent stars and gossamer clouds streaking the sky. "I can leave now if you'd like. Since it's all in order."

A frantic hand grabbed hold of Elliot's shoulder and he met panicked eyes. "Please don't. I want you to stay. Please."

Elliot melted like he'd sunk into a hot bath, resolve no stronger than a wisp of steam. Still, he gave it one more attempt. "You might not wish I did so in the morning. If you recall any of this." Warren's eyebrows lowered and drew together. Elliot oughtn't be so cryptic. "While you sleep, inhibitions lower, defenses peel away. It's far too easy to say or do things you'd regret on waking."

"Puh-leeze." Warren rolled his eyes. "I wouldn't regret

anything with you. You're the most interesting man I ever met. If I could've, I would've spent so much more time talking to you. Maybe never would've stopped. Told you all my secrets too."

Warren's gaze was so sincere Elliot had to repress a grin. "Perhaps you wouldn't, but are you typically so free with that sort of praise when you're not seducing someone? Or are you only expressing those thoughts because at this moment you don't possess the foresight to consider consequences or how you might feel about saying it later?"

Lips pursing, Warren stared out at the grass. He was quiet for long enough that Elliot got lost examining stars, attempting to pick out half-remembered constellations. Finally, Warren said, "I get what you're worried about. Probably wouldn't be so easy for me to admit I wanna spend time with you out there, or that I hate I never got the chance. At least not out loud."

"Exactly."

"But..."

"Yes?"

"This is a dream right?" At Elliot's nod, Warren continued. "If it's a dream, will I even remember it tomorrow? I don't usually, except awful snatches lately."

"Then probably not, no. Most people I've had occasion to interact with haven't remembered much. Our encounters seem to remain locked in the subconscious."

"Right. So what's the big deal. I won't even know if I say or do anything dumb."

"It's wrong because it violates your right to privacy whether you're consciously aware of the violation or not, Warren. Your mind ought to be safe. And *I'll* remember. That's not right."

"Didja think my mind was safe when you showed up?" Warren

asked, his stare far too perceptive as a hint of fear crept back into his voice.

Elliot sighed. His shoulders slumped. Damned if he did, damned if he didn't. Guilty no matter which way he turned. "No, however—"

"So stay, then. Keep me safe in here, because it's sure as hell not gonna be safe if you're not with me. At least in here it can be easier if I've got you to keep me from dreaming about what it'll be like over there. I don't want to admit it and seem weak but I'm scared, Elliot. I'm so scared, all the time."

How could he say no to the pleading in Warren's voice? Or to the distress plain as day on his face? "All right. I'll stay to keep away the nightmares and help you rest peacefully."

Warren smiled triumphantly, then it dimmed. "Will you come back tomorrow? It's been hell every night if I'm being honest. I really don't want to be alone. Please come back?"

Elliot waffled. He oughtn't agree to this. Warren was already confessing things Elliot suspected he would hate revealing in the waking world. Christ, he knew better.

"I'll do my best," he said. Warren brightened, throwing himself at Elliot. Almost knocked Elliot over as Warren tucked his face into Elliot's shoulder and wrapped his arms around his neck in enthusiastic thanks. It startled a chuckle out of Elliot. He allowed himself a brief embrace before pulling away. "I'll come back if we can agree to abide by some rules."

Warren made a show of rolling his eyes again as he sat back, but the brilliant smile never left his mischievous lips. "Rules?"

One word. One word and the smug flirt made it into precisely the opposite of what Elliot had meant it to be. Grant him mercy. In any other circumstance he could think of a thousand witty responses. Those would only get him in trouble with his conscience, so he kept his voice from conveying how much he'd like to offer a vastly different sort of reply.

"Indeed. Rules such as: we refrain from touching one another. Absolutely no physical intimacy. I won't take advantage of you in that way, not here." He struggled to disregard the disappointment on Warren's face. An immensely difficult task. "Further, if you tell me to leave I will. If you tell me not to return, I'll stay away. Nothing you say here will be held against you, now, or in the future. Nor will I expect anything from you in the world outside."

"Can't say I like the first rule," Warren said, sounding reluctant. "But if it means you'll come back, I'll learn to live with it."

This was a terrible idea. A terrible, horrible, genuinely awful idea. The kind of idea that would inevitably incinerate them both and salt the scorched earth. It was bound to have unintended consequences. But when Warren looked at him so gratefully, Elliot couldn't bring himself to regret whatever accident of fate had deposited him here. He'd been wondering how Warren was faring since they'd parted outside The Hotel La Salle in the early morning hours. Curiosity that only deepened whenever they'd encountered one another at a distance in the weeks since. Now he might see that curiosity sated.

There was always an infinitesimal chance this wouldn't lead to utter ruin.

CHAPTER SEVEN

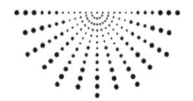

THE GROUND SHOOK IN violent tremors that rattled Sully's teeth. Thunderclaps reverberated overhead unnaturally often, so loud his ears hurt. Sully shielded his head and squeezed his eyes shut tighter. Dirt sprinkled him with every impact, the entire structure a breath from collapse. He'd be buried down here, crushed under the rubble.

Better than facing what was outside. Screams, cries, the rapid blasts of heavy gunfire. He was a miserable coward. They needed him. He was supposed to pick up his damn gun and—

The blasts halted abruptly. Decay, death, and damp earth replaced by something…soft?

Fluttering open his wet eyes, lashes catching briefly before parting, a figure swam into focus. Beautiful, blond, and polished in the same gray suit Sully pictured him in so often. His thoughts went fuzzy or the world around him did, remade the way Elliot wanted it to be. Gone were the garish images and sensations

Sully's mind had cast up of an inevitable future, replaced by soft and luxurious surroundings.

He found himself on an ornately carved rosewood settee, deep blue velvet plush beneath him and at his back. A lovely dark fur pelt appeared across his lap. Sully startled at the sight of his own slightly shabby black cuffs. He was in his finest suit, the clothes he'd worn on the night they met. The plain dark green tie Anne gave him for Christmas last year was snug at his throat. Sully reached up and loosened it and unbuttoned the collar, reeling from the normalcy.

A fire burned cheerfully before him in a beautiful white stone fireplace, throwing dancing shadows along creamy mint-colored walls.

"Am I dreaming again?" he murmured, glancing around. Elliot perched on the settee facing Sully with one long, well-shaped leg folded beneath him.

"Correct."

"You came back." Relief made Sully's grin stretch. Elliot had given him every indication he would, but Sully didn't put much faith in words. Men lied all the time—to their friends, their partners, and most emphatically to the men they fucked. He'd been called enough sweet names in the dark and ignored outright or worse during the day to be deeply acquainted with disappointment.

"I'm sorry I was late," Elliot said. Wonderfully considerate.

Sully lifted a shoulder, nonplussed. "Can't expect you'll always be asleep when I am. S'pose I'll have to get used to dreams like this. We're not even over there yet and I'm already cracking up."

Elliot frowned, his full mouth pinching. "You're doing nothing of the sort. I expect most soldiers are having nightmares, it's natural."

"But it ain't. That's the problem." He hadn't meant to let that slip. *Secrets are secrets for a reason. Even if you want to spill them.*

"What do you mean?"

Sully bit his lip, uncertain. What'd Elliot tell him about saying things too easy in dreams? Maybe he shouldn't.

But if he didn't talk about it here, now, who else would he be able to talk about it with?

No one that's who, because he wasn't about to voice his fears where he'd face scorn and judgment. Not even in letters to Anne. She was distraught enough over his circumstances, he couldn't burden her further. And as much as Edie was his friend, she was also his boss. He didn't want her thinking he was defective. What if she thought he couldn't work cases when he made it home?

"Look, you had the secret about the whole dream-thing—"

"Dreamwalking," Elliot supplied.

"Right, dreamwalking. And I... the night we met, you asked if I was always confident of my reception. And I said something flippant probably, but the real answer was yes. I know because I feel things," Sully announced in a rush, muscles tensing in anticipation of Elliot's inevitable recoil.

He arched one light brow. "Yes, well, some of us are better at sensing the interest of other men."

Sully's face flushed with heat. Apparently his grand revelation wasn't as revealing as he'd thought. "No, you crackpot. Emotions, it's other people's emotions I feel. It's a skill. Been able to do it since I was a child. Maybe since I was born. Dunno. I can't remember ever not feeling them."

Two brows up now, Elliot examined Sully's face. Did he think it was a joke? Sully met his scrutiny with seriousness.

"You're an empath?" Elliot asked. "I've met one or two, but they're mostly twitchy sorts. You seem steadier."

Sully almost laughed, would have if nerves weren't wriggling in his guts, twisting them all up. "You might be too if you felt what we do. But have you really? Met others like me I mean?"

"In Paris, a lovely French woman. She was a bit eccentric. And in Edinburgh, there was a gentleman with eyes you wouldn't believe, but he couldn't stand most people. Including me. He said my feelings were too loud."

"Huh. I haven't ever met anyone else who is a—what was that word you used? Empath? I guess I wouldn't know if I had. It's not like I go around blabbing about it." He was rambling and couldn't stop, but it wasn't as if there was a book that laid out the vast variations in power or what each type was called. Since he didn't like to discuss this particular skill, he hadn't ever asked anyone. Ma hadn't known the word, or she would've used it. "Can't say I've met many skilled individuals I trust in the first place and then, like you said, we've all got secrets, don't we?"

"We do indeed. Why don't you trust those you do meet?"

"Oh, I meet them through my job. The types of cases the agency sends me out on aren't to get to know good friendly folks. I foil criminals mainly, using their skills to steal, cause havoc, sometimes far worse. We consult with the police. They don't know they're dealing with magic, just that Edie gets results. But generally if it's not a serious crime, it's a warning from us and we keep tabs on them. Those types aren't prone to heart to hearts. And even if they were I don't trust them."

"Right. That does make sense." Elliot shifted forward to rest his forearms on his thighs. "We've gotten off topic. How does being an empath relate to your night terrors?"

Sully released a gusty sigh. How could he say the next part without sounding like a coward? Even with his inhibitions lowered he struggled with himself.

"I'm picking up on everyone's worry and fear and excitement, and I can't even get away from it in my sleep. I'm already dreading what it'll be like over there with so many people hurt and suffering, dying and scared. It's almost knocking me off my feet here and half the fellas I meet are thrilled they're going."

The official draft had only just gotten underway as far as the public knew. Those whose magic had brought them to the attention of the government knew differently. Men like him and Elliot had been approached and informed of their precarious positions, forced into signing up. He'd expected more to be like them, reluctant, but this group proved otherwise. Within the first day it became abundantly clear they were caught up in patriotism and fighting for their country, signed up out of some sense of civic duty Sully lacked. It was hard to feel patriotic about dying for a country that required him to hide so much of who he was.

"Doesn't exactly sound pleasant."

"Guess I'll get used to it after a while. Adjust and whatnot. But what's it gonna do to me if I get used to feeling all that pain?" Sully shivered. He'd barely let himself consider any of this, let alone spoken it. "I might not remember much of my dreams when I'm awake but I remember the terrifying sensations and feelings. I wake up feeling like I didn't sleep at all. Like I'm not resting and replenishing properly. It's only going to get harder."

"Warren."

"I'm not trying to guilt you into coming back all the time. I just…" Sully shook his head, watching the fire. He tried to drag his thoughts away from this. He didn't want to talk about himself anymore. It was too pathetic, showing off his weak spots. "Never mind. Tell me about you. How has it been for you? Every time I see you, I wonder how those soft hands are doing."

Elliot looked like he didn't want to talk about himself either, but he finally answered. "Unpleasant. I despise rules, I despise discipline, and I despise men who think I'm too delicate to be capable of fighting. My hands will never recover, but I can live with that."

The left corner of Sully's mouth twitched up, teasing, and relieved Elliot submitted to the change of topic. "You're stronger than you look. I thought so the night we met."

Elliot pulled a face. "I'm not *small*, you're just built marginally larger." Sully snickered. "Oh not like that. I'm still taller than you, even if I'm slimmer." A muffled laugh shook Sully's shoulders. At Elliot's grin, Sully's heart thumped in his ribcage.

He's too attractive when he does that. How's anyone think around him, let alone figure out what to say back?

"I think this whole process is far more tedious and trying than it needs to be," Elliot said, turning serious. "I understand the basic principles at heart: break the soldiers down, build them up as a cohesive, stronger unit. But really, must we live in such difficult circumstances prior to being shunted across the globe and dying in the muck?"

That froze Sully to the bones faster than an icy winter sky opening up in a torrent. "Don't talk like that. You're not allowed to die, got me? And it's not so bad. Plenty of people got it worse. 'Least we've got beds, roofs over our heads, and three meals a day."

Wrinkling his nose, Elliot shifted to lean away, placing his arm along the back of the rosewood. "You have a point, but they aren't me. I'm not at all used to shared living quarters. How on God's green earth does one find a moment's privacy?"

Sully couldn't help a wry smirk at that. "Oh, there's ways. You'll get used to it."

Elliot grimaced. "I suppose I must, but you ought to know it's under extremely heavy protest."

Covering his mouth to hide a smile, Sully shifted so his position mirrored Elliot's, resting his back against the arm of the settee. "Were you spoiled all your life then?"

Elliot's lips curved upward, mostly amused, a little self-mocking. "Compared to most? Undoubtedly. It's hard to fathom many people having more than I did. My childhood was unpleasant, nonetheless. I was small, shy, and sensitive. You must know how boys generally react to those attributes. I grew and things got better. I was sent to school when my mother felt I was sufficiently capable of restraining my magic. My father would've preferred to send me sooner but sending me late was preferable to revealing my nature."

"What was that like? Being sent away for school?"

Elliot's face tightened.

"Frightening at first. I didn't know what to expect. My brothers told ghastly stories. In the end, I enjoyed the experience. My peers liked me—or at least enjoyed looking at me. One can never be quite sure which it is, can they?" Elliot rubbed at his jaw, and Sully's gaze followed his long fingers massaging over flawless skin. "And I did decently. I was never caught getting into trouble. Caught is the important word in that sentence. I got up to all sorts of—anyway I'm terribly boring, going on about myself."

"No, I'm fascinated," Sully murmured, and he was. Images of Elliot younger and infinitely more vulnerable flashed before his eyes. What trouble had he gotten into? What was he like back then? What interested him, made his heart race or tears prick at his eyes? Sully suddenly, vividly, wanted to know him inside and out. He couldn't decide what to ask first.

"I daresay," Elliot replied dryly.

"I'm serious. You're so…" Sully groped for the right words and found none to encompass the interest he felt.

Elliot's smile was scornful. "Self-obsessed? I am aware, trust me."

"No, that's not what I was going to say. Not that it's not true." Sully grinned at Elliot's scoff. "I think I was gonna say that you're so intriguing. I want to know all about you."

Elliot's eyes lit up, lashes flickering slightly. "Flatterer."

Rubbing the back of his neck, Sully hunched his shoulders. "Hardly. No one would accuse me of that."

"I just did."

Sully glanced upward and forced himself to sit straighter. "But I'm not. Flattering you, I mean."

There was a short silence, and Sully watched the muscles in Elliot's face move, surprised he couldn't interpret the expressions. "I suppose I can't deny I'm equally interested in you."

Sully's skin tingled. He was hardly interesting.

Orphaned twice over, barely eking out a sustainable existence, he was a disaster more often than he wasn't. The interest on Elliot's features seemed genuine. Sully's eyes were too wide, he blinked and shifted as if he was only getting more comfortable. Inside something warm and fragile curled around his heart.

"So, can you make this dream into anything?" Sully asked, a wild attempt to deflect attention.

Elliot's expression was quizzical, and no wonder when Sully jumped to an entirely new topic without warning. He probably seemed odd. "I can."

Licking his dry lips, Sully pushed up to stand, the fur pooling around his feet. "How 'bout instead of just sitting around, you take me to some of the places you've visited. You said you traveled a lot, right? There's got to be somewhere more entertaining than this room."

Elliot seemed thoughtful, lips forming an obscenely attractive pout, then his face brightened. "Excellent idea. Let's start with Paris. You'll love it."

CHAPTER EIGHT

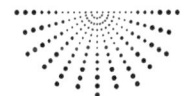

AUGUST 15, 1917
Camp Devens, Massachusetts

IN THE AFTERNOON, ELLIOT was appointed to lead a group of soldiers in a race through the obstacle course in an all-out fight to the finish. Usually they held themselves back, not actually allowed to injure one another. They'd just been informed that wasn't to be the case today. Their group rankings were going to determine assignments in Europe. The first to cross the line would be teamed with French Army soldiers in elite units who would operate away from the front lines. The slowest would be leading enlisted soldiers at the front, concealing their magic to the best of their ability unless it was required to combat skilled German soldiers.

Elliot's gut twisted. He didn't want to do either of those things, but he didn't have a choice. He had a team to think of. Hoffman, Swift, and Bellona were counting on him as their leader in this race and he couldn't let them down. Each of them deserved to be on an elite team where they wouldn't be involved in the heavy fighting at the front lines, where they stood a higher chance of survival. And if they got through this race first, he could deliver that.

Considering the four of them, weighing each skill, Elliot focused on choosing a plan of attack. He had five minutes to form a proposal and communicate it to them. Scenarios tripped over one another as he played them out.

Finally, he motioned the others closer and pitched his voice low and quiet. Bellona was by far their best shot at winning, she could transport up to two with her as far as she could see. "Right. I suspect our greatest chance will be for Bellona to transport Swift and me far enough ahead that I'm able to get a wide start on the others and make my way to the finish. They'll return for you," he said to Hoffman, who could prevent others noticing him so long as they didn't know where to look. "As I tackle the remainder. If necessary, I'll hold anyone who approaches the finish back until you arrive, though I don't anticipate any such occurrences. No one else can transport."

Bellona nodded her agreement. Hoffman scowled, but that wasn't unusual. Swift grinned broadly. "I assume I'll be along for the ride, shielding?"

"Precisely." Elliot glanced at Hoffman, his heavy dark brows drawn down low with irritation. "Does anyone have any suggestions?"

"I can't wait at the start," Hoffman grunted, crossing his arms. "The others will be anticipating it. They all know we've got her, and they'll expect we'll use her, so they'll be on the lookout for me hiding. Putting me out of commission to keep you from winning is their only shot and I'll be easy pickings for most of them." He said that last part with distaste, as if the idea he wasn't stronger than every other cadet in the program was a sore spot.

Hell. Hoffman was right. Everyone knew the team Bellona was on had the largest advantage. Thus far, she'd won more than she'd lost. Only a few critical moments existed where their opponents wouldn't know where Hoffman was, then they would be on him with the intent to incapacitate him and prevent their team from crossing the finish together. Elliot's mind bounded ahead, searching for a solution.

"I'll stay behind," Swift volunteered. "They can't hurt me. Well, they could if they worked together long enough, but so long as Bellona's quick, I should be fine."

Elliot knew from experience just how resilient Swift was, but there would be a lot of people targeting him. It rankled to leave him behind and yet it was the only option. If Elliot remained alone he would be easily overcome, if he stayed with Swift, he would weaken him considerably.

Evaluating Swift's face for any signs of discomfort, he was met only with big, trusting eyes. Elliot sighed inwardly. Swift was so young it was hard not to be overprotective, hard to remember he was capable. "Right. One jump should take her moments, then Hoffman and I will make a mad dash from there to the third obstacle where Bellona can fetch us after she's returned and brought you to the finish."

All parties agreed just as the whistle sounded to get in position. They lined up with the rest. The terrain before them was a baked field of dirt, heat rolling off the earth in shimmering waves beyond the first obstacle, a five-foot shallow ditch. Past that was a two-minute run to the next challenge and a few rows of hurdles. Those unlucky enough not to be teamed with Bellona would have to traverse the ditch and run to the hurdles. By then, Elliot and

Hoffman would be on their way to the bar fence, safely moving at a pace that would keep the others from catching them.

"All right!" Shouted a Captain off to the side of the starting line. "Don't forget what you're fighting for and do try not to kill anyone."

The whistle blew sharply three times in rapid succession. They were off. As Bellona grasped his hand, glowing vines sprouted with alarming alacrity from the ground around Elliot's feet, winding up around his legs, trapping him.

"Fuck," Elliot swore, lowly. The magic in the twisting violet vines clamped down on him, holding him fast. He was stuck and even Bellona couldn't whisk him out of them.

She cursed under her breath and dropped down beside his feet, pulling at the roots in an attempt to free him. "Forget me," Elliot said to Bellona. "Get Hoffman out of here."

Bellona nodded and they disappeared. A small hand slipped into Elliot's. He raised an eyebrow and glanced down at Swift, who grinned at him. "I've been experimenting with this."

Both of Elliot's brows rose. "With holding hands?"

Swift snorted quietly, grin slyly shifting into a smirk. "If I hold on to someone, I can extend my shield more easily. It's stronger that way, and it frees up some of my concentration."

Now wasn't the time for Elliot to remember someone else who'd told him something incredibly similar in extremely different circumstances. "Right."

Elliot weighed up whether the tradeoff of losing the use of one of his own hands was worth it, but he didn't have time to come to a decision. Some of the cadets had surged forward, counting on their peers to neutralize Elliot's team or with plans of settling for second place. The remaining men, at least twenty of them, advanced.

Squaring his shoulders, Elliot prepared to fight one-handed as Swift knelt beside him to tug at the roots holding Elliot in place. At least Swift's shielding had somehow stopped them growing further.

The onslaught began all at once, a boulder careened toward Elliot and slammed into the shield. A shimmer of red light sparked around it, stopping its forward momentum. It bounced off and thumped down, harmless. Swift grunted, his hand squeezing Elliot's as psionic energy crackled inches from their skin. Sparks of red and blue showered to the dirt from the sustained contact.

The ground beneath their feet rumbled in warning. Swift's eyes flew wide as the earth between them speared upward in a wave. Forced apart, the grip of their fingers broke as Swift tumbled backward. The unstable ground thrust Elliot toward the waiting mob. *Christ.*

He brought his hands up and huffed in a breath of liquified air, lungs struggling with the humidity. Sweat dripped into his eyes as his gaze darted around to determine who was the most immediate threat. There were far, far too many.

"Stone!" Swift shouted from behind him, voice panicky. A second later a small boulder smashed into Elliot's shoulder. Or it should've. Instead it gently tapped him and fell beside his feet.

Swift. Elliot smirked at his would-be attackers. "You'll have to get closer than that," he told them, wriggling his fingers. He noticed a few men shifting uncomfortably, clearly remembering sparring matches with him. "Any takers?"

"Not if I've got anything to say about it," Bellona said, suddenly beside him. Elliot glanced over at her, standing there with Swift. A grin split Elliot's lips just before Swift's eyes widened.

"No," he shouted, grabbing Elliot's hand, reinforcing the shielding around him as a jolt of telekinetic energy zapped along the shield's edges. An unnatural gust of wind and icy pellets blasted against it, sputtering more sparks.

"Focus on Bellona," Elliot demanded, inclining his head to where she was kneeling at his feet, struggling with the vines. "Without her, we'll be trapped."

Swift nodded and released his grip on Elliot, resting both palms on the bare skin on either side of Bellona's neck since her hands were occupied. She stiffened a moment, chin ducking as though she might laugh, then relaxed.

Finally, a cadet who was brave enough stepped forward, a man Elliot recognized as Ferris. His stern mouth twisted upward as he concluded he stood a chance. Reaching out a hand, two of his fingers collided with the shield. His eyes closed in intense focus. A glowing red line zigzagged down the front accompanied by the sound of crackling glass, Swift sagged slightly, his knees buckling before he pushed himself upright again, tenuously maintaining control.

"Hurry, Bellona," Elliot encouraged in a strained, urgent voice. He bent to tug at the vines as well, and they freed one foot. A meaty fist collided with the shield, Markham's superhuman force behind the blow. In combination with Ferris's psionic assault, the shield shattered in a burst of glittering crimson fragments.

Elliot straightened as that same fist aimed for his face. He narrowly dodged it, slapping his palm down on the swinging knuckles. He shoved enough horror through their connection to drop Markham into the fetal position at Elliot's feet, trembling like a warning to the others.

"Almost got it," Bellona muttered. Elliot wanted to tug at his foot, but it might tangle him further, so he trusted her to free him. Still his guts clenched unpleasantly as potential attackers circled closer.

"Swift, are you all right?"

"Dazed for a second, but don't worry I've got it." The shield was already back up, sparking all over, tiny scarlet fault lines snaking through the air around them. They didn't have long. Ferris placed two fingers on the shield once more. The ground rumbled and shook.

And then the bloody vines around his ankle began growing again.

"Damn it all to hell," Bellona muttered.

The shield shattered as a volley of rocks headed their way much too fast.

"Hell!" Swift shouted. He threw up the shield again, but it wouldn't hold for long. Elliot doubled over, blocking Bellona with his upper body and covering his own head with his arms. He heard the shield shatter once more and braced for impact. When it came it wasn't what he expected. A body forcefully collided with his, nearly toppling him over. Elliot opened his eyes to see Swift unconscious, a cut on his forehead oozing blood, amid a pile of rubble.

The little shit threw himself in front of those rocks without his shield up. Damn and double fuck.

"Come on, come on," Bellona muttered under her breath. Suddenly he noticed, she had peeled the vines away from his leg. Though they were still fused from the ankle down.

"Christ. Get the laces, leave the boot." She pulled a knife from her belt and wedged it beneath the laces, sawing away from his foot. It sliced through slower than he'd have liked but fast enough that he yanked his foot free before the vines were able to crawl up and prevent his escape. "Now!" he shouted.

Bellona's hands smacked down on Elliot's arm and Swift's shoulder. The world became a series of quickflash images: the hurdles, the dusty run, the bar fence, another run, the climbing wall, run, the balance beam, and finally an uphill scramble. They found Hoffman struggling up the side, sweat dripping down his face, fighting for breath as he climbed.

"Take him, leave me," Elliot insisted. Seamlessly, she let go of Elliot's arm, and latched onto Hoffman. Elliot scrambled up the course, the sound of others shouting behind him much closer than he'd have liked. They'd taken too long at the outset. His one missing boot was a detriment he had all but forgotten until he was running lopsidedly with one socked foot, debris in the dirt scratching at his soles. He gritted his teeth and pushed through it, mostly to the top when Bellona appeared at his side again, mock saluting him as she latched onto his arm and flashed them to the finish.

His team crossed together, Hoffman and Elliot carrying Swift, who was drowsy but regaining consciousness. A redheaded officer blew his whistle four times, signaling their arrival. Elliot faintly heard Hoffman grumble something that sounded positive about his performance, but he was too focused on his injured teammate to celebrate victory.

A medical team quickly triaged Swift, and now that the adrenaline of the fight and the race was seeping out of Elliot, guilt clawed and writhed in his belly. Swift had taken that injury for him. If he hadn't, Elliot might be the one unconscious and without a doubt they would have lost with his foot tangled as it was.

He would rather have lost.

The idea of someone, a friend in particular, hurt due to him was abhorrent. Elliot had the sickening feeling he'd better get used to it.

This was only the beginning.

CHAPTER NINE

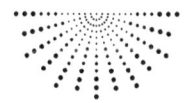

A GENTLE BREEZE RUFFLED Sully's hair. The tall green grass around him swayed and rustled. In the distance a mountain range towered, lush and vibrant with trees and life. He breathed in slowly through his nose, taking in the scent of fresh wilderness and summertime. He'd never smelled air so clean in his life. At camp, they weren't in a city the size of Chicago or New York, but with so many men crowded so closely and facilities that were hastily built, it certainly didn't smell half so wonderful as this.

The weight of Elliot's head resting on Sully's outstretched thighs was a pleasant connection. Months of time spent in each other's company had relaxed Elliot in miniscule degrees until the rule prohibiting touch shifted into a silent agreement that physical contact was permissible if it was innocent.

Sully absent-mindedly hummed a quiet tune, stroking his fingers through Elliot's silky flax hair. They hadn't spoken much tonight, but something about the haunted look in Elliot's eyes when he appeared led Sully to drag him down into this position, cradling him as much as he thought Elliot would allow.

Now those beautiful, heart wrenching eyes were closed, dark blond lashes fanning over his smooth sun-pinked skin, almost glowing white where the light caught them. His perfect rosy lips downturned in the faintest pout. Sully's mouth flooded with moisture. He swallowed, forcing his gaze to the mountains before he could surrender to the strong impulse to lean down and capture those soft lips with his.

"Where are we today?" he asked instead.

"Italy, near the Dolomites. That mountain range there." Elliot was quiet for a moment, his lashes cracking open to reveal blue as the sky that stretched wide and clear above. He turned his head slightly to take in the spectacular view. "I was here years ago with a lovely Italian painter. I posed for him in the grass with the mountains behind me, and spent hours basking in the sun while he painted. It took him a week to declare the painting was finished, and I suspect it only took so long because he kept cutting his work short to thoroughly tumble me."

A burning sensation simmered in Sully's gut. He frowned to himself at the reaction.

"It's very pretty here." Sully noticed Elliot's intense focus on him. "And I can see why he'd be so distracted," he added, glancing slowly along the length of Elliot's body and back up to meet his longing gaze. Sully's breath caught in his chest, and he ached with wanting.

Clearing his throat, Elliot turned away again, looking out at the scene before them. "I don't expect it's nearly so pleasant here anymore." His expressive face clouded over as he spoke. "I'm glad I'm not going back, I don't think I could stand to see what's become of the places I knew, or the people I loved there."

"What happened to the painter?" Sully asked, bitter curiosity prompted by the revelation Elliot had been in love at least once before. He wished he had the same experience, but he'd assumed fleeting and anonymous fucks were how it had to be. And then Elliot went and spoke so easily of love. What would it be like? To be in love with a man. To have those feelings returned.

"Luca and I fell out, it was never meant to be more than a summer romance on either of our parts. Though we lost ourselves in it for a time, when it ended, it was the way most things between us did—with a passionate explosion." Elliot's gaze went distant, caught up in a recollection Sully couldn't see. "I continued occasional correspondence with his cousin Pietro who was my friend first. We studiously avoided any mention of Luca until Pietro informed me they had both enlisted." Elliot shut his eyes, a furrow pressing between his brows. Sully refrained from smoothing it away with conscious effort. "A few months later, Luca wrote me a hastily scrawled letter. An apology for how our friendship ended. A request for forgiveness. I immediately wrote him back, but days after Luca's letter arrived, another came from Pietro. Luca was shot while laying barbed wire. He said it was quick but he would say that, wouldn't he? No one's going to tell you if it was a painful, drawn out affair."

"Probably not."

"No."

They were silent for long moments, both lost in thought. He was afraid to ask about Pietro. Afraid of the answer and of bringing up more pain.

It was hard not to compare circumstances, not think of the future, of the dark, shapeless, terror-clogged void of madness and violence waiting to swallow them whole too. Or of the upcoming voyage across the Atlantic through icy waters that would be infested with German U-boats trying to sink them before they ever set foot on foreign soil.

Elliot's thoughts must have taken the same direction. "Have you heard when you'll be going over?"

Sully swallowed nervously. "Another week before we head to New York and wait for deployment. You?"

"Next week, precisely the same. I was selected to lead a special operations unit comprised of three members of my class and two French Army officers. I've been promoted to Captain of all absurd things."

Sully's eyes widened. He knew from talking to Elliot that he was smart, clever, and could take charge of at least one man anyway. Still, it seemed to crystallize everything Sully didn't like to think of. How they were both headed toward drastically different, uncertain and frightening times. "Congratulations. You skipped right over Lieutenant, first and second. That's..."

"Awful decision-making? Three months of classroom learning, play acting soldier, and forcing myself to use a skill I swore I never would unless I had no other choice, and I'm deemed fit to determine the fate of five of my fellows? Even the month of training in France won't qualify me. Then I see the others in my class, and half the cadets are hardly old enough to be living on their own without their mothers. I shudder at the thought of them fighting, let alone leading men. They're all swagger and the confidence of youth. At least I've been thoroughly disabused of the foolish immortality of the young. I suppose I can be counted on not to assume it will all turn out because our side is the right one. As if there's truly any such thing in war."

"Aw hell, don't get me started on the fools." Sully groaned, massaging his temples. "Excited to march off to battle, thinking it makes them men."

"What about you? Where will you be stationed?" Elliot asked, something desperate in his voice Sully couldn't interpret.

Leaning back, Sully rested his palms on the soft grass. "France is all I've been told. Somewhere at the front. When we get there, we have another month of training for trench warfare. Learning to use real guns."

Elliot shot upright, staring at him incredulously. "Real—wait—what do you mean real guns?"

Sully shouldn't smile, but Elliot's indignation on his behalf was endearing. "Well, they haven't got enough of them, so we had to practice with wooden ones. You must've seen us marching 'round with them."

Elliot's brows were drawn down in fury, his pale cheeks suffusing with outraged red. *Why does anger look so good on him?* "Yes, but I don't know, I assumed you were at least being taught with real ones. You can't be serious!"

"Just the way things are," Sully said with a shrug. No use in wasting time being furious on his behalf. It wouldn't change anything. "Not like they're sending us out into the trenches without learning at all."

"No, but—"

"And anyway, at least I finally got a couple uniforms and a pair of boots that fit."

Elliot's brows pushed down lower, his lips pressed tight. Guess that didn't seem like much consolation to him. It did to Sully after marching around with the shoes he came in for so long. With some difficulty, Elliot mastered himself again, muscles losing their rigid set. "Yes, I've seen your new uniform. Quite the sight."

Tilting his head slightly side to side, Sully couldn't suppress a grin. "You're one to talk, I'm half-tempted to forget the risk whenever I see you in them, just walk over there and lay one on you. Might even be worth the court martials if anyone saw."

"Without a doubt." Elliot sounded troubled once more. Sully wanted him to be happy, the way he was in here. Wished it could be a safe place for both of them. "You still think of me when you're conscious?"

"Lots. Probably too much since I don't remember enough of this to make sense of it. Just think I can't get over you."

Elliot chewed on his bottom lip. Sully wanted to reach out and run his fingers through Elliot's hair again. He didn't think it was a good time to. Elliot's conflicted expression made him think over what he'd said. Should he not have admitted it?

"I know you were teasing but it still bothers me that you don't know," Elliot said softly. "I've tried to find an opportunity to speak to you for months now, but there's never enough privacy, never a reason for our paths to cross naturally. This would be so much easier if you remembered. Or I could be sure of your reaction to my approach."

Sully shook his head. "I promised I'd keep you safe the night we met, and I know I'd damn well do it now too. If I could be sure no one would see through the illusion, I'd have approached you, even without any of this stuff going on in my head."

"The crux of the problem," Elliot acknowledged. "With so many skilled around, it's damned near impossible to guess who's perceptive enough to see past your illusions."

Sully hummed his agreement. "But if you spot a chance to get me alone, take it. Don't like the idea of you feeling guilty. I'm the one who asked you to stay. I'm the one who keeps asking you to come back." Pausing, Sully reflected. It was true, but he knew himself enough to know that admitting it or having to face up to it outside this charmed place wouldn't be easy. Relying on anyone else was a foreign and unwelcome sensation. He couldn't tolerate it most of the time. The only person he could rely on was himself. "Just break it to me gently. I hate to say it, but I might not take it as good as I'd like. Not at first."

"Reassuring, truly."

"Sorry."

"Aren't we all. Distract me for now. Tell me how you're doing. Have you let yourself make any friends yet?"

"Mostly I keep my mouth shut, keep to myself. There is this one kid—could've sworn he was barely old enough to be here, turns out he's nearly my age—and I can't help mothering the brat. He's trying to hide it, but he's nervous as hell and it itches under my skin."

Elliot smirked at him, something false about it. "Getting under your skin, is he? Might you have feelings for the 'brat'?"

"Ha, no." Sully rolled his eyes. Was Elliot jealous? Suddenly, something that should've occurred to Sully months ago smacked him square in the face the second the words left his mouth. He didn't *know* if Elliot was jealous or not because he couldn't *feel* it. He couldn't feel any emotions emanating from him. Hadn't this entire time. How was he too boneheaded to notice? He was practically missing one of his senses. If he hadn't been so overwhelmed by everything he might have noticed sooner.

Had some weird phenomenon of Elliot's magic caused it or was it because they were inside Sully's mind? Either way, it was frightening. And sort of exciting.

A flash of memory tugged at Sully. His lips twisted up as he said, "Not remotely the sort of man I'm interested in."

"No? What sort's that?" Elliot asked, playing along. A thrill zipped over Sully's skin. He remembered too.

"I think you'll simply have to share a drink with me to find out," Sully quoted back to him, pitching his voice low and coy as Elliot had.

Laughter doubled Elliot over, his eyes sparkling. "God, tell me I didn't sound like that."

"Oh you did." Sully grinned at him, his own laughter bubbling up. "But I liked it." The desire to actually see Elliot, out there, in the waking world swelled and pressed in. "I don't know how it's possible to miss someone you only knew for a night in reality, but it feels like a lifetime in here. And I do. Miss you, I mean. I wish I could go back to that night and relive it, the way your lips felt, the way your mouth tasted." Sully reached out and slid his thumb over Elliot's lips, watched his eyes go wide and hazy. "How it felt with you pressing me into that cold rough brick or against those soft, soft sheets." He pushed his thumb down on Elliot's bottom lip hard enough to part them. A flicker of tongue darted against the pad, and Sully groaned. He smoothed the dampness over Elliot's lips, leaving a shiny trail, heat slip-sliding through him with startling force.

Sully's gaze darted down to the obvious bulge in Elliot's pants and lingered there, recalling exactly how wonderful that cock was. He started to lean forward, cradling the back of Elliot's head, guiding him closer, intent clear, desperate need reflected right back at him in vibrant shades of blue.

Then Elliot abruptly pulled away, rubbing a hand over his mouth. The yearning on his face slowly overwhelmed by determination. "I want to, Warren. You can't possibly understand how much. I can't though. I'm sorry. I can't."

Sully sighed, disappointment cooling the rush of blood and anticipation. As much as he wished Elliot didn't feel that way, he understood. With a rueful smile, he raised one shoulder. "It was worth a shot."

Elliot smiled back, eyes tinged with sadness or regret or some similar emotion that twined around Sully's heart and squeezed it.

Standing, Elliot held his palm out to Sully. "How does skipping rocks sound? I know a lovely little pond that's perfect."

Sully grasped his hand and levered himself up. "That'll have to do."

CHAPTER TEN

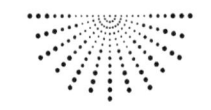

THE AUGUST WIND GUSTING through the night air almost made the heat bearable. Except every time it died down, it left Sully burning twice as hot in its absence. The dark expanse of the sky stretched overhead, scattered stars sparkling. The silver moon hung low in the trees.

Sully strolled down an eerily deserted path, the shivery sound of the leaves disturbed by the breeze and his own quiet footsteps cracked an occasional dry twig.

He shouldn't be out after curfew, but it was his last night here, and anyway, one little use of power to keep anyone from noticing he was out here couldn't hurt anything. What was the worst they could do? They were already sending him to hell on earth, with a detour to the second last place he wanted to go first.

The idea of being back in New York even for a short time sat uncomfortably on his chest. Too many memories, good, bad, and horrific haunted the city. Things he didn't want to think about, people he couldn't remember without dredging up debilitating pain when he desperately needed to be strong. He didn't have the time or patience to sort out his own emotions when everyone else's had been increasingly weighing on him, fraying his nerves.

Sully pinched the bridge of his nose and massaged. Selecting a tree that seemed suitable, he wandered over and leaned against it. He huffed out a breath and struggled to empty his mind.

There was no use worrying. He was going to New York whether he liked it or not, same as he was going to France. There was nothing he could do to stop it. If he couldn't block out the memories here, how would he do it with the once familiar scents, sounds, and sights of the city surrounding him?

Long minutes passed as he stared through the gray shadows of trees and brush until his mind felt marginally better shielded. Whether it would hold up was anyone's guess.

Sully finally pushed off the tree and looked up at its robust branches. He'd never climbed one, and the brief playful urge to try struck him. Just as he reached up for a handhold, a confusing whirl of emotions skittered across his senses.

He glanced back down the path and noticed a familiar form frozen in the moonlight before it shifted and moved toward him. Even without the moon, Sully would have recognized the feel of Elliot. Over the past months, he'd become so attuned to the sensation, to the odd guilty pleasure Elliot vibrated whenever they crossed paths. It frustrated him endlessly, wondering what made Elliot feel guilty. He hadn't picked any up the morning after their encounter, so he didn't understand what triggered it or why it got more intense as time wore on and they marched closer to deployment.

Sully had to be misinterpreting the emotion. Maybe it wasn't guilt at all. Sometimes he leapt to the worst conclusion from raw emotions. He couldn't help it.

As Elliot stopped an arm's length in front of him, Sully's pulse sped and his stomach fluttered. It was pathetic how excited he was. Automatically, Sully wove an illusion around them, made sure they wouldn't be spotted. He hoped.

For a silent moment they just stood there, Sully unabashedly drinking in the sight of Elliot in his uniform, feeling Elliot's eyes on him too.

"You look good," Sully murmured. His gaze caught on the glimmer of silver bars on Elliot's shoulders. "Wow. Captain already. You must be doing great."

Elliot ducked his chin, hiding his face with the brim of his service cap. Sully would've bet he was blushing. Embarrassed by his success? Because there was no way it was the comment about his looks. He had to be used to people pointing out how beautiful he was. "Not terribly. Listen, Warren, I've been wanting to speak to you."

Sully didn't fight the smirk on his lips. "Never would've guessed with all those stares you sent me. Lucky for you I was paying attention, kept anyone else from noticing too."

His eyes went wide. "You did?"

"Mhm…" Sully shifted closer, drawn forward against every self-protective instinct. It was late, no one else was out here. And Elliot kept showing up right when he needed a distraction. How many last nights were they going to get? "Made you a promise once, didn't I?"

"You did," Elliot said, his voice soft and warm. His white teeth sunk into his bottom lip and Sully was a goner.

Reaching up, he traced his fingers over Elliot's jaw, the faintest trace of day's end stubble tickling his skin. Elliot's eyelids flickered, drifted slowly shut as Sully leaned in, brow pinching in a heartbreaking, conflicted expression as dizzying flashes of emotion chased around him. The strongest was want. It pulsed along Sully's nerves, pushed out common sense.

Elliot's breath was hot against his lips. Their mouths met in the barest brush. Just once. And Sully ached with it, how good it felt, how right. Then Elliot flinched away, his apology taking a moment for Sully to register.

"I can't do this. Not without talking to you first. There's something I have to tell you." There was that guilt again, cloying, and overwhelming. Sully was sure of it this time, and it was confusing as hell.

"Okay." Something skittered across Sully's senses, and he cocked his head. "Hold on." His tone must've conveyed seriousness because Elliot didn't say another word.

Focusing intently on the source, Sully discovered a giddy sort of excitement not dissimilar to the way everyone at camp felt most of the time. A sadistic undercurrent turned his stomach. Laced into it was something hot and angry. There were multiple sources, three, maybe four. *What in the hell is that?*

"There are people nearby, heading this way," Sully whispered. His heart hammered in his chest. He ought to pull Elliot deeper into the woods with him, forget he ever felt anything out of the ordinary. It was none of his business what those soldiers were doing. They could finish their conversation out of earshot. Then he could get his mouth back on Elliot's, burn off some of the desire he couldn't seem to shake.

The ominous feeling that if he did, he'd regret it permeated him. Maybe his mind wasn't capable of determining exactly what rose the hairs on his arms, but it felt like trouble. And he couldn't ignore his gut. "Stay in the shadows. I've got to see what's happening. Something's wrong. When it's safe to come out, I'll give you a sign."

"Warren, wait—shit."

Sully took off in the direction of the strange emotions. There was a commotion. Rustling, muffled curses, a grunt of pain that matched a flare of annoyance.

"What's wrong? Didn't think I'd be such a challenge?" A voice Sully recognized shouted. Allison, the one other soldier Sully didn't mind chatting with. Sully's eyebrows flew up, surprised. "Expected you'd have the advantage, huh? Ain't that bad luck."

A shaky trickle of fear from him pushed Sully to action. He jogged forward, it sounded as if Allison was facing several attackers, somehow holding his own. Sully needed to disarm the crisis as quickly and quietly as possible before they all got in a whole hell of a mess.

Rounding the next bend, Sully threw up an illusion just as he came into view, impersonating an officer.

Allison, as suspected, was engaged in a fight. He was winning against four much larger men, moving a lot faster than anyone ought to be able to. Little bursts of speed allowed him to duck out of the way of punches and land his own. Sully would've been more impressed if he hadn't seen Allison manipulating the air around himself for months.

One of the men snuck up behind Allison, a rock in his meaty hand, split lip glistening with blood. If it wasn't for the impending braining, Allison had been doing good for himself. A vicious stab of anger blossomed in Sully's gut at the dirty fighter, and he sprang into action.

"Privates!" he barked out sharply, and all of them froze. He almost smirked at how quickly they all snapped to. "What, precisely, am I witnessing here? Because what it looks like is four men ganging up on a fellow soldier. Does that strike any of you as appropriate?" A chorus of no-sirs met his question. "I don't give a good goddamn what any of you thought you were doing, it's over. Do I make myself clear?" he growled. The four burly attackers were pale, nodding and chirping out their agreement. Allison's head cocked slightly, a knowing gleam in his eyes. "You four," Sully pointed at them. "Get the devil back to the barracks and thank your lucky stars I don't have the time to deal with you further. If any of you approach this soldier again with anything other than utmost respect, I'll have you dishonorably discharged immediately, and don't think I won't. I don't care how badly this army needs men, it doesn't need the kind who turn against their own, you useless maggots. Now get the hell out of my sight before I decide to have you thrown out forthwith."

Was that too much? It was probably too much.

All four men practically pissed themselves thanking him and rushing off to the barracks. As soon as they were out of sight, Sully dropped the act. Allison's eyes went unfocused for a half a second as he adjusted to what he was seeing, and then he let out a bark of ecstatic laughter.

There was a scrape on Allison's cheek. His shirt appeared to have been stretched by grasping hands. He didn't even have pants on, only the shorts he'd been sleeping in.

"What the hell were they doing?" Sully demanded, harsh with fury. Did he need to track down and eviscerate the sorry bastards?

Allison looked down at himself, then up at Sully, his eyes comically huge. "Oh, no, no, not what you're thinking. Dixon was livid I beat his time today on the course. Says I musta cheated." The way Allison smirked made it clear he had. Sully rolled his eyes. What'd happened to the nervous, shy kid he met his first day here? "Hey, it's the last day. And that foul-mouthed asshole has had it out for me from day one, so I worked even harder to win. I didn't need to cheat."

"Oh, really? So how come he thinks you did?"

"'Cause he hates that I'm better than him at anything, thinks I jumped the gun. Which is bunk by the way. I'm not a cheater. I manipulated the air to move myself faster, jump higher, like always, maybe pushed it a little farther than I shoulda. Takes the life right outta me, using it that way, but I was mad enough to. That's how they got the jump on me in the barracks. Never would've let 'em get their grubby meathooks on me if I'd been alert, but I was out cold."

"So, what? They decided to kick the snot out of you, and you just let 'em drag you out here?"

"Lay off. There were four of 'em and everyone else was asleep. One of them got his stupid hand over my mouth. And by the time I realized what was happening, they already had me outside."

Sully tiredly rubbed a hand over his face. "Yeah, and if I hadn't come along your brains would be scattered all over the dirt right now. That louse was about to smash in your skull with a rock."

If anything Allison's grin grew wider. "Guess I'm lucky you came along then, ain't I? Though I can't believe you risked impersonating an officer. Are you out of your mind? What if someone saw through it?"

"Almost no one ever does." He recalled the strange look on Allison's face earlier. Sully jabbed a finger at him. "You did though, or not exactly, but you knew it was off."

Allison shrugged, arms lifting wide, palms up. "It's the air, I can sense things through it. Movement or mass or something like it didn't line up to what you were projecting." He frowned, considering. "It was *wrong*."

Shite. That meant he couldn't hide Elliot from Allison, and he couldn't let him go back to the barracks alone in case Dixon and his buddies were waiting for him. "Not many people even notice that much. We ought to head back before we get caught for real."

"Ought to," Allison agreed. "But c'mon, if you can do that, can't you just do it again?"

Narrowing his eyes at him, Sully crossed his arms, irritation flashing. He was losing out on what could be his last chance with Elliot, and he hated it. Like hell he was gonna stay out here with Allison while Elliot had to wait in the shadows for them to leave. "Can, but I'm not going to. If I've got to keep an eye on them and you, I want some damn sleep first."

Allison appraised him, then gave in with another shrug, seeming to accept Sully's offer of protection. Not that he apparently needed it much. However reluctantly, Sully did care about Allison's welfare. Somewhere along the way, he'd become a friend. Sully didn't have many of those for good reason. Now two people he was attached to were headed into danger. Damn it all to hell. This was why he was better off not letting anyone get close.

As they headed back down the path, he sent a signal to Elliot. Used an illusion to write letters in the air for him, "Sorry, got to go. Be safe."

He wished there was time for more.

CHAPTER ELEVEN

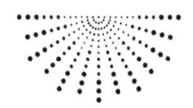

October 24, 1917
Fienvillers, France

THE HOUSE ASSIGNED AS their living quarters and base of operations was utterly silent save the odd creak in the chill fall wind. Elliot ought to be sleeping. He was finding that difficult at the moment, so he stared up at the unblemished ceiling. Moonlight filtered through the dirt-streaked window and lent the atmosphere an ethereal glow. He could almost imagine he was somewhere else instead of in a foreign country on the eve of his first true test of leadership. He was obsessively occupied with their mission objectives and the plan they would be setting in motion.

After a month of training with Sergent Michel Charbonneau and Caporal Léon Remonet, two French Army soldiers assigned to Elliot's team, they were a cohesive unit. Tomorrow their hard work would culminate in their first assignment together.

Two days previous, during the latest offensive campaign in the area around Passchendaele they'd received reports of German soldiers getting back up and continuing to fight after receiving mortal wounds. Officially, it was written off as the fevered imaginings of soldiers in the chaotic cesspool of porridge-thick mud and death and shelling, confused as they fought for their lives and failed to gain ground.

Unofficially, they suspected a German necromancer had been at work. Rapidly gathered intelligence suggested the suspicions were correct and offered a possible location to infiltrate for more information. Planning for the mission was rushed, but solid. What they could prepare for was done. All that was left was to do it.

They were due to commence after dusk, and Elliot regretted the promise of an entire day ahead with nothing to do aside from second guess all of his decisions.

The only thing guaranteed to cause their failure was if he lay there awake all night worrying himself into nervous exhaustion.

Blowing out a deep frustrated breath, he flung his arm over his face and attempted to turn his thoughts in a more pleasant direction. Which inevitably led him in a single direction.

A sly smirk and flashing hazel eyes filled his mind. He let his mind play over a memory so vivid that he was very nearly standing on that Chicago sidewalk once more, an urging hand in his hair, Warren's soft mouth closing hard on his. His heart stumbled in its rhythm, precisely as it had then, a swell of dazed emotion rising in his chest. Elliot drifted to the last time he'd seen Warren in person, the briefest press of their lips. How sweet it had felt right before the guilt at not getting to the point faster slammed into him. Now it was too late to tell Warren. He'd missed his chance.

"You're not helping yourself here," he whispered into the darkness.

Rolling over onto his stomach, Elliot made himself

comfortable. At least he had a real bed here, his own room. Some peace and quiet. Many had it far worse.

Warren probably has it worse.

Elliot's chest tightened and he swallowed, hating that thought. Hating even more that it was true. He would move mountains to have Warren somewhere safe if there was any way he could. There wasn't. What if he never got the chance to speak to Warren in real life again? What if one night Elliot went to sleep and Warren just wasn't there anymore? Didn't exist anymore?

The morose turn his thoughts had taken was less helpful even than the memories. He sighed and turned onto his back again, restless and frustrated and afraid. So damned tired of being afraid.

Eventually, his lashes drifted shut. When he opened his eyes, he was inside a ship, only it was all wrong. The porthole was on the roof—or, no, the room was on its side. Frigid water lapped at his waist, all the more uncomfortable in contrast to the stifling hot air suffocating him.

Warren stood in the far corner, trembling. A girl no more than thirteen with long brown hair the same shade as Warren's clung to him, arms wrapped tightly around his neck, her face tucked up against his shoulder, muffling her terrified cries. Warren whispered something to her, protectively cradling her slight form, his words reassuring despite the slight waver in his voice.

The water rose in a sudden gurgle, waves jolting up to Warren's shoulders. The girl screamed, the sound cutting through Elliot, reminding him to act.

He lifted a hand and made it all disappear, furious with himself for letting it go on so long. He should've stopped the nightmare as soon as he arrived, but it hadn't been the typical scene he walked in on in Warren's dreams. He'd been distracted.

A memory or something his mind conjured to torture him with? Perhaps a combination?

"Anne!" Warren shouted, tear-filled eyes flying open as the dream shifted and the girl disappeared. His gaze focused on Elliot and he sucked in an agonized breath, a dire plea for help on his face. Closing the distance between them, Elliot reached out and Warren collapsed into his arms, gasping for air. Elliot held him tightly as if he could fix this if he only gripped hard enough.

"Sorry," Warren mumbled, hands curling in the back of Elliot's shirt, pulling the material.

"Shh," Elliot rubbed his palm over Warren's spine in firm, broad strokes. Something lodged in his throat and ached in his chest at the broken sound of Warren's apology. "Catch your breath. It's over."

"I'm sorry, I can't—can't stop sh-sha—" Warren squeezed him harder, and Elliot felt wet lashes brush the side of his neck, damp breaths warming his skin. The dull ache behind his ribs sharpened. He wished he could ensure Warren never dreamt anything so awful ever again, wished he could make that promise, but their sleep could hardly be counted on to align when they were in training, let alone when they were at war. All he could offer was a temporary reprieve now and then. Never as long as he'd like. Never as long as Warren needed him. But Christ, he wanted to promise.

For a week, when Elliot had been at sea and Warren had still been waiting to deploy, they'd hardly crossed paths. Being unable to offer solace had been sheer torture for Elliot. Here he was, once again limited in his ability to provide assistance. It was a minor miracle of late they'd been meeting more frequently and for longer periods.

It struck him then, how odd it was that no matter when he

dragged himself off to sleep, he discovered himself in Warren's dreams. That wasn't usual. But was it cause for concern?

"Warren," Elliot started, a suspicion he didn't like nagging at him.

"Hmm?"

Running his hand absently up Warren's back, worn thin material slipping beneath his palm, Elliot asked, "When did you last wake?"

"Dunno. 'S all a blur," he said, voice thick and muffled, clearly struggling for control of his emotions.

"Were you hurt? Sick?"

"No."

Frustration bubbled up in his chest and he fought it down. Warren wasn't being evasive on purpose, he simply didn't grasp the importance of the conversation. His mind remained on whatever scene Elliot had interrupted. *Perhaps if we address that first, he'll be more forthcoming.* "Was this real?"

"Sort of," Warren mumbled. For a moment, Elliot feared he would pull away and change the subject, but he pressed himself closer instead. The vulnerability of the act made Elliot's throat tighten. "Did you hear about what happened to the Eastland?"

Everyone had. Even without the letters from his sisters during his visit with a friend the summer of 1915, he would have seen the headlines. The SS Eastland had rolled over onto her side while tied up at dock in the Chicago River. Loaded down with over two-thousand passengers, the disaster had been monumental. By his recollection, the death toll had been over eight hundred—the horror inflicted upon the survivors unimaginable. Elliot's stomach rolled sickly. "I did, yes. Is that where we were?"

"Yeah. We were there. My Aunt Maggie and Uncle Thomas had

gone below to see friends. Anne and I were out on the upper deck. I was trying to decipher the anxious tension in the air when the boat started listing. At first, they all assumed it was a joke, but I could tell something was wrong. Just didn't know how wrong until it all went straight to hell. The panic and fear and grief was overwhelming. Thought I was gonna pass out, but I couldn't. I had to save Anne."

"Christ." Elliot rested his cheek against Warren's hair, wanting to lend him comfort, lacking the words. What could he possibly offer to provide even a modicum of relief? The thought of all those bodies in the water, all those people drowning, and among them Warren, feeling everything, it nearly ground Elliot's heart to bloody pulp.

"People said we were lucky, after we were dragged out of the river." Warren's matter-of-fact tone no doubt masked heavily shielded pain. People uttered such inadvertently cruel things when they offered sympathy. "We hit the water intact, somehow hadn't got clocked in the head by debris or struck by other people. Hadn't been crushed or drowned, trapped inside, like the people on the main deck."

Like his aunt and uncle? "Did they—"

"No one ever told us how they died. If I hadn't been so busy trying to figure out the whys and I just trusted what I felt, I could've saved them too. But I..." He shuddered. "I barely kept Anne from drowning, and I try not to think about how much worse it could've been if she hadn't stayed with me."

"I'm so sorry," Elliot said softly, inadequately.

They were quiet for a while, Elliot trying not to consider all the ways Warren's life could've been snuffed out before they'd ever met, all the ways it still could be. The odds that in all likelihood, it would be. Elliot felt like he couldn't breathe. He instinctively tightened his hold on Warren and had to make himself relax his grip.

With a parting sigh, Warren stepped away, a false smile pasted on though his eyes remained haunted. "So where are you taking me tonight?"

"Where would you like to go?"

Warren's lips pushed out in thought, his head tilting slightly. Then he gave a genuine grin. "How about the place we met?"

Elliot's heart tripped over itself. Biting down on a smile, he lifted his palm and concentrated, changing the world around them. He'd give anything for it to be this easy to make things better for Warren all the time.

CHAPTER TWELVE

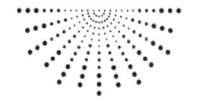

ELLIOT GROANED AT THE feel of soft bedding as he crawled beneath the covers, muscles sore down to his bones, every inch of his skin too tight and heavy. Even if this mattress was absolutely abysmal compared to those he formerly took for granted, it was several large steps above the cold wooden floor he'd achieved a few grateful hours of sleep on during their mission. *Our successful mission*, he corrected, shuffling around until he found the least painful way to lie still.

No sooner had he closed his eyes than he opened them in the middle of a pitched struggle between two ragamuffin boys surrounded by a dozen others. They were in some sort of empty lot, dry dirt and weeds surrounded by tall brick buildings. A city, but not Chicago.

Something recognizable though, somewhere I've been. Is this Warren's dream? he wondered, swiftly followed by, *Who else?*

"Alright boys!" he called. "Stand down!"

Neither paid him any attention, fists flying, fingernails clawing and grabbing. Right then. Elliot stuck out a hand and froze the dream. One of the boys, with a grime-covered face, blood trickling from a gash on his cheekbone, smashed his small fist into the face of the much larger boy to no effect at all. That seemed to capture his interest, and wide, confused, hazel eyes met Elliot's. That was Warren all right. Elliot's mouth tugged up into a crooked smile. *I suppose he's always been scrappy.*

With a wave of his hand, Elliot dissolved the world around them and fashioned it into the parlor in his childhood home. Light golden wallpaper with cream colored scrollwork scaled the walls lined with dark bookshelves. Beneath a chandelier sat a beautiful piano. Comfortable chairs were lined along the wall beneath a large family portrait opposite to the white stone fireplace.

As Elliot lowered his arm to his side, Warren's form went wispy and he shifted into his usual appearance, glancing around the room curiously.

"Haven't thought of that in a while," Warren muttered, rubbing his knuckles though no marks remained.

"Should I ask?"

Warren rolled his eyes. "If you take me somewhere I can collapse first. I'm exhausted. Feels like it's been one bad dream after another for ages."

Prickling awareness tingled at the base of Elliot's neck. "Of course." He waved his hand theatrically and they were seated on a plush settee before the gently crackling fire. Warren slouched instantly, his chin tucking to his chest, arms crossing as if it took all his effort not to melt straight into the padding. "When you say it feels like one bad dream after another—"

"Hmm? Oh that. It's nothing. Just nightmares is all. I knew you couldn't always be here when I fell asleep, but I guess I didn't think too deeply about how awful it'd feel."

Elliot's brow furrowed. He wanted to ask about the dream earlier, but this was troubling. He couldn't let another opportunity to discover what was happening pass by. "Warren, tell me the last thing you remember being awake for." Raising his eyebrows, Warren looked at him skeptically. "Please think. It could be tremendously important."

Rubbing his forehead, Warren's eyelashes fluttered down in concentration. "It's hard to remember. We finished training. They couldn't decide where to send us, and then we got our orders. I'm going to serve at a listening post somewhere near Ypres. They think I'll be able to feel when there's movement from the Germans."

A slight trickle of relief seeped into Elliot. "So you haven't arrived at the front yet? You haven't been hurt?"

Warren's lips pursed. Elliot struggled not to be distracted by the display. "Don't think so. Why?"

"Were you sick at all? Feverish?"

Warren's brows drew down as he tilted his head, peering at Elliot in complete confusion. "No. I was fine. Anxious because…"

"Because?"

Stroking his thumb along the rosewood arm rest, Warren hesitated. He drummed his fingers on the thigh of his faded black wool trousers. "I could feel the pain and despair distantly from where we were training. It was distracting, sort of painful, and we were farther away than I'd ever felt anything before. I was worried that up close it would be overwhelming. I mean, it already hurt and we weren't even near."

A new possibility occurred to Elliot. One he didn't like at all. "When was that, precisely?"

"What do you mean? It was yesterday."

"The date, Warren."

Warren's troubled expression darkened. Displeasure now, beyond bewildered. Elliot didn't blame him. "Twenty-second of October. What? Why do you look like that?"

Dread shifted into fear. Elliot rubbed at his jaw, the slight prickle of stubble scraping against his fingertips. "I look like this because it's not the twenty-second. It hasn't been for days now."

Warren sat upright at that, arms crossing defiantly. "I don't understand. It must be."

How could Elliot jolt Warren out of this? His mind raced, spinning in circles with no answers. "It isn't. Today is the twenty-eighth, in fact. Or it was when I fell asleep."

Warren's eyes widened, paling as his lips parted. After a slight pause he shook his head, disbelieving. "But then why can't I remember?"

"I suspect you've been unconscious. You're always here when I fall asleep no matter when. Yesterday I thought something might be wrong."

Warren's cheeks suffused with a bit of color, dark brows drawing down over sparking green-bronze eyes. "Unconscious from what? I was fine!"

This was tricky. "You mentioned concerns surrounding the potential for overwhelming pain. Is it possible your mind recoiled when you were brought nearer to the front?"

"I'm not a weak little coward," Warren growled, body tensing as if he was preparing to launch to his feet. "You think I'm too afraid to fight? I've never ducked out of a fight in my life."

Elliot gripped Warren's forearm to stop him, to reassure him. "Of course you aren't. I know you're not. Moments ago I watched you wallop a boy twice your size and you couldn't have been more than eight."

"Six," Warren corrected. "I was big for my age."

"Yes. I wasn't, and I reacted much poorer than you did in similar circumstances. So believe me, I realize you're anything but a coward. I'm discussing a physical response to the massive trauma inflicted upon your mind by the bombardment of pain and suffering."

Warren seemed mollified as he contemplated it. "If that's what happened, they've got no way of knowing what's wrong with me. What if I'm trapped here till I die? They can't keep me alive forever if I'm not gonna wake up."

"They damned well better keep you alive," Elliot muttered, heart suddenly pounding, chest tight, face hot. "I'm not an expert on any of this. I might not even be correct. You're the first empath I've been this close to."

There was a tight silence that stretched longer than Elliot would have liked, but Warren never dropped his gaze from Elliot's.

"It feels true," Warren finally whispered, looking away, shoving a hand through his hair and leaving it in disarray. "I think you *are* right. If that's the case, this is going to be difficult to solve. But maybe if I..."

"What?"

Warren seemed uncertain. "I've never tried it on this scale, so I wouldn't swear to it, but my sensitivity to despair is exaggerated. When you experience certain things as an empath, it opens a deeper level of feeling. It's as if you discover new ways to feel pain." He sighed, a bone deep weary sound. "And even if I wasn't absurdly attuned to despair, the weight of feeling everyone at once is hard, you know? I can never close everything out, but I can dampen some things if I'm focusing enough. Mostly I don't bother 'cause it wears on me, trying to control it. Dividing my energy between keeping an emotion away and working the rest of my magic turns into a balancing act. Once I recover, if I make the wrong move out in the field and I pass out, I'll be a sitting duck. And whoever I'm supposed to be working with, they will be too."

"I don't like the sound of that," Elliot said. He noticed he was still holding onto Warren and released him, staring up at the ceiling, reaching for alternatives that simply didn't exist.

"Me either. And all of that is if I can find a way to wake up in the first place. I don't have a damn clue how to get myself to be alert long enough under all the pain to realize what happened, isolate the emotions keeping me under, and tune it out as much as I can."

Elliot watched the flames dance as he considered something. He'd never attempted it, but it might work. He had to make it work. "Tonight might be something new for both of us. What if I jolt you awake? Could you do it then? And will whatever you do last? What happens the next time you sleep?"

"Don't know. Like I said, I never tried it on this scale, but in theory? I think so. I've numbed myself to feelings for a while in the past. It's always hard when they come back, hurts worse. But..."

"But you don't have much choice."

Warren pulled a face. "I hate not getting a choice."

That petulant tone made Elliot smile softly. "I know."

"He stole my friend's papers," Warren announced, a non-sequitur Elliot didn't follow.

"Who?" he asked.

"The older boy, Sean. He was bigger than us, and I wasn't there when he got to Michael, or else I'd have protected him. I wasn't great at illusions then, but I'd gotten us out of a few scrapes with them before. When I found him, Michael had a black eye and a busted lip, he didn't even have to tell me who did it. I was angry enough to storm over to Sean and pick a fight."

"So, you're telling me at six not only were you selling papers, but taking on all comers?"

Warren grinned ruefully. "Told you I was big. Ma always said I was too clever for my own good. I fudged my age when anyone had the brains to ask, and I bought my papers fair and square like anyone else."

"Did you win the fight?"

Warren's laugh shook his shoulders and lit up his eyes. "No. Didja see the size of that lug? But I got in enough good hits that Michael and me weren't worth the trouble after that."

"Brave boy."

Warren smirked, lifting one irreverent shoulder. "Been called worse."

They smiled at one another, and then Elliot turned serious. He reached over to cup Warren's jaw in one palm and brought their foreheads together, shutting his eyes, wishing he could pass on whatever strength he had. "Braver than I, by far. You can do this. I know you can. You told me once I wasn't allowed to die. Under no circumstances are you allowed to die on me either, Warren. Do you hear?"

CHAPTER THIRTEEN

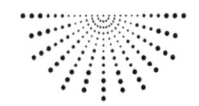

November 27, 1917
Havrincourt Sector, France

AFTER HE'D WOKEN IN a hospital on October twenty-eighth with the unexplained instinct to lock away his awareness of pain and despair, it had taken nearly three weeks of recovery before the doctor, the only skilled one on staff, cleared him for duty. He decided Sully was no longer compromised by the emotions that had debilitated him in the first place or too weakened by the muscles he had to rebuild. They both knew it was a slight stretching of the truth, but the pressure to get Sully out into the field had swayed the decision.

He'd done his best to erect a strong wall in his mind, dampening the intensity of the onslaught. It was a fine line between devoting his energy to holding it up and maintaining enough vigor to be an effective soldier. Ineffectiveness was a surefire way to cop it and wind up staying in France indefinitely, buried beneath blood-soaked soil, so he learned fast how to get by.

All he'd thought of during his recovery was where Allison and Elliot were. Whether they were all right. Not that he would likely ever know if Elliot was. For all he knew Elliot was dead already. Sully cringed away from that thought.

Bull, I'd know. Maybe I'm cracked, but I'd swear it.

Snatches of absurd dreams between horrific nightmares were nothing to cling to as far as proof went, but he was willing to grasp at any straws at all if it meant he didn't need to consider that somewhere out there, Elliot might have ceased to exist.

This war was brutal enough. Had taken enough from him. He'd been out in no man's land more times than he could count in the last ten days and seen gory mangled death and wanton destruction on a scale he never could have anticipated. He'd been the only thing standing between groups of soldiers and German snipers who would have picked them off in seconds. The result of his constant creeping exhaustion, the risk that he might collapse if he didn't cool it on the illusions, was lives saved. That justified any cost as far as he was concerned.

The tepid coffee in the tin Sully held hardly warmed his icy fingers. It was as quiet as it ever got around here, which meant not quiet at all, but not so loud his ears rang. He sipped at it as he wandered down the line of the trench, along dry dirt walls, ducking low out of rapidly acquired habit to keep his head down so it didn't wind up with a hole in it. Walking past soldiers, some of them asleep against the back walls, others crouched and smoking, Sully scanned face after face, searching for Allison. They were due to participate in a large forward offensive the next day. It was a massive, ambitious undertaking that would see the Brits using tanks to crush the impenetrable barbed wire defenses that stood between their troops and the goal: taking back the town of Cambrai. Supposedly, it was a critical target and would serve a major blow against the enemy if they were successful.

He ought to be anxious about what was to come, the soldiers around him radiated varying degrees of concerned tension and excitement at the possibility of a real score in their favor. But he was much more subdued. It was slowly getting easier to push out his reactions to those around him and bury his own stress and fear in order to focus on the work at hand.

A short soldier headed his way and Sully let out a tiny exhalation of relief.

Allison's smile was hollow, face lined with weariness and smudged with dirt. Even his uniform was dusty. Sully's wasn't any better. He was so covered in grime he could feel old blood and mud beneath his fingernails and coating his skin. Must've smelled awful, but everything here did. The two of them had been out here on the front line too many days with no relief. The only respite Sully got these days was when he closed his eyes and let himself escape into the privacy of his mind.

"You look half-asleep on your feet," Allison observed.

"When don't I? Didja just get back?" Sully asked as they met in between two huddled groups of soldiers and leaned against the wall of woven branches side by side.

"Yeah, they had me listening to the wind again, seeing if the Germans got any idea what we're up to."

Sully sent him a grim smile. "You any better at understanding them?"

"You'd think after this long and all the time they spent trying to teach me, it'd be child's play, but no. I can get the general idea most of the time, but I've never had much call for learning other languages, and it turns out I'm shit at it."

"They had me listening too," Sully said, leaning forward in a poor attempt to stretch his back. "All quiet. Feels like any other day over there."

White teeth flashed in the dark in a sharp smile. "Good. That's the impression I got too. Maybe we got a chance after all."

Sully shrugged, then sipped his cold tea. What he'd give for milder weather. And some goddamn coffee. "Maybe."

"Shouldn't you be sleeping? Replenishing the old reserves for tomorrow?" Allison asked, a chiding tone to his voice.

Sully narrowed his eyes, face heating slightly. "Yeah, well."

"Oh," Allison said, pouring it on thick, acting like he made some grand discovery, the little shite. "Were you worried about me?"

Sully grimaced. "Wasn't. Shut up. Not even a bit."

Allison bumped his shoulder into Sully's bicep. "You absolutely were, you big softie."

"I wouldn't have to if you'd be more careful about letting the soldiers notice you're skilled!" Sully hissed, making sure they weren't overheard even as he recognized he was being harsh because he was embarrassed. "Some of them would rather get shot by a German than showed up by a witch."

"Is that what they're calling me now?" Allison asked, voice melodic with amusement. "I don't even have a broomstick."

Getting Allison to be serious was worse than pulling damn teeth. They weren't witches of course, witches didn't exist, but that didn't make idiots who saw magic and didn't understand it any less likely to want to burn them at the stake. Or shoot them in the back. "It's not funny, asshole. You do remember what they used to do to so-called witches back home, right? There's a damn reason we keep it a secret."

That finally got Allison's back up. "Yeah, well, if I ain't scared of German artillery, I ain't gonna walk around scared of some rinky-dink bumpkins I'm supposed to be working to protect. I'm here 'cause I've gotta be, 'cause I've got a job to do, and I'm gonna do it how I want. They can buzz off."

Sully sighed and rubbed his aching forehead. "Would you believe I ever thought you were scared of your own shadow?"

Allison chuckled, relaxing again. "I'm small and know it. Helps if people think I'm not a threat. But I'm not about to risk my life on the battlefield to keep up that illusion. Speaking of the battlefield, I did see somethin' weird today."

"Oh?"

"Sergent Davies, the skilled one, he just came right up out of the trench and started walking toward the Germans. Heard some shouts for him, but he ignored 'em. Got shot right between the eyes in under a minute."

"Hell," Sully muttered. "What the fuck was he doing up there?"

Allison grimaced. "Word is he was getting court martialed."

"For what?"

"Got caught with an officer, if you know what I mean." Allison sounded sympathetic. A chill raced down Sully's spine, he hadn't known Davies was like him.

It wasn't the first time he'd heard about someone taking a bullet to spare themselves or their family the embarrassment of a court case. It never stung any less—the reminder that this was the only option for a lot of people who got caught.

He was in the rare position that his boss back home knew he slept with men and didn't care. Edie preferred women herself, and she'd clocked him almost as fast as she'd noticed he was skilled. She'd never fire him for it. He hadn't told Anne, but he liked to imagine she wouldn't hate him. He hoped she wouldn't. Didn't want to find out any time soon. "The poor sap," he mumbled, not thinking.

Allison raised an eyebrow, then his expression smoothed. "Damn shame. He was terrible at cards; I won every time we played."

"You were right about one thing," Sully grumbled tiredly, ignoring the comment.

"Yeah, what's that?"

"I ought to be sleeping."

Huffing a laugh, Allison tapped him on the arm. "So go flop. I'll see ya tomorrow."

CHAPTER FOURTEEN

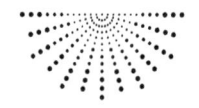

BULLETS BLASTED INTO THE cobblestones behind Elliot as he barreled full steam down the street. Chips of plaster flew off houses as shots narrowly missed him.

Fuck, fuck, Christ.

It wasn't supposed to go like this.

He pushed himself harder toward the stone fountain looming up ahead, skidded behind it, and ducked down low. He counted out bullets and reloaded his pistol.

Footsteps pounded closer. Four, maybe five German soldiers were closing in, hot on his heels. He peeked around the gray stone column and flinched back at a shot that nearly struck him.

On one hand, his brilliant diversion had certainly yielded results. On the other, he hadn't expected to get separated from Hoffman in the pursuit. They'd found the necromancer who kept plaguing the western battlegrounds—Leutnant Alwine Albrecht. They were supposed to catch her off-guard and capture her alive if possible. Rumor was, she was working on something that could

IMPERFECT ILLUSIONS

change the course of the war. Things had deteriorated rapidly when she'd spotted their approach.

"Captain!" Swift's voice shouted from his right. Elliot glanced over and saw him crouched behind a house, in an alleyway. Swift leaned out a little further at something behind Elliot, shouting his name, throwing out his shield, palm outstretched for him.

No, no. He's leaning out too far.

Two loud pistol retorts rang out, one after another, Elliot tensed, expecting one in the back that never came. He opened his eyes as a third rang out from Swift's direction, and saw Charbonneau standing there. It took him a moment to recognize the slumped form at Charbonneau's feet was Swift, and that Charbonneau had shot the man behind Elliot right after a German had gotten Swift. His furious gaze met Elliot's. He shifted his stance, firing at the soldiers pursuing Elliot. Providing cover.

Please let Swift be all right. I told him not to risk himself like that. Not for me, not for anyone. Christing shit.

As he was about to make a mad dash across the street to them, a small hand landed on his shoulder. Bellona's, he recognized fast enough he hardly jolted. And then Hoffman opened fire, four quick, precise shots, and it was silent save the distant sound of many boots rushing in their direction.

The second Hoffman stopped shooting, Bellona transported them to Swift. Elliot's throat clogged. Charbonneau had dropped to his knees, cradling Swift. Blood seeped darkly from the left side of Swift's chest. He was struggling to breathe, face pale, eyes hazy and panicked, locked on Charbonneau's. Elliot's heart shriveled and sank.

He turned to Bellona, "Get them to the safe house. There are medical supplies there." The anguished glance she gave him said too many things he didn't want to believe. "Now. Hoffman and I will make our way to the vehicles and secondary location so we aren't followed, get us when you can. *Go.*"

She released him and obeyed orders, leaving behind nothing but a puddle of crimson on brown cobblestones. Elliot couldn't tear his gaze away.

This is my fault.

"Captain," Hoffman, shoved at his shoulder, pushing him down the alley. "We need to go before they catch up. He'll be all right. He has to be."

Elliot tucked away his pistol, his hands clenching into fists as he staggered into a run alongside Hoffman, fingernails digging painfully into his palms. He swallowed against the lump in his throat, fighting for air.

This is my fault. All my fault.

It was a blur until they were hiding the car among brush and stumbling through dense woods to a small cottage that was hardly standing. Inside, Elliot slumped onto a rickety chair. A sudden heaviness weighed him down. He sagged forward, resting his arms on his thighs, hands hanging limply between his parted knees. His head was too heavy to hold up so it drooped forward as he squeezed his eyes shut.

They aren't medics. He can't possibly survive without one. Swift is going to die. He's going to die, and it's my fault. Charbonneau's going to watch him die. Because of me.

Elliot lost track of time, forcing back hot tears.

Neither he nor Hoffman spoke. They simply waited.

CHAPTER FIFTEEN

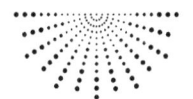

A SOLDIER TANGLED IN barb wire was bleeding and screaming, feet away from Sully. The earth shook with the brutal force of shells pounding into dirt, great plumes of the stuff blasting high in the air, raining down like a hailstorm. Lightning streaked the sky and lit puddles and rivers of scarlet pouring over the ground.

A threatening yellowish cloud rolled toward him, wisps rising up, skimming over the ground, reaching for him.

Sully's breaths came in fast gasps, but he couldn't get enough air. Blinking, he tried to clear his eyes. His fingers fumbled for his gas mask.

Fuck, fuck, fuck. Shite. I'm not—
I can't—
Oh God.

The world around him froze in an instant, and Sully sucked in a ragged breath of air, his hands flying to cover his mouth as he slammed shut his eyes and shook his head. Trembling muscles suddenly weak.

A dream.

Thank God, thank fucking hell. I could kiss him.

Sully let out a shaky laugh and opened his eyes. Looked around to find Elliot. He was sitting cross-legged on the grass several feet away, silent, gazing away at something far off. Sully's gut twisted. Something was wrong. Something happened. Mouth dry, Sully cleared his throat and swallowed tightly. "Elliot?"

"Mmm." It wasn't even a word, and in here Sully couldn't sense emotion, but that hum was agony. It reached beneath his ribs and crushed his heart in a punishing fist.

"You all right?" Sully asked, pushing up to his feet. He cautiously approached.

"Peachy," Elliot muttered, but he didn't move. Didn't sound peachy either. He sounded like all the light and good had been sucked out of the world and the only remains were pitch black ruins.

Sully lowered himself onto the ground in front of Elliot. He tried to think of something to say, the right question to ask, but for all his ability to read emotions, he was never any good at managing them. No matter how hard he tried, he always said the wrong thing. He asked too many questions, or not enough, and the consequences could be dire.

The image of his mother's weary face at the train station when he was eight years old swam to the surface of his mind. There was the churning sadness he'd written off as grief, the way her green eyes glistened as she pulled away from kissing his forehead, her thumbs brushing softly over his cheeks.

Jaw clenching, Sully watched Elliot tug up tufts of green grass, the warm orange sun behind him setting his pale hair aglow, every strained line of his body screaming that he was in a fragile state. He needed to know what was wrong. He wanted to—needed to—make sure this time.

"Elliot, look at me." There must have been something sufficiently commanding in his voice because Elliot complied, blue eyes full of anguish so deep Sully's stomach lurched. "Talk to me. What happened?"

Elliot's lips parted, and his eyes went glossy. He shook his head and lowered his gaze again as his tears fell, inhaling a raspy gasp as his face flushed dark. That was the last straw. Sully reached out and grabbed Elliot's shoulder, jerking him forward. Elliot leaned into the momentum, let himself be drawn into Sully's lap. He burrowed his face against Sully's neck, breaths heaving hot and damp against the bare skin there. Wetness soaked into Sully's collar. He held Elliot crushed to him as he sobbed. His own heart pounded out of control with fear, sick with worry.

Sliding his hand into the back of Elliot's hair, Sully massaged the nape of his neck. Tried his best to soothe him.

He wished he could feel what Elliot was going through, wished he could make sense of it. A million horrible thoughts flitted through his mind. Sully didn't want to give voice to any of them.

Instead, he ran his panicked fingers through Elliot's soft hair. Tried to calm himself as much as he was calming Elliot. Sully wouldn't be any good to either of them if he couldn't focus and help. "Elliot, talk to me. Please. Tell me what happened."

Elliot made a choking sound and tightened his arms around Sully's torso. "I... I... He..."

He who? God help the poor fucking bastard if someone hurt him. Sully would kill him. "Elliot, you got to concentrate. I need to know you're okay. Please. Who hurt you?"

"Not me." Elliot shuddered, words thick and painful. "It wasn't me. Should've been me."

Guilty relief trickled through Sully. If he wasn't sitting, his knees would've given out. It was awful he felt relieved at someone else's misfortune, but the tension in his shoulders released. He exhaled slowly, deliberately quiet, and pressed his lips to Elliot's flaxen hair and made soothing sounds when Elliot couldn't add anything else. Sully's pulse slowed from frantic rushed beats into a slow steady cadence.

After his tears ran dry, Elliot still didn't release Sully. He remained slumped as he was, clutching at the back of Sully's jacket, breaths evening out. Which was fine. Sully would've been reluctant to let him go anyway. He wanted the solid warm weight of Elliot against him, a glowing, inescapable reminder that he wasn't hurt. Not physically. "Tell me when you can."

He felt Elliot's nod, his hair brushing silk against Sully's cheek. Several slow inhales passed, then he mumbled, "It was Swift. Ollie. He was so young, Warren. He was invulnerable, for Christ's sake. He should have been fine. He would have been *fine*—" Elliot's voice cracked. "It should have been me. I should have bled out, not him. I was in charge. It should have been me."

Sully ached, frozen all over at the thought of Elliot dead.

No, it for damn sure shouldn't have been you.

He kept his voice soft and comforting. "I'm sure you did everything you could."

"Well it wasn't enough," Elliot said in clipped tones, though he didn't move away. "I was never qualified for this. I oughtn't be making these decisions. I was supposed to protect them. And I failed. Like I fail everyone."

That's bunk. It's bull.

Sully drew back to stare defiantly into Elliot's eyes. "And how much worse could it have been if the person in charge didn't give a goddamn shite about them? If they were under someone who didn't cry at their loss? Wouldn't lose a wink of sleep if the lot of you were snuffed out of existence?"

"Warren—"

"No," Sully growled, on a roll now, unable to bite back the words shredding him up. "I'm sorry about your friend, I am. But I won't tell you I'm sorry it wasn't you. And it could've been if you had to follow someone else's orders. It could've been you, and I'll never be okay with that. I told you you're not allowed to die, and I damn well meant it, Elliot. I love you, you sapskull! I never did that before, and I'm not gonna lose you now that I went and did it. So don't talk like you should be dead because you shouldn't."

Sully's heart pounded, pulse roaring in his ears. Had he really said that? Out loud? Elliot sure as hell wasn't kidding about feelings spilling out easier in dreams.

Blinking a couple times fast Elliot's mouth opened slightly, his cut glass blue eyes glistened. *Ah, shite.* Sully made him cry again. He should've kept his big stupid mouth shut.

"I...Warren..." Elliot seemed to struggle for words. Sully's heart beat faster, a thread of fear and worry seeping in. What if Elliot didn't feel it too?

Silence stretched on, blue eyes studying Sully's, flicking from one to the other, as if Elliot was trying to see into the core of him. Then something despairing flashed in Elliot's expression. He leaned forward, chin tilting in a clear invitation. *Yes.*

"Sullivan! Wake up!"

Sully jerked to awareness as a boot jostled him. "Hmm?"

"Time to get your arse out of bed and into boots."

Groaning, he levered himself into a sitting position on the cot he'd managed to find. "'M up," he mumbled, rubbing sleep from his eyes.

His lips tingled with the vaguest sense he dreamed of Elliot again. Something bittersweet and longing stirred in him. He wished he could sink back into sleep. Instead he squared his shoulders, determination settling in his bones as he rose.

~

ELLIOT WAS NURSING A headache at the kitchen table where he'd apparently fallen asleep last night. Resting his elbows on the table and hanging his head in his hands, he stared at the bleached wood as the sun rose in the sky, stretching orange and shadows over it. Outside, a crow cried out a mournful sound. Elliot sighed tiredly, the memory of Warren's mouth so close to brushing his faded into stark reality.

The gin he'd consumed last night as they grieved Swift's loss soured his stomach.

Swift knew the danger when they went on an assignment, they all did. Perhaps Elliot had been foolish, naïve, to assume their skills and planning would keep them safe, but it had thus far, and it wasn't bloody fair for it to fail now.

Life's not bloody fair either, is it?

His muscles ached, his chest scraped raw, and his throat scratchy. He didn't know how long he sat there, fighting back tears he couldn't afford to let fall. If he started crying again for Ollie, he might not ever stop.

So he wrote instead, words pouring from his heart like warm blood onto dirty paper in pencil scratches. *Sunlight wreathed in golden hair, a spill of sun-kissed freckles. They matched your boyish smile, contradicted your tested mettle. You laughed when we couldn't. Fought like you'd never be stopped. And so we thought you never would—until fate proved us wrong.*

You traded your life for mine, and it was no bargain. Life, and love, and time—all things that should have been yours, not mine.

The front door opened and shut quietly. Light footsteps Elliot knew briskly traversed the wooden floor behind him. He thought he'd been the first to wake. Apparently he'd misjudged. Scooping up the papers he'd been writing on, he hid them away in his pocket like tucking his heart back inside his chest.

A stack of files dropped unceremoniously on the table beside his elbow with a loud thump. He winced and glared up into Bellona's grim face. "What are these?"

"Courtemanche says you're required to choose a replacement today. Says these are the top ten skilled soldiers. Some officers, some enlisted, but they're all extremely useful in some way. He says you need to decide quickly. We have to train them up in a few weeks so we can get back out there while things settle down for the winter. The Germans are getting awful quiet. That's not good."

"It never is." Elliot sighed, grinding his palms into his closed eyelids. This was too soon. He didn't want to choose someone new, didn't want to be responsible for anyone else. "Right. A replacement."

He ran his thumb along the edge of the file on top, gaze unfocused.

"Captain?"

"Yes?"

"You'll need to open it unless you've developed a new skill I've not been made aware of."

Elliot narrowed his eyes at her. "Terribly clever. Go do something useful instead of pestering me."

Bellona patted his shoulder affectionately and left the room. Silence rang once again.

The throbbing in his head increased as he leafed through the first six files. There wasn't anything *wrong* with them as choices, but they weren't Swift.

He pushed them to the side and opened the next.

Name: Warren Thomas Sullivan

Elliot's heart skipped a beat. He shoved the irrational reaction aside. Warren wasn't as common a name as John, but it certainly wasn't rare. He continued to skim the page.

Next of kin: Anne Margaret Doyle (cousin)

Elliot's brows shot up. Now what were the odds of that? Another Warren with a cousin Anne who happened to be skilled? They must be low. Mustn't they?

It couldn't be.

But what if...?

He dove into the file, pouring over every detail, skimming until he came across irrefutable proof. Corporal Sullivan had been unconscious for his first six days at the front, condition undiagnosed, status recovered. This was without a doubt his Warren. *His Warren.* Right there on paper. The possibility of choosing him dangled over Elliot's head but he couldn't make such a decision on the impulse to see a former lover, no matter how many dreams they shared. No matter how much Elliot longed to shift those encounters into the waking world. To explain himself and hopefully earn forgiveness for the trespass. This was life and death for all of them, he had to make the best choice, not the one he selfishly wanted.

Elliot read on.

At the end, he came to several conclusions: Warren had been taking every opportunity to put himself in harm's way, to get between German bullets and Entente troops. He'd been putting himself at risk, going out with stretcher bearers to aid in concealing them from German snipers. He'd done enough to earn not one, but two promotions in such a short span of time.

The file indicated that Warren was dedicated, so much so that he had to be ordered to retire most nights, half-asleep on his feet when it became apparent he was a danger to himself. Elliot's stomach twisted over the idea that someone else he cared for was prepared to sacrifice himself on the altar of altruism.

He closed Warren's file and breathed deeply through his nose, attempting to be rational. To make a proper decision. After a few moments, he sifted through the rest of the files, carefully weighing the options. He narrowed it down to four including Warren, and three others he'd never met. Staring at the cover page of each file, he tried not to let the longing in his chest pull him in the direction his heart so desperately wanted to lead. He tried not to think about Warren's words, *"And how much worse could it have been if it was someone who didn't give a goddamn shite about them?"*

Did Warren's commanding officers 'give a goddamn shite' about him? What if they didn't? He was working with regular troops for the most part. His commanding officers were not skilled and might not even truly understand what magic entailed. The general public still didn't believe in magic, and if they did, it was the devil's work.

Governments, those who made it their business to know, had generally left the skilled unbothered in recent times, until the war made them decide they needed an advantage. Had Warren's superiors been educated at all on the skilled? If not, they were probably prejudiced at worst, unaware of his needs at best. What if they were indifferent to his safety? Concern gnashed at Elliot's gut. He massaged the bridge of his nose and forced out a sharp huff.

It wasn't fair to let that make his choice.

Since when is anything in this godforsaken war fair? It never was and never will be.

Warren was qualified. Skilled. Useful. Elliot knew he'd fit in. He attempted to convince himself those were the only reasons he placed him above the others. Clenching his jaw, Elliot resigned himself to self-recrimination at some future date. Guilt could wait it's damned turn. The man he loved was in desperate need of saving.

Whether it was decent or not to have fallen in love with a part of Warren that no one else could see, he'd gone and done it. He couldn't stop himself.

He'd have to box up those feelings. It would be so much harder since he'd heard Warren say the words last night. Elliot had to remember the Warren who loved him wasn't the one he'd be face to face with soon. In the waking world, life would've left defensive wounds on him, he would have different ways of interacting, processing. He wouldn't be entirely the same, not at a surface level.

If Elliot was any kind of moral person, he'd confess to dreamwalking immediately and then create distance between them. He would be Warren's commanding officer. He ought to act like it and be proper. For once in his life he could do the right thing, the good thing.

CHAPTER SIXTEEN

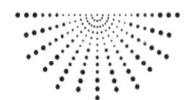

Bourlon Wood, France
November 30, 1917

THE LAST TWO DAYS dug into their tenuously held position in Bourlon Wood had been chaos. More shells than Sully could count were fired into the trees at them, blasting craters into dry, frozen earth and shattering the unblemished land.

It was nothing compared to this morning.

First light had hardly broken when the Germans stormed them, heavily engaging their troops in a relentless firefight. They broke through the surprised British line to the south and spread in surging tides. The fighting was fierce, brutal. Sully did everything he could to provide his side with an advantage, confusing Germans when he was able, running messages when he had to.

Moments ago, he'd been plucked from his attempts to hold off nearby snipers. On General Townsend's orders Allison came to fetch him. Sully reluctantly complied, wincing as the German snipers resumed picking off men when Sully could no longer exert his illusions on them. Impotent rage curdled his stomach.

This had better be fucking important.

"Excellent," Townsend said, nodding when he saw them. The reek of his desperation pressed up against the already taxed dam in Sully's mind. A slight trickle of relief right behind it. Probably that Sully hadn't been killed before he could be of particular use. "Precisely the men I require. Urgent reinforcements needed, got to get the message through. I've dispatched men twice, and haven't heard from anyone since."

Those odds sounded awful. How cut off were they? Didn't matter. Between his illusions and the burst of speed Allison could give them, they would make it. They should have been the first damn choice.

Sully tried not to think about how little sleep either he or Allison had gotten over the last few days, how much of his concentration was focused on keeping the suffering and terror surrounding them from overwhelming him.

Townsend withdrew letters from his breast pocket and handed one to each of them which they placed in their own. "Quickly now. Every moment counts."

As if they needed telling. The two of them clipped out, "Yes, sir," and took off at speed. Serving as a runner was dangerous and unpleasant, but it removed them from the immediate deafening sounds of the battle. Sully's fraught nerves had several long minutes to recover.

Tense in front of him, Allison's compact form was made lighter as he harnessed the air. Sully did his best to keep up. If it weren't for the occasional boosts Allison sent, he'd have been left in the dust.

They wove through tall bare-branched trees, onto a packed dirt road, feet slamming into the dust and propelling them along the path. Up ahead Sully sensed a lurking threat. He created an illusion to distract them. Concealed himself and Allison as they flew past.

Struggling for air, and muscles aching with strain, they made it past several groups of Germans. There wasn't time to dwell. He was tiring out mentally and pushed himself to remain sharp.

Up ahead, the captured German trenches came into view. The broken bodies of fallen British soldiers, discarded and bloody, littered the roadside. Sully sent up a short prayer to a God he didn't believe in these days.

One of the bodies twitched.

"Did you see that?" Allison asked slowing.

"We can't stop," Sully said breathlessly, though every instinct he had insisted they couldn't leave a man alive out here to bleed to death.

"But we can't just—"

"We gotta."

"Heeelllp meee," The fallen soldier's voice groaned. He was trying to push himself up, the one next to him, twitched too, with an echoing plea. Fuck.

Allison stopped, giving Sully a look. So much for focusing on their objective. As they approached, Sully caught his breath, his senses reasserting themselves with the influx of oxygen to his brain. A sudden tingle at the base of Sully's skull spread ice-cold down his back. There wasn't any emotion coming from those soldiers. Nothing but a void.

"Allison, stop! Shite. It's a trap. There's a necromancer somewhere nearby." Sully widened his senses, using his magic to search for them.

There.

He looked back through the trees, just as a sneaky flash of pride caught his attention in the opposite direction.

No, no, no.

Sully launched forward tackling Allison to the ground as a sniper's bullet whizzed past them, passing through the space Allison occupied seconds ago. Allison's gasp rang almost as loud as the gunshot. They were exposed. Sully's illusion wasn't strong enough to conceal them. He was running through energy too fast.

Moving them on instinct, Sully scrambled. He guided Allison toward a crop of trees for shelter. Dirt flew up in tiny bursts around them until they were hidden from view.

"Fuck," Allison muttered under his breath, voice pinched.

Sully looked down at where Allison was sitting, his back against a tree. He was about to tell him to shut up, when he saw it. Dark red was seeping from the olive wool at Allison's right shoulder, near his collarbone. Sully's gaze flitted to the strained grimace on his sweaty, sickly pale face. "Fuck," he agreed, crawling forward.

For all they knew the sniper was closing in on their position, and Allison was shot.

He's fucking shot. I should've concentrated harder on the illusion! Shouldn't have let this happen. What the hell am I supposed to do? Put pressure on it? Or do we make a run for it? What do I do? What do I do?

"Go," Allison whispered, as Sully crouched in front of him, staring helplessly at the wound. "You've got to deliver the message." He rubbed at the perspiration on his forehead with his left arm and winced at the movement. "I'll be fine. You'll come back. If it's just you, he won't even see you, right? The problem is you trying to hide us both at once when you're run ragged, and you got nothing left to give."

Bile rose in Sully's throat. If he left Allison like this he was good as dead. They both knew it. The sniper would finish him off the second Sully stopped protecting him. He'd be left here, vulnerable, bleeding, waiting for the shooter to put him out of his misery. No. "Like hell I'm leaving you," Sully hissed.

Allison huffed a breathless sound. Was he actually laughing? The stupid bastard. Didn't he know what he was asking? "They need reinforcements, Sully, you don't got a choice."

Sully glowered at him. *Bull.* "Always got a choice and I'm sure as shite not making that one. Both of us or neither."

Allison scowled right back. "Then we'll die."

"No we won't, Allison. I'm not leaving you. I can do this." This was going to sound foolish. He pushed down his embarrassment. Could handle any joshing if it meant not leaving his friend behind to die. "I wasn't touching you. That makes it stronger."

Allison let out a laugh, then grimaced, eyes squeezing shut. "Seems like a lot of effort you're putting in here just to touch me. If you wanted to hold my hand, you could've just asked. You're not really my type, but like they say needs must."

Sully wanted to smack him upside the head, the sapskull, making stupid jokes at a time like this. He was *hurt* for fuck's sake. "Shut up for once in your whole damn life! Just trust me."

Allison frowned, palm pressing gently against his wound as he grunted. "Even if you get us past him, I'll slow you down. Something's broken. Can't lift my arm. Doubt I can run."

Sully sized up the options. He rolled his eyes heavenward. "Can you still do your thing with the wind? Make us lighter?"

"Probably," Allison hedged, then his dark eyes narrowed on Sully's face. "You can't be serious. That's going to look fuckin' ridiculous."

"Stow your pride, sapskull. Is it really worth your life?"

"Maybe." If he could, Allison would've petulantly cross his arms. "No, you are *not* carrying me."

A bullet hitting the dirt in a violent spray a few feet away shattered the false sense of security they'd briefly indulged in.

"On second thought," Allison muttered, struggling to his feet. "Fine. But I hope you're prepared to conceal a lot of cursing."

Sully ignored that and warned, "This is probably going to hurt."

"Didn't think it would be a grand ol' time, did I?"

Sully turned around and crouched a bit, his back facing Allison. Nothing happened. He let out an irritated sigh and looked round. "You gonna make me wait like this all damn day or what?"

"Oh sorry, just considering whether this is more or less dignified than how I thought you meant to do it."

"Will you shut the hell up and get on so we can get out of here?" Sully growled.

"Fine."

By some miracle, they made it past the sniper and the crawling, groaning corpses. Allison's good arm across Sully's shoulders, he clung to him in a death grip, his legs tucked snugly around Sully's waist. If anyone could see them or hear the pained grunts and foul words that Allison whisper-shouted at him the whole way, they were bound to laugh, Allison was right about that.

The boosts Allison gave them as Sully leapt over trenches kept them from falling in, and finally, they crossed into safety. Once he handed Allison off for medical treatment and relayed the need for reinforcements, he found an officer he could tell about the necromancer. Then Sully was ordered to rest before he was allowed back into the field.

He was walking through gelatin, muscles barely holding him

up. When he found a place to lie down, even his concern for Allison wasn't enough to keep him awake.

Three days later, the decision to retreat to a more defensible line was made. They would retain enough gained land that it could loosely be called a victory. Never mind they'd failed miserably to achieve the objective. The cost in terms of lives lost was tragic.

All for a few miserable goddamn miles of frosty ground.

Some prize.

~

THE NIGHT WAS DARK and oppressive. The frigid bite of the air made Sully tremble as he pressed a finger to his lips in a shushing motion, his other hand clasped Private Smith by the side of the neck. Crouched in a shell hole, musty ruined earth, acrid cordite, and smoke filled their nostrils. Made it hard to breathe. Sully's entire body ached with effort of staying upright. He could hardly focus on what he was supposed to be doing—casting an illusion that kept them hidden. He and this soldier who'd been next to him when their plan fell to fucking shite.

Sully wasn't even supposed to be here. Orders had come from above and he was being reassigned to some special French Army unit of skilled soldiers. Only he'd been sent out for one last mission after barely enough sleep to function.

If he'd been more focused, less exhausted, he might've recognized the sensation of the German alertness. The anticipation of an impending assault had been there, but he'd been too busy following orders to pay it any mind. His limited resources were occupied weaving an illusion as wide as he could possibly stretch it. Making the Germans believe they were still engaged in a firefight, stretched every scrap of him thin as the rest of their troops began a calculated retreat.

It hadn't lasted ten minutes when the Germans charged them. He'd watched as the man to his right was shot in the chest, and Sully had doubled down on his efforts, pushing out more energy than he ought to, impossible to maintain. The Germans faltered for a moment, but it didn't stop them. They shook it off too fast, squared their shoulders, and marched forward into the false suppression fire he was showing them.

They knew.

It was the only explanation. Betrayal and impotent fury burned in Sully's gut. They were lambs to the slaughter, those left to pull up the rear. He'd grabbed Smith, standing to his left, and pulled him into a nearby shell hole, concentrated his illusion on a smaller area, concealing them. Then he wasted bullets fruitlessly attempting to give their troops a chance to retreat, but they'd stood ground.

In a matter of moments all was lost. The British were overrun, surrounded by enemy troops pushing forward. Guttural German shouts rang out around them. It was all Sully could do to maintain the tenuous illusion keeping Smith and himself hidden.

Darkness helped. He made the shadow deeper. Slowly drained his reserves until he'd been forced to clap a hand on Smith to keep him inside the illusion.

Sully didn't know if Smith understood what was happening, but he was scared enough to follow Sully's lead. Thoughts sluggish, he struggled to come up with a plan to save them. If —*when*— they left this dank hole, they were separated from their own troops by innumerable Germans ready to cut them down the second Sully's illusion faltered. They'd doubtless be on the lookout for him if they'd known enough to march right through his false firefight. Whether someone sold them out, or they'd picked something up with their listening posts, they'd known.

This is bad. I'm fucked. We're fucked. I couldn't save any of them, and I won't be able to save this poor sap either. He'll die just like the rest, and so will I.

A shout caught his attention. Sully's brows shot up. He had to be hallucinating. What idiot would be out here yelling his name for all the world to hear? Was it a trap? Did the Germans know his name? But even if they did, there was something familiar about that voice.

No.

Could it be?

Sully shifted. Smith sucked in a panicked breath. Giving him a reassuring glance, Sully slipped to the edge of the hole and peered over. The stillness of the forest was eerie. Moonlight cast the world in glowing shades of gray. Headless trees threw long shadows over charred frosted earth, but nothing moved. Distant gunfire echoed, but there wasn't a single person in sight. No voice calling him.

He must've imagined it. But, they might not get a better chance. If they stuck to the shadows, maybe they could skirt the firefight. What else were they supposed to do? Wait for a laughable figment of Sully's imagination to charge to their rescue?

No one was coming. No one was even looking for them. If they were going to survive this, they had to act.

He was about to say so when out of nowhere two people appeared, suddenly standing a few feet away. Smith made a startled squeak before clapping his hands over his mouth.

"Perhaps we ought to wait for daylight?" A feminine voice asked. Was that a woman in a male soldier's uniform? "He could be anywhere. If he's using an illusion to conceal himself, we won't spot him. And if he's dead, there are too many of them to examine each one in the midst of the fighting."

"He's not dead. He's too smart for that," Elliot said.

Sully stared. How? What?

This can't really be happening. He can't really be here. You're cracking up, Sullivan.

The woman braced her hands on her hips as she stared at Elliot. "And you know that from reading his file?"

"I—" Elliot seemed to catch himself. "Yes."

"Would you care to attempt that in a more believable tone?"

This was real, even though it was goddamn impossible. And Elliot needed a rescue too before he stepped in it. Sully dropped the illusion. "Looking for me, huh?"

The two of them flinched at the unexpected voice, both tensing momentarily before Elliot grinned at him. Even in the faint moonlight it was glorious, the most beautiful thing Sully had ever seen. A warm feeling spread in his chest, so much deeper than it should've, winding under tissue and bone. A crushing tightness gripped him, at odds with the wild flutter of his pulse.

"Corporal Sullivan?" The woman asked.

"That's me, ma'am." Abruptly, he remembered the German soldiers all around. "It's dangerous to be out there like that. I can't keep up an illusion around you, maybe you should get down."

The woman nodded and climbed into the crater followed by Elliot after he'd glanced around. Checking that no one was approaching?

With a small burst of renewed energy, Sully concealed them all. He turned to Smith, who was plastered back against the dirt wall. "It's okay. They're on our side."

"They appeared out of thin air!" Smith hissed with dismay.

"Would you like to be saved or not?" The woman asked, scorn dripping from her clipped words.

"Bellona," Elliot chided. "The boy's in shock. Try not to frighten him all the way to death. I'm sure this has been enough of an ordeal."

"They're safe," Sully said, infusing his voice with certainty. Why was he so convinced he was in the clear? Just because of Elliot? He hardly knew the man. What was it about Elliot that after spending one night with him, Sully felt completely secure?

Memories swept over him. Intense longing threatened to drown him. So much emotion flooded in all directions. He had no hope of picking apart which were his or even what they were. He was too damn exhausted.

A battle waged in Smith, reflected across his features. Sully felt him come to a decision, relax a fraction.

"What now?" Sully peered at Elliot for guidance. The naked heat in Elliot's eyes was near incendiary. He looked like he had thousands of ideas, none of them remotely related to their immediate situation. Sully fought the responding blush that rushed to his cheeks. Then Elliot reined himself in, expression settling into neutrality.

"Right. Well, Bellona can only take two at once." He contemplated them. "Corporal Sullivan isn't likely to leave a man behind, even temporarily."

She raised an eyebrow and Sully practically heard her ask *how the hell would you know?* How did he? How would Elliot explain? They were from entirely different worlds. Their circles would never have crossed. It was obvious as the differences between their uniforms.

Could they say Sully had worked for him? Investigated something on his behalf? Maybe she wouldn't ask?

"He's right, I won't leave Smith here undefended." Sully resolutely crossed his arms. If all he did today was save one man, he might be able to tell himself he wasn't useless. He might be able to look Anne in the face again when he got home. Might not feel like such a damn coward. "I stay behind, you two take him. I can conceal myself easy enough."

It wasn't entirely a lie. He could hold out a while longer. If they were quick about whatever it was they were doing. No one had to know how weak he was, how he was pushing himself too far keeping this entire conversation silenced.

Elliot's expressive mouth pursed. Sully saw the argument coming before he opened it. Bellona got there first. "I'm not leaving you behind, Captain. Not alone. Corporal Sullivan is correct. He has the best chance."

Jaw clenching and unclenching, Elliot glanced up at the night sky. Sully followed his gaze; twinkling stars dotted the dark blue. Smoke drifted around, obscuring them in patches. "Bell, you'll do as I say." She narrowed her icy eyes but didn't fight him. She didn't have grounds to since he outranked her. "Get the private to safety, I'll remain with Corporal Sullivan. He can conceal us if need be, and the longer you spend arguing, the greater the danger."

Bellona scrutinized Sully. He tried to seem like he had no idea why Elliot would want to stay with him either. Suspicion lit her eyes, and Sully cursed internally at Elliot. He had no idea what game Elliot was playing, but it was obvious their connection shouldn't be made blatant. It wasn't the most dangerous part of being out here, but it could still get a man discharged in humiliation. Or more likely in Elliot's case, court martialed.

Or would it be like Allison's injury, not even bad enough to see their kind relieved of duty? Sully's insides squirmed uncomfortably as Bellona continued to examine him. Finally she huffed an irate sigh.

"Right then," she said to Smith. "With me. And you." She fixed her fierce gaze on Elliot. "We are going to speak about this later, and you are *going* to explain yourself."

Elliot nodded. "Be safe."

She inclined her head slightly. "And you don't be stupid."

Sully was impressed she had the guts to talk to him like that.

A moment later she vanished from sight along with Smith. Sully stared at the space they'd been. "Huh. Can't say I expected you to show up here, saving people willy-nilly."

"Warren," Elliot whispered. Sully looked at him, heart flayed open at the tender way he said it, so many feelings swelling inside of him that made absolutely no sense. It had to be relief after almost dying. Had to be. He was just confused.

Then Elliot's hands cupped his face and those once silk-soft fingers were calloused and dry, and Sully couldn't breathe with aching for him. Elliot must have changed so much in the last months, every hardship he endured altering him in ways that might never be reversed. Same as Sully had been.

"How are you here?" Sully asked, words full of too much meaning. Too much wonder.

Elliot's intense gaze held his. An electric shock traveled through Sully's weary body. It sped his heart and made his legs buckle before he caught himself. "I came for you."

In a surge of motion, their mouths met. Crashed into one another, frantic. Elliot kissed him and it was like that first desperate time. Sully could almost feel the brick at his back as he yielded to the sweet pressure of Elliot's tongue, parting his lips. Barely enough sense left in his mind to throw up an illusion concealing them. He would never leave Elliot unprotected. He'd made a promise. He didn't break those.

When they drew back, Sully gasped. Cold air rushed over where Elliot's hot mouth had been. His whole body tingled, his knees on the verge of giving out. Elliot's strong arms were all that kept him upright. "God," Sully sighed.

Elliot flashed a satisfied smirk. "I cannot tell you how many times I've thought of doing that again."

Something soared in Sully's chest. Elliot still thought about him.

"Me too," he admitted sheepishly. He tried and failed to suppress a yawn.

"Boring you, am I?" Elliot asked with a touch of wry amusement.

"Un-unh." Sully yawned a second time and alarm flitted across Elliot's face.

"You're overworking yourself."

It was nice Elliot was worried about him. Sully liked it. Liked the warm caring feelings wrapping him up as surely as Elliot's body was.

How did he know about Sully's limitations? Faint awareness prickled.

"Read about that in my file did you?" Sully sagged a little more in Elliot's arms. Elliot took his weight easily, still stronger than he seemed.

A strange expression Sully couldn't interpret tightened Elliot's mouth. There wasn't enough space in his mind or power to parse it. He was tired. So damn tired. Sleep was reaching out with open arms, curling around him, weighing him down.

"Mmm. Bellona ought to be here any moment, you may as well drop the illusion."

He couldn't give in. Had to stay awake a little longer. Had to protect Elliot.

"Said I'd keep you safe," Sully mumbled.

The world went dark. He thought Elliot called his name, but he couldn't have opened his eyes for anything.

CHAPTER SEVENTEEN

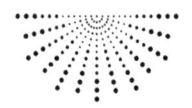

ELLIOT SAGGED AGAINST THE cold wooden wall of a hastily constructed medical building, a small one room cottage really, his breath puffing in front of him in wispy white clouds. Closing his eyes, he tipped his head back and fought to steady himself. Warren was going to be fine. Doctor Browne assured them he simply needed rest to recover. It wasn't like the last time. It wouldn't take days.

He couldn't prevent himself from reliving the moment Warren collapsed in his arms, dead weight he'd been forced to lower to the ground. He was cradling Warren's head when Bellona returned. She called his name, but he hadn't been able to tear himself away from checking if Warren was all right. When she'd called him by his given name, Elliot jerked his gaze up to meet hers, and her eyebrows flew up at whatever she read in his face.

He'd forced himself to respond normally, to push his features into a neutral expression, but he suspected it was far too late for that.

They hadn't spoken of it in the intervening hours with Warren unconscious inside the building and waiting for Doctor Browne, who Elliot gathered was either skilled or in the know, to have a few spare moments.

Many cases inside, and in the dozens of similar buildings, were much, much, worse. Warren had been at the bottom of everybody's list. With no external injuries and a magical root to his problem, Elliot was surprised Doctor Browne found time to see him at all.

The doctor was dead on his feet, his flaming hair in irreparable disorder, and glasses slightly askew in front of exhausted aqua eyes. But he seemed competent and wasn't outwardly hostile while Elliot explained what happened. After a rushed exam and diagnosis, he'd given the nurse instructions and moved on to the next patient.

Elliot was only in the way. He couldn't stand there staring like some lost pup at a man he wasn't even supposed to know, so he'd slunk outside.

A few more moments passed and the tightness in his chest eased ever so slightly. He focused on the way Warren had been ecstatic to see him. Fervently hoped that didn't change when they actually had a full discussion.

Speaking of discussions, a presence settled beside him against the wall.

"You and I are due to talk," Bellona said, her arm brushing his. He was probably infusing that simple action with too much meaning, but it felt like a sign of support.

Elliot scrubbed a hand over his numb face, his muscles aching with fatigue and strung tight. "Can it wait?"

Bellona's dark brows lifted, her gaze skeptical. "Certainly. If you'd rather have this discussion with Corporal Sullivan awake and listening or in a house full of officers trained to observe absolutely everything."

Elliot groaned. Those were infinitely worse options. "I can't precisely speak freely out here either," he informed her, eyes darting to soldiers and nurses passing them.

"Then, isn't it a wonder that Courtemanche thought ahead to at least ensure we had a place to bed down tonight, and unlike the barracks you've been assigned, I've been given a private room usually reserved for dignitaries. It's rather lux for the front. I'm told they didn't know quite where to place me, and I'm to be grateful for Général Courtemanche's thoughtfulness in insisting I not be sent to sleep with the nurses."

"They'll probably be watching to make sure you don't bring any men in," Elliot attempted to argue, if he could put off this conversation indefinitely that would truly be ideal.

She rolled her eyes at him, dropping a hand onto his shoulder. Of course she wasn't going to let it go so easily. She was, quite possibly, the most stubborn person he had ever met, impossible to deter. "Then for heaven's sake, let's not get caught."

"Wait! Not here." Elliot searched the vicinity, eyes darting over shoddy wooden buildings in rows on either side of the wide dirt path. "There," he said, nodding to the shadowed recess between two of them near the end of the row. "I'll wait for you there. Take a small walk and come around the other side. Let's not attract too much attention, please."

Once they'd safely met again, Bellona made a rapid series of calculated transports until they found themselves in the shadows of the building she was assigned. Getting inside undetected proved rather easier than it would have if she had actually been a dignitary and not simply afforded the comfort of one based on her position as Courtemanche's favorite. Not that he begrudged her the respect she richly deserved.

Bellona switched on the electric light as they entered. There was an actual bed, albeit not luxuriously constructed. It was made of a simple wood, no ornamentation. The rest of the room contained sturdy matching furniture. An armoire for suits or uniforms to be hung in, bedside stands, a chair and small table for dining at near the square window. Lacy yellowing curtains covered the glass, obscuring the room from view.

"Very fancy," Elliot said, examining everything and wondering who had stayed here prior to Bellona.

"And not at all what we've come here to speak about," she replied archly.

"No." Elliot wrapped his arms around himself, an old habit when he felt vulnerable. It made him appear immature, but he couldn't seem to stop.

"You know him, Stone. He knew you. How were you planning to conceal that from me?" Bellona asked, her eyes containing barely disguised hurt. She didn't understand why he wouldn't trust her. Why he *couldn't*.

Sending her a regretful smile, Elliot gently lifted a shoulder. "In all honesty, I hoped it might not be so obvious. We only met once before I left for this damned war, and he doesn't—shouldn't —remember the times we've crossed paths in, er, dreams."

Bellona cocked an eyebrow. "Dreams as in…?"

"As in I dreamwalk, and I'd appreciate it if you kept that to yourself as well. But as for Sullivan and me, we hardly know one another."

Bellona's gaze narrowed, her hands landing on her hips in a pose that strongly reminded Elliot of his sisters. "I'm not utterly daft, you know. I've eyes. And they saw the way you looked at him.

Any person of moderate intelligence could tell you're fond of him."

"I wouldn't call it fond," he said, face heating. He cursed himself a thousand times for putting Sully in the position that their connection might be discovered. And his stumbling over his words wouldn't convince anyone. "We really did only meet just before I left. I swear. There's nothing—whatever you're thinking—it's nothing to do with him. It's only me, if you absolutely must be disgusted by anyone. If you feel the need to report anyone. He's only ever been a friend and—"

"I wish you'd stop lying. And for God's sake stop worrying I'll report anything. No one mentioned any such thing. What you say in this room never leaves it." Bellona crossed her arms and sank onto the bed.

Elliot stared at her, stunned speechless for a moment. "Pardon?" he managed, and on the whole, at least that made sense.

"Don't be so uptight, Stone." Had he entered another reality? As if anyone in his life had ever once accused him of that before. Libertine? Yes. Uptight? Never. "If you enjoy men, and he enjoys men, I don't give a toss. I'm not utterly unaware of the world or cloistered away. I've two younger brothers in this war, and I love them both dearly. One of them, Peter, he's that way too. And I'll tell you the same blasted thing I told him when he turned up in my room with tears in his eyes at sixteen and confessed because he couldn't bear hiding it any longer: It's nothing to be ashamed of, some men simply prefer other men." Of course he believed that. He was only shocked she did. Society in general certainly didn't. She paused and tilted her head in consideration. "I suppose it stands to reason that some women prefer women, and perhaps some prefer both or neither. Who am I to judge? I aim to fix things, not ruin them."

Something released in Elliot's chest, a shaky influx of relief followed by elation. It was an enormous comfort that in a world so dedicated to eradicating every facet of him, some wonderful, decent people, accepted him as he was.

"Thank you." His voice was a little raw. Clearing his throat first, he added, "I'm not ashamed of who I am, and I don't believe there's anything sinful in love or even pleasure. I'm simply cautious. Not everyone believes as you do. Here it's even more dangerous." More often than not, Elliot felt as if his bones might give out with the weight of the world and all the mounting expectations pressing in on him. "I'm glad you know, truly. But it's so much more complicated than that."

"All right, tell me," she said, settling back against the wall and patting the mattress beside her. And that too, reminded him of May and Hazel. The three of them sitting in May's bed, listening to her read them stories, giggling, and trading increasingly implausible tales of their own adventures until Mother would scoop him and Hazel up to deposit them back in their own beds, a kind smile on her face, smelling of flowers and all things wonderful. God, he missed them all.

Freeing himself from the recollection, Elliot crawled onto the bed next to Bellona, arms once again brushing. He spared a thought for the impropriety of getting into bed with her, but he never had paid much attention to propriety. Nothing untoward would occur.

Elliot closed his eyes and considered what he ought to say. The government didn't know about his ability to dreamwalk, he hadn't told anyone here. Not even his team. It was too private. He'd wanted to keep that one thing about himself out of the government's hands. But Bellona's suspicions over what lay between him and Warren were enough to land him in hot water if she was so inclined. And instead she'd been accepting. She'd offered friendship he sorely required.

This was an opportunity to show trust. Could he let himself trust her?

"I won't judge," she said softly. "But you need to confide in someone, and I need to be able to trust you. Tell me what you can."

Slowly nodding, Elliot let out a breath, and expelled the entire story. The guilt, and the need, and the pain he could already feel headed for him like a freight train when Warren inevitably confirmed he didn't remember any of the last months. The determination he had not to make things awkward while Warren was adjusting.

"I'll tell him," Elliot added hastily. "Of course I will, but he's already got so much to deal with and now this on top of it all."

Bellona's gaze was sympathetic. "The right answer, if there is one, certainly isn't obvious to me. All I see are mines in every direction and the slightest false move…" She shook her head. "Are you sure you've made the wisest decision, selecting him?"

"Yes," Elliot said forcefully. Then, "No. Of course I can't be sure. The Warren I know is only a part of him, not the whole man. Though what I knew of him was wonderful. Chicago on a night out isn't the same as France at war, granted. But you saw his file."

"It was impressive and risky. The things he can do will certainly be useful, I won't deny that. But how will this affect you? The others? Him when he discovers the truth?" Elliot couldn't take the concern in her voice.

Shoulders drooping, he buried his face in his bent knees like a child instead of the grown man and leader he was meant to be. He was trying his best in these circumstances, he was, but his whole life he hadn't been accountable to anyone. Now that he was bearing responsibility, he loathed to disappoint. The problem was, he couldn't seem to stop doing it. "I thought of that, I swear. And I don't have the answers. I wish I did."

"But you chose him anyway." Bellona's voice was soft, full of understanding he didn't deserve in the least.

Elliot sat back up straight, looking her in the eyes, wanting her to know he was telling the truth. "He's qualified. He'll do his job. Wa—Sullivan, he doesn't do things by halves. And he'll excel at this, I know it."

Bellona sighed and patted his arm. "You know I trust you. Even your somewhat questionable judgment. But tread lightly, Stone. Human emotions are disastrous enough without adding an empath into the mix."

That warning rang in his ears as he snuck back to the barracks later, and again as he lay in the dark in a room full of strange snoring men, waiting for sleep to claim him.

CHAPTER EIGHTEEN

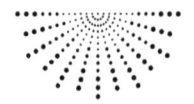

A LOW PAINED MOAN to his left greeted Sully as he drifted toward wakefulness. He winced at the disgusting smell of whatever room he was in. Forcing his eyelids to open, he blinked at the bare wood ceiling. Cold sunlight streamed through the one window in this too-crowded room full of injured and anguished soldiers. For a moment, he panicked, taking stock of all his limbs, trying to determine whether the unbearable pain he felt came from himself or the mangled people surrounding him.

Steaming up his defenses, Sully steeled himself against the clawing, nauseating mass of suffering. It was them. Not him. He exhaled slowly in relief.

"Finally up, are you?" A young nurse asked him, approaching his cot. Her apron was covered in stains he was uninterested in examining, so he looked up at her face. Wisps of her wavy golden hair had come loose from the tight bun she wore, glowing in the sunlight and softening her otherwise severe style.

"What am I doing here?" he asked in a voice that scraped his parched throat, then remembering his manners, added, "Sorry, I'm just confused. Nurse?"

She smiled kindly at him. "Nurse Jackson. Nothing to worry about. You were unconscious when your handsome friend brought you in. Doctor Browne said you'd be free to go as soon as you were up and able. How are you feeling?"

My handsome friend? What friend? Allison's still injured.

"I'm a little tired." He wracked his memory for the night before. Remembered being hunkered down with Private Smith, beyond that it was a blur. "I think I'm all right."

She offered him a vibrant grin that eased the exhausted strain around her wide hazel eyes. "That's wonderful to hear. We don't get much of that. Captain Stone asked if you recovered before he returns, that you report to him."

Captain Stone, his new commanding officer. Sully struggled to recall anything about meeting the man, but there was nothing beyond a fuzzy headache. He wasn't surprised given how low his reserves had gotten.

Once the nurse cleared him to leave, Sully figured he had some leeway before he'd be missed, and besides he smelled like everyone else in this shithole. Showing up reeking of who knew what filth would make a terrible impression.

Sully retrieved his kit and made his way to the baths. Climbing into warm water and washing off was all he could think of. The fact he'd be in a giant vat with a bunch of other equally grimy men no longer disgusted him on the same level it once had. Anything was better than the filth of the front lines or the gore of battle.

After he was sufficiently scrubbed and dressed in the single spare uniform he owned, Sully sought out Allison. If he was going to leave today, he owed his friend a farewell in person.

The little wooden building serving as a convalescence ward for

Allison and five other wounded soldiers was one of many. Sully entered the building and offered the nurse a polite smile. She pursed her lips, forbidding, protective of her resting charges, but didn't stop him from going to Allison's bedside.

There wasn't anywhere to sit and hardly room to stand between cots, which made it awkward, but Allison opened one eye, then the other as Sully approached. He shifted, trying to sit up in his bed, and grimaced at whatever it did to his wound.

"Don't hurt yourself on my behalf," Sully said dryly. "Just came to check on you before I leave. How are they treating you?"

Allison sent him a dazed sort of smile. It seemed they weren't short on pain medication today. "'M, all right. Nurse Jopling's real nice."

The nurse let out a snort of laughter she quickly pretended hadn't come from her as she busied herself with another patient.

Sully gave Allison a lopsided smile. "You're tougher than you look, I guess. Don't say I never said anything nice about you."

Allison smothered a yawn then mumbled, "You're nice too."

This time Sully was the one who broke into a laugh. "Uh-huh. So, I came to say goodbye. Been selected for an assignment elsewhere. It'll be a while before you're back in the field anyway, but watch yourself. Okay?"

Allison's brows pinched. He was so small in the cot. So vulnerable. It made Sully feel like shite, like the lowest scum that he was getting out of here and leaving him behind to fend for himself. "Y'feel bad going?"

Annoyed at himself because that was exactly it, Sully sighed. What happened to not forming attachments? "Mm."

"Stupidest thing. 'M glad one of us is getting out." Allison yawned again, unapologetically. "Jus' write sometimes. Might even miss you around."

Heart aching, Sully gave him a smile. He was never good at goodbyes. For someone who felt so many emotions on a daily basis, he was the worst at expressing them. "Second I get a chance to. Take care."

Allison tried to roll his eyes, but they sort of drifted shut instead. "Gonna. You too."

With a short nod Sully gently patted Allison's good arm. "Sure thing. See you around, Allison."

When he left, Sully found an officer he recognized to ask for directions to where he could find Captain Stone. Captain Stargel shrugged. "Haven't the foggiest. The lieutenant he came with might, though."

The building pointed out to him was off the beaten path, in an area reserved for important people. Sully knocked on the door and waited, hands loosely held behind his back. The door opened, and all the air rushed from Sully's lungs. Pale blue eyes, so permanently etched into his memory that he hadn't forgotten a single detail of them, held his gaze.

"You're...?" Sully didn't know what question he was trying to ask. Finally, he settled on, "I'm looking for Captain Stone."

Elliot's pretty pink lips twisted in a cheap approximation of a smile. "You've found him."

Sully blinked twice. His exhausted mind scrambled for a proper response. Concern, warmth, and a confusing mass of something all tangled in longing and guilt radiated from Elliot. "I don't understand."

"Why don't you come in? We've got quite a lot to discuss and the sooner we leave the better."

Elliot was Captain Stone, Sully's new commanding officer and the man who requested his reassignment. Following him inside, Sully turned the information over in his mind. He didn't like the conclusions he was coming to. What was Elliot expecting?

There was a woman with pitch-dark hair pulled back from her face, sharp eyes watching him intently. She was seated on a chair near the window, in a man's uniform. Something about that jogged memories he hadn't been able to grasp earlier. They'd appeared unexpectedly and he'd—Sully's eyes flashed to Elliot. Those velvet lips were just as soft as he remembered them being in Chicago. His heart stumbled, heat rising in his cheeks, and his chest tightening.

The woman cleared her throat as awkward silence gripped them. "Right," she said, when it became obvious neither of them was going to speak first. "Lovely to meet you Corporal Sullivan." She stood, holding out her hand to shake, and Sully accepted. Her grip was firm. "Lieutenant Bell, though the boys have adopted that one's silly nickname for me. I'm sure soon enough you'll do the same."

"Bellona suits you," Elliot said with an unrepentant grin in her direction.

Despite her exasperation, she exuded fondness for Elliot with a strength Sully envied. His closest ally in Europe was lying in a bed wounded. Hell knew when he'd see him again. If he ever would.

"Nice to make your acquaintance, Lieutenant," Sully said politely, and she gave him a friendly nod in return.

"Right, I'm off to ensure we're properly kitted out for the return journey. Don't suppose you know how to ride a motorcycle?"

Sully stared at her, incredulous. Did she? "Uh, no. Never had a reason to learn," he said, feeling suddenly underprepared for this assignment.

"Sidecar it is," she declared, resting a hand on one cocked hip. "Don't worry, we'll teach you at the house."

"The house?" Everything was happening so fast, Sully's head spun. A thousand questions battered him, and he could feel his temper igniting. There was something secretive passing between Bell and Elliot. Not Elliot. Captain Stone. Here he was Captain Stone. First names would absolutely not be passing between them. And he needed to wrap his mind around the fact that the man who starred in every fantasy he'd indulged in for months was now his superior officer. He didn't like the way it made his skin itch with apprehension. It would be too easy to slip up and give them away.

"Our headquarters. Near Amiens, on our side. Far enough away that we can work without interference. Anyway, I'm sure Captain Stone," she said his name pointedly, accompanied with an unsubtle stare. "Will fill you in. I'd best be off."

What's that about? She mad at him for something? What did he do?

With a last polite incline of her head she was off. Sully was left to flounder for some thread of a thought to grasp at. He turned to Stone, crossing his arms and reclining slightly against a bare wood wall.

"Start with why the hell you chose me for a team there's no way I'm qualified for," Sully suggested, the aggression in his voice making his head ache. Made his heart ache too, but he was doing his best to pretend it didn't.

"That's utterly preposterous. If you weren't, they would never have sent me your file. You are perfectly qualified." His defensive posture gave him away. There was something Elliot wasn't saying. It was there in his mood too. He was all over the place, so Sully couldn't get a read on what he was hiding, but it made his blood boil.

"That doesn't answer the question," Sully bit out.

Elliot worried his bottom lip, considering Sully as if he was weighing the impact of his words before he committed to them.

Suddenly, Sully didn't want to hear whatever lie Elliot was about to blurt out. It was obvious, now that he was starting to parse the mix of emotion filling the room, desire and longing, right there beneath much more intense nameless things covering them. He clenched his fists.

"Let me guess, Elliot, you figured since I fucked you once on the other side of the world, I'd be more than happy to fall right into your bed in exchange for a job away from the heavy fighting." Sully gritted his teeth and sent Elliot a spiteful stare. "I got news for you, I've never sold myself before and I'm not starting now, so you can take your assignment and shove it right up your—"

"Christ, Warren. That's not it!" Stone cut across, face red with anger, emotions a roiling mass of frustration and darkness. "I wasn't—I wouldn't—I'm not after that."

Sully scoffed, throwing his arms out from his sides, palms up. "Right, just happens that I'm the best guy for the job? Me? A screw up who's barely useful to anyone because I'm always one push too far from collapse? Bull. If you read my file, you would know—"

"I know you've been taking risks, bigger ones than you ought to, just to keep the men around you safe," Elliot cut in, voice reasonable and urgent, like he thought this was a better alternative to the unseemly insinuation Sully had made. "I know you push yourself to your limits every day and are never given enough time to recover before you rush right back out there again. So don't tell me I don't understand how useless you are when you're the one who fails to understand how *valuable* you are."

Recognition lit up in Sully's mind, fueled his flaming temper, shoved reason right outside and locked the door behind it. "Ah. So that's what this is about. You think you can just swoop in and rescue me from myself, like I'm too stupid to know what I'm doing."

Elliot's brows drew down. His fists curled in tight balls at his side. "Well do you? Honestly, Warren, do you? I thought you wanted to get back home to Anne. Didn't you tell me you would do anything to? Because it appears you've lost sight of that."

Sully's nostrils flared as his breath quickened, responding to the rising tension between them. "Of course I want to make it home! Of course I don't want to leave her alone. But for fuck's sake Elliot, have you been out there? How many men have you seen die right in front of you? How many body parts have you seen blown clear off? I'm doing my job, same as every other man here. I'm not any better or worse 'cause of what I can do or who I am. They deserve to be safe as much as me. Why shouldn't I ride my limit? I watch less people die that way."

Elliot's anguished eyes pierced holes into Sully's heart. Tendrils of fear licked the air. "Christ. And what happens to you?"

"Why should you care?" Sully asked flatly, stance defiant. "You've got no right. We fucked once. That's all. You don't get a say in what I choose to do because you had your cock in me."

Stone shut his eyes, a despairing clench of something not quite pity, but close enough to tick Sully off more, permeated the room. Choked Sully's throat up and he cleared it angrily.

"I don't want to fight you," Stone said, quiet, opening his eyes, pleading blue all lovely and poignant and focused directly on Sully.

It's not fair he's got those damn eyes. Even when I'm fucking furious I want to stare in them forever. "So don't. Tell me the goddamn truth, Elliot. What do you want from me?"

"I swear I don't expect anything more than hard work. Everything in me says you can excel in this role. You're smart, resourceful, and you've got skills suited to deception and infiltration. You would be an asset, one we need desperately if we're to stop an attack that could see the Germans turn the tide of this war before America has a chance to shore up the Entente troops."

The sincerity underlying those words, the honest pleading in his voice begged Sully to believe him. Sully's rage tempered to a simmer. Stone wasn't lying. He really did believe all those things. Maybe Sully had jumped to the wrong conclusion. His constant exhaustion wore on his patience and made him quicker to burn hot. What he needed was to think without all the feelings between them distracting him.

There was no time to press Stone for more information as a quick rap of knuckles tapped on the door, then Bell stuck her head in.

"Hate to interrupt, but that pompous old windbag who didn't want Sullivan going anywhere? He's on a war path. I suggest we sneak off while we can and let Courtemanche deal with the rest later."

"Of course," Stone said straightening, then he bit his lip in a shy gesture that plucked at Sully's chest. That wasn't fair either. Sully was supposed to be angry, not thinking about the marks those teeth left behind and how much he wanted to run his tongue over them, to taste Elliot's seductive mouth. "Will you still be joining us, Warren? If you feel you can't, I understand. But I wish you would. We truly do require someone like you."

Sully hesitated. He was frustrated. In the dark on too much. Was he furious enough to turn this down? His chance to get farther away from the carnage wearing him down day by day before it spat him out raw? What would even be left of him when he finally returned home if he went on like this?

His anger couldn't be worth staying. As part of Stone's team he could be useful. Useful in a way that wouldn't necessarily leave him undamaged either but might not destroy him quite as rapidly.

At least I might be able to breathe unrestricted. At least I might be able to think straight. But there's one thing needs saying.

"Sullivan," he corrected, uncompromising. "We do this, you need to remember who I am to you here."

Something pained crackled around Stone. Sully frowned at it, but a second later it was locked down. A wound he obviously didn't want Sully nosing around in.

"Right," Stone said. "Yes, obviously. Shall we, then?"

With a sigh, Sully followed them outside. He really hoped he wouldn't regret this.

CHAPTER NINETEEN

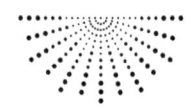

FIVE FUCKING MINUTES LATER, Sully was full of fucking regret. Bouncing around in a sidecar attached to a metal death trap as it barreled along at high speeds was definitely considered unsafe when your entire body was exposed to the elements. He tried closing his eyes, except that was even worse. Then he couldn't see the million ways they might die, and Elliot—Stone, damn it—had the nerve to feel exuberant.

Exuberant. He's fucking thrilled.

The sensation bubbled over Sully's skin like fizzing soda.

How dare that bastard enjoy this?

If Sully was in control at all, it might not be so bad. As a passenger, he hated it with every single part of his motion-sick body. If they made it all the way to their destination without Sully losing the meager contents of his stomach all over the road, it'd be a miracle. Cursing every time he was jolted, Sully shot daggers with his eyes that Stone failed completely to notice, his full attention being on where they were going. Which, all things said, was a good thing. Even though it irrationally made Sully angrier.

Plus he was freezing his balls off. The wool uniform and jacket he wore, while stifling in warmer weather, failed completely when ice cold wind was blasting him all over. His fingers were practically about to fall off in his olive wool gloves.

The only highlight to this awful trip was that the pressure on the dam in his head gradually decreased the farther they drove until it was hardly even a blip, and finally, it melted away completely.

By the time they reached Fienvillers, it was stretching into the afternoon. Every muscle in Sully's body was cramped with tension. He clambered awkwardly from the sidecar and stood on shaky legs, relieved and slightly faint. Bell and Stone exchanged amused glances that incensed him further.

"All right?" she asked, patting at the wild strands of her dark hair that had come loose as she removed her leather cap; he didn't think there was any hope of salvaging it. Sully probably looked even worse for wear and wouldn't be surprised if he was pale as fresh snow.

He narrowed his eyes. "Yeah. Peachy. You both always drive like maniacs or was that special just for me?"

The two of them chuckled. Sully's stomach warmed at the sound of Stone's deep laugh. Why were his reactions to Stone so intense? Why the hell was Sully so fixated on him after all this time? They'd had one night of desperate, clinging, toe-curling, mind-blowing sex, that was all. One.

The vivid sensation of Elliot moving inside him, their foreheads pressed together hit Sully square in the gut. And then that hardly even a kiss before they left camp, the way his pulse raced when their mouths met...

Sully rapidly doused those thoughts before he embarrassed himself. Okay, before he embarrassed himself more.

"You'll get used to it," Stone said with a blinding smile. The ride apparently having relaxed him. "It's much more enjoyable when you're driving."

Sully didn't doubt that. "Right." He grabbed his kit bag and rifle. "Now what?"

"We'll introduce you to the team and get you settled," Stone said, lacing his fingers behind his back and stretching his arms. The muscles more defined than Sully remembered them. *Much more defined.*

Jesus, stop looking.

"Let you recover," Bell added, then sent him a teasing smile. "Feed you once you stop being quite so violently green."

The house was a decent size made of white stone with a sloping tile roof dusted in the lightest coating of powdery snow. The plain rectangle windows were framed with faded wooden shutters that might have once been stained dark, it was hard to guess what color they were originally meant to be. Time and lack of care had transformed them into a dull sort of gray, on the verge of falling right off.

Woodsmoke from the chimney and fresh winter air mingled. Sully tried not to make a show of inhaling it. God, it was good to be away from the horrible smells. You got used to it, but now that he was out here, he didn't know how he'd ever stood it.

They brought him inside where three men were sitting around a worn wooden table, playing cards. Two of them were French Army, their light blue uniforms said as much, though the state of them was deplorable. Buttons undone, jackets left open, hats absent—things Sully would've been reprimanded for. The other one was in much the same state, though he was an American, his olive drab jacket also hung wide. The dark bristles thick on his unshaved cheeks and jaw added to his rugged appearance.

"I see you've made yourselves useful in our absence," Stone said haughtily. Two of the men laughed, the pale American and the dark-skinned Frenchman. The other Frenchman, still summer tanned, shrugged; his eyes remained determinedly on his cards, refusing to so much as look at them. Light brown hair fell over his forehead. His shoulders were tense and a sad sort of anger emanated from him, knotting Sully's stomach.

What's his story?

The friendly Frenchman smiled brightly at them, his deep brown eyes dancing. "A little rest and recuperation never hurt no one." He had an American accent, something slightly southern that wasn't quite masked by hints of a French one. "This must be our new recruit, no?"

Sully smiled. He liked the warmth the man exuded. "Corporal Warren Sullivan. You can call me Sully, everyone does. Good to meet you."

"Caporal Léon Remonet. Likewise. That grumpy fuck is Lieutenant Charlie Hoffman," he pointed the second man who'd laughed. Certainly not the one Sully would've pegged as the grumpy one, but he did have a reserved air about him. They exchanged polite nods. "And our Frenchest member over here is Sargent Michel Charbonneau." Light brown eyes glanced flatly up at him, then dropped to the cards again. He rearranged them as if he wanted nothing more than to play a game, but Sully sensed a roiling resentment that almost knocked him off his feet. He couldn't grasp why since they'd never even met before. Looking to Stone for guidance, Sully hated that he felt the insecure need to seek him out.

Stone met his eyes, then returned his gaze to Charbonneau. He paused, grimacing as if he knew he was about to push a boundary and would rather be doing anything else. "Right. I suppose you're busy, so I'll just show Sullivan up to—"

Charbonneau's chair scraped across the wood floor and crashed backwards as he vaulted to his feet. "Tu fais chier! I'll not share a bed with him. It's a large enough house, put him somewhere else. Put him with you or in the kitchen for all I care. Ol—Swift is hardly cold in the ground, and you think he can be replaced so easily? Well, I do not. And I cannot bear to spend every second reminded by—by—"

Remonet's hand landed on his shoulder and he murmured something that seemed to deflate Charbonneau's fury enough that he stormed from the room, stomping out the front door and slamming it behind himself. You could've heard a pin drop when he left. Sully's recently loosened grip on grief let him feel the full force of Charbonneau's mourning and he ached with it in a way he wasn't even certain he still remembered how to.

Guess I'm not permanently numb after all. Don't know whether or not to be glad of it.

"Crap," Hoffman muttered. "That was...something."

"He's," Remonet began to say, then frowned in the direction Charbonneau had stalked off in before addressing Stone. "I'll talk to him."

Stone nodded; his lips pressed together in a thin line. Remonet followed Charbonneau, and Stone sighed. "Fuck, that could've gone better."

Sully rubbed at the remaining ache in his chest. "What now?"

Elliot's expression was tense, a clear plea in his eyes. "You can't room with Bell, and there are only four rooms. Her, Charbonneau, Hoffman and Remonet, and er, mine."

"So, you want me to room with you?" Sully thought he might

rather the kitchen. If he hadn't felt the eviscerating grief, despair, and fury from Charbonneau, he would have wondered if the whole scene was planned. Exactly how long ago had the man he was replacing been killed? Did Stone even have time to think of the consequences to Sully's presence here? The uncomfortable panicking he was doing while anticipating Sully's reaction spoke volumes. There wasn't another choice, not without making it obvious to everyone in the room he had issues with Stone. That would raise more questions than either of them was prepared to answer. "Guess if you don't mind, I don't have a problem with it. Never been in an officer's quarters before."

Hoffman choked out a laugh and Bell echoed him. Stone gave Sully a wry smile. "Ah, shall I show you the height of luxury then?"

Sully shifted his pack on his shoulder and pretended his stomach didn't flutter at the prospect of being alone with Stone. This was ridiculous. *He* was ridiculous. He was not happy to have Stone to himself, damn it. He wasn't happy to be with him at all.

Even as he thought it, Sully knew he was lying to himself. Still didn't like it. He wasn't remotely ready to move on. He had a right to be mad. Whether his pesky body perked up at Stone's voice or not was beside the point.

Up a narrow wooden stairway, onto the second floor, there was a small landing with two chipped white doors on either side. "Bell's is the far left, next to her Sw—Charbonneau. This one is Remonet and Hoffman," Stone said as they passed the first door on the right. "It used to be Remonet and Charbonneau, but they traded because Charbonneau snores and Swift..." Stone paused with his hand on the door, then pushed on. "Didn't mind the noise. I knew he was taking it hard, we all are, and I should've talked to him before you arrived and spared you that scene. It's just that this all happened rather fast."

"I'm sorry for your loss."

Sighing, Stone opened the door and led Sully inside. "If I had your insight perhaps I'd have spent more time considering how to room us all without injuring him further." Sully's heart clenched unpleasantly at the reminder Stone knew his secret now. *How differently will he see me? Is he already on guard? He is. Remember how he forced down what he was feeling back there?* "I suppose I could suggest he room with Remonet again and you with Hoffman. Then you wouldn't be stuck in here with me."

Sully stemmed his panic and refocused on their conversation. "I don't think that's a good idea. Not tonight anyway, he's…" Charbonneau's gnashing, furious pain was a pit in Sully's stomach. Whatever his own issues, it wasn't worth causing more harm to someone already suffering so deeply. "Better to let it lie for now."

Stone took off his cap and tossed it on the bed, ran a hand through his hair. Sully tried not to be distracted by strands of wheat colored silk slipping through his elegant fingers. There was a distant glaze in Elliot's sun-bleached blue eyes. "I do realize this sounds incredibly pompous, but for the longest time I was all but certain Swift…he seemed to fancy me is all."

Sully felt a stab of jealousy that wasn't fair to anyone chased quickly by a flash of guilt and annoyance at himself. God, he was jealous of a dead man, and for what? Still, he couldn't help but ask, "Did you fancy him?"

Stone quickly shook his head, his gaze on Sully once again entreating. "We were only ever friends and he never outright said it, but I was positive there were hints, which I summarily ignored because of course I was—" His voice cut off, pink flooding his face.

He was what? How was he going to finish that sentence? Sully desperately wanted to know and didn't at the same time. Stone abruptly wandered around the bed to stare out the window.

The bed.

The sole bed.

The one they would have to share.

Sully could've kicked himself, he was so oblivious sometimes. These were small country house rooms. Nice for what they were, roomy even by some standards—by his standards back in Chicago and luxurious beyond the pale by his standards at the front—but he hadn't fully considered what that meant.

"You were…?" he prompted in an attempt to take his mind off the looming prospect of being *in that bed* with Stone later.

"Nothing," Stone said, still not facing him.

Sully let out a huff of air and sank down onto one corner of the flowery quilt, determined not to let his discomfort show. "Maybe he moved on when he realized you weren't interested."

"It appears so. I'm glad he was happy while it lasted. I take it you noticed…" Stone swallowed, and Sully wished he couldn't feel how much he hurt.

"How Charbonneau feels? Yeah."

Stone nodded slowly. "Look, there is something else we should discuss—" A clatter from downstairs cut him off, and Stone groaned wearily. "Right after I go see what the devil is happening now."

∽

THE HOUSE WAS STILL, silent save for the odd creak of the wood settling in the cold. Elliot sat alone at the kitchen table. The navy knitted fisherman's sweater he wore over his long-sleeved shirt did little to keep out the chill. The fire in the woodstove was low, soon to sputter out for the night. A kerosene lantern provided the only illumination in the dark, shadows clinging to the edges of the room.

Warren had retired hours ago, exhausted from his ordeal and the journey. After the distraction of the post arriving, there hadn't been enough privacy to continue the conversation he desperately needed to have with Warren. So he put it off, convincing himself that Warren needed rest more than he needed the truth tonight.

Elliot should have told him all of it anyway. This wasn't a secret he could keep. The longer he concealed it, the more likely Warren was to be furious. He couldn't pretend he hadn't known there would be consequences to indulging the two of them in Warren's dreams. It was only that he hadn't expected they would catch up with him so soon.

After the way Warren reacted to discovering Elliot was his new commanding officer, the tension brewing with Charbonneau, and the awkward evening spent planning for Warren's rapid training and integration, he was too exhausted for another blow out.

Besides, there was no real privacy here, not with all of them crammed into this little house. If Warren raised his voice, everyone would hear and everyone would know. And while Bellona had been accepting, and it appeared Charbonneau would theoretically also be inclined to look the other way, the rest of his team might not.

Proof of an improper relationship with another man in and of itself could be enough for a court martial, especially as an officer. The risk of prosecution was infinitely greater if you were an officer carrying on with an enlisted man. He didn't think his sisters would cut him out of their lives even if he was convicted, but their father certainly would and his brothers might. He would rather not find out. Whether or not they personally despised his choice of bedpartner, every last one of them would be disgusted by the public humiliation a court martial would entail and the unfavorable attention it would draw to their family.

He needed to talk to Warren to explain what had been happening in his dreams, but he didn't know when or how. That, he simply couldn't go up to bed and face. The moment he fell asleep, he would be in Warren's mind. With the way things were between them, Elliot doubted he would be welcome. Not by a conscious Warren.

Neither could he trust himself to turn away when he fell asleep and inevitably discovered he was once more in Warren's nightmares. Leaving him to suffer hadn't been an option before. Why would it be any more palatable now? It was difficult enough to remain awake, knowing he was breaking a promise to a man who wouldn't truly want him to fulfill it.

So he sat here, staring at the darkened window, raking himself over the coals of his guilt.

The kitchen door creaked open, letting in an icy draft of winter air, and Elliot sighed soft frustration. The second reason he wasn't in bed stumbled inside from wherever it was he'd holed up with the emergency bottle of gin. Charbonneau blinked in the glare of the lamplight.

"Do shut the door," Elliot intoned in a clipped voice. "It's cold enough in here, thank you."

Charbonneau grunted something vaguely pejorative, though he complied. He stumbled a few unsteady steps inside, then grabbed onto the kitchen counter to hold himself upright.

"Sit down," Elliot ordered. "We need to speak and now strikes me as the ideal time."

Charbonneau gave him a sullen stare Elliot assumed was a rebuke. He kept his gaze on Charbonneau until he relented, muttering under his breath in French that Elliot understood perfectly and chose magnanimously to ignore. If he was going to talk to someone so obviously corked, he'd have to put up with mumbled insults. Through sheer luck, Charbonneau made it to a chair and slumped heavily in it. Bloodshot eyes blearily rested on Elliot. "What is it you want?"

"What I want is exactly as I've stated. I wish to speak to you. With you." Elliot knew what he wanted to say, but he was feeling his way in the dark. He wished, rather suddenly and vividly, that he had Warren's skill instead of his own. "I recognize you're grieving, I do. I know what Ollie meant to you. You were close. And I think you were quite a lot more than good friends."

Charbonneau bristled. Tried to launch to his feet but tripped right back down. "It is none of your affair," he growled, voice raising.

And Elliot was mucking it up already. Fantastic. He held out his palms in a placating gesture. "I'm not attempting to admonish you. I'm attempting to tell you I understand. I won't judge you if you speak freely."

"There is nothing—" Charbonneau winced, and covered his eyes with one hand in a blatant attempt to conceal the despair on his face. Even drunk he was obstinate. "Rien to discuss," he lied through his teeth, the denial likely fueled by instinct and self-protection. And perhaps Elliot ought to let it go until he was sober, but they didn't have *privacy* for these sorts of conversations when everyone was awake. It needed hashing out. Now.

Charbonneau couldn't be allowed to take his grief out on

Warren, no matter how much Elliot empathized with that grief. Animosity between members of his team could get them killed. This needed to be rooted out before it festered.

"There is," Elliot insisted, his chest aching with the sick knowledge he could easily have been in the same situation, with no one to speak to. No one who understood him. "And I'm sorry I didn't acknowledge it sooner. I could have—I don't know..." Elliot scrubbed at his scalp and fought to do the one thing he was usually good at, finding the right words. "We have more in common than you think."

Charbonneau flushed red, his face twisting with rage as he struggled to get up again. "If you are saying that Ollie—that you and he—"

Elliot's stomach plunged and his lungs froze. "No! Christ, man. Let me speak. I'm not saying that at all." Could he possibly cock this up more? "I know you're not this dense when you're sober."

Charbonneau's brows drew together, and he looked like a confused, lost puppy as he wearily ran a hand through his once cropped brown hair. Now it was overgrown and shaggy. Like all of them, he sorely required a cut. "And you are not usually so god damned shit headed at making sense."

Cracking an unwilling smile, Elliot rubbed at his jaw. "If you'd actually listen to me instead of wildly jumping to conclusions, you would know I'm saying I have similar *interests*." Elliot glanced over his shoulder to ensure they were absolutely alone, then whispered, "You prefer men? Or you enjoy them at least? I do as well. Swift was more than a teammate to you. He was...yours. Wasn't he?"

Charbonneau let out a shuddering breath, glistening eyes dropping to the table in front of him. After a tense moment, he gave a faint nod.

"Is there anything I can say or do to help?" Elliot asked. "Absolutely anything?"

Skeptically, Charbonneau glanced up at him with one dark brow perfectly arched. "Can you turn back time and fix it?"

"I wish I could."

"Then no." They were silent for a while, Elliot miserably searching for something to say, Charbonneau seeming lost in his own thoughts. "We all have sacrifices to make in this godforsaken whoreson of a war. I've lost so many I lose count. The only thing to be done is continue." Charbonneau's expression was grim, and he held Elliot's gaze for a long moment before his focus drifted. "That is all."

Elliot's guts twisted and clenched. "If I could go back and trade places, I would. I hope you know I would never have sacrificed him."

"Ta gueule," he spat, hands flying up in exasperation. "C'est pas possible comment que t'es stupide. Of course, je le sais." Charbonneau pinched the bridge of his nose and let out a gusty exhale. Elliot could see the restraint it was taking him not to keep cursing and was oddly touched. "He is your first loss as commander. I would say to you it becomes easier, for some it might," he trailed off, examining Elliot with all the intensity of a drunken man forcing himself to focus. "For you I suspect no."

"No," Elliot agreed, and as much as it splintered his heart he would never wish not to feel this. He didn't want to become immune to loss. He wouldn't like himself very much if he did. He swallowed hard against the emotion welling in his throat. "I can't bear to think of losing anyone else either. I'll keep doing everything in my power to see you all through to the end of this. I don't want anyone else sacrificing themselves on my behalf."

Charbonneau nodded, and if he was thinking what Elliot was,

about how he'd so roundly failed already, at least he had the grace not to say it. "You will do what you can."

"Right," Elliot steeled himself for another outburst. "And that includes looking out for Sullivan."

Charbonneau waved a hand at Elliot dismissively. "I don't blame him, if that's what this is about. I'm not so stupid as that. How could I explain why I was angry? Without saying."

Elliot nodded, relieved. "I don't want to have to ask this, but I have to know that when the time comes, and we're in the field again, you'll be focused on what must be done. Can you swear to me you'll inform me if that isn't the case?"

Charbonneau's mouth pressed into a firm line, and a spark of indignation lit his eyes. "Absolument."

Inclining his head in appreciation, Elliot added, "And if you need to talk about anything, it's entirely confidential."

"Pas maintenant," Charbonneau said, hardly managing to stifle a yawn. He stared at a spot over Elliot's shoulder. "Perhaps not later, either. I do not know. Talking is..." He flapped a hand.

"Right. Let's get you up the stairs without breaking your neck, yes? That sounds like a suitable alternative for the time being," Elliot suggested, taking his cue for a change of subject to a safer one.

At that, Charbonneau cracked a half-smile that Elliot returned. He hoped the fact that Charbonneau didn't have to button up his feelings entirely might help in some way. Even if he didn't want to speak of it, perhaps simply knowing he could would prove a relief.

CHAPTER TWENTY

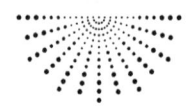

WAKING IN BED ALONE again after tossing and turning through nightmares, Sully tried not to feel disgruntled. Traces of horrible scenes full of pain and terror clung to him whenever he surfaced, until Stone finally crawled in at God only knew what time each night. Then he was gone again by morning.

Sully squeezed his eyelids tighter to block out the light and wished he could convince his body to fall back asleep.

Three days and he was still bent out of shape over Stone because there hadn't been time to resolve anything. Because Stone was clearly avoiding any moment alone while they were both conscious.

Why couldn't he forget about all of it for five minutes? Why did he have to keep agonizing over Stone?

It was one night! It wasn't even that good.

Okay, so that was a dirty fucking lie, but who cared? It was still only one night! One.

And a few months of borderline obsessive thoughts, not that anyone was counting.

Sully didn't want to feel any particular way about the fact that he'd been plagued by an inability to sleep restfully for the last few nights until there was a warm body inches away from his. Or that he'd slept so deeply he didn't have a single nightmare once Stone was beside him. He didn't want to be angry about it, or confused, or questioning his sanity. Much preferable was ignoring it all together.

Yeah, he could just ignore the hazy recollections of an Elliot Stone who never existed but somehow filled his mind while he drifted somewhere between asleep and awake. An Elliot who recited poems in lilting tones as they lay on a grassy lakeshore after skipping stones. He had impressions of Elliot laughing at himself and insisting the poems were awful, but they sounded lovely to Sully.

Didn't happen. He hardly even talked about his poems at the hotel.

In his dreams Elliot's arms were around him, holding him tight, and his heart near pounded out of his chest at that intimate embrace. Elliot's soft hands were a ghost along Sully's wet cheeks. *"You're dreaming, love."*

And, okay, sure, he'd called Sully love when they were fucking, but lots of people talked sweet when they had their cock in you. Sully hadn't *actually* cried that night. He held back those stupid tears by the skin of his teeth.

None of those fuzzy fantasies were real. They were Sully's mind grasping at the last emotional experience—the only emotional experience—he'd had with a lover and sticking him in sweet scenarios that drowned out the horror he was experiencing. He wasn't a doctor or anything, but it made a sick sort of sense.

And if his boneheaded brain thought that was a kindness rather than a cruelty, then the joke was on him, wasn't it?

Yawning, Sully reached up over his head. Fingers brushing the wallpaper, he stretched his back, and glared balefully at the sunlight streaming in the dirt-streaked windowpane, dust floating through golden beams. If he could roll over and get five more minutes, he was sure he'd be able to face the day. Mostly sure.

Unfortunately, the clatter of the household rising kept him from it. He was due for another day of slogging through what the team had lovingly—and he used that word in the most sarcastic sense—taken to calling his initiation, rather than training.

Two days ago he'd been forced onto a motorbike with only enough instruction to ensure he might not kill himself right away and been relieved to find out he was a fast learner. First. Bell got him to practice on the relatively straight drive leading up to the house, then they went farther afield, Bell leading, Sully following. She'd put him through his paces, and by the end of the second day he was maybe not hitting on all sixes, but he sure wasn't going to fall off and make a real mess of himself all over the packed dirt road. Not through a careless mistake anyway.

Today though, Stone was taking over Bell's duties. Apparently, he wanted to evaluate Sully. There had to be more to it. Stone had been acting squirrelly since the day Sully got here, but other than some heavily repressed flashes of guilt, and one quickly suppressed burst of longing, his emotions were too muddled to get a good read on. Whatever it was Stone felt when he was around, it was complicated, and it was eating him up. The dark circles beneath Stone's eyes rivaled his own. Sully wasn't sure whether he felt good or bad about Stone's turmoil because his own thoughts on what was happening between them were just as rife with inconsistencies.

Stone was every bit as attractive and alluring as the night they'd met, and he didn't appear to have been attempting to gain any favors from Sully. Neither was Stone babying him, which was the thing he'd started to worry about when Stone let it slip that he thought Sully was acting recklessly. Those two things didn't come up again. Which went a long way toward easing some of Sully's anger.

That wasn't the whole story though. The secrecy and the things Stone had locked down were hiding something big. And until Sully knew what that was, he needed to keep his guard up. Had to focus on the job and on his usefulness to this team. They came first.

If there was one thing he learned on the front lines, in the stinking cesspit of pointless deaths, wanton destruction, and putrid decay, it was your squad mates were all you had. You protected each other. He had a duty to them, and he'd fulfill it no matter what his emotions were chirping on about.

After this morning's ride with Stone, he'd spend the afternoon doing everything from showing off his skills, to working out plans with the others for their skills to mesh with his in ways that might be useful for deception, infiltration, or destruction if need be.

So far, they'd discovered he and Hoffman made a formidable team of scouts. Sully could cast a wide whisper thin illusion to give them as much coverage as possible, and then stick close to Hoffman to ensure no one saw deeper. Even when the others had known for a fact where they were standing, no one pinpointed them, or noticed anything beyond what Sully showed. Hoffman had given him a nod of approval and what passed as a half-smile on his taciturn face. According to Bell that was nothing short of a declaration of affection.

This afternoon he and Charbonneau were to work on

combining his illusions and emotional insight with Charbonneau's enhanced speed and strength. There had to be a way to use it to get him hidden, kept in shadow through a dangerous situation perhaps? Or concealed so he could neutralize anyone on guard before the poor sap knew he was done for.

At some point before nightfall, it would be a free-for-all sparring match with Stone serving as the referee. None of them were taking it easy on him. Sully preferred it that way.

"Sink or swim," Bell had announced with a teasing grin.

So he'd swum. He had the bruises and a couple of superficial cuts to prove it. And they already felt more cohesive as a group. He couldn't deny that.

A rap of knuckles at the doorway pried him from his musings.

"Mm-what?" he mumbled.

The door cracked hesitantly. Sully realized with an internal groan that Stone was giving him a chance to cover up whatever untoward thing he might be doing. This day was already off to a wonderful start.

I'd have to have the energy for that, which I don't thanks to you.

"Excellent, you're up. Could you be ready in ten? I've packed breakfast if you can hold off eating."

Sully wet his dry lips and made a conscious effort to wake all the way up. "Sure. Can I at least get a cup of George? Need the pick-me-up before I'm much use."

"Of course. I'll heat up some instant while you get dressed. Does that sound all right?"

Shoving down the pleased sensation warming his stomach, Sully nodded. "Thanks."

Stone closed the door behind him on his way out, and Sully dropped back down onto the pillow with a disgusted grunt. *Stop it before you lose control. It's only coffee, Sullivan. Not a proposition.*

Sully pried himself out of the warm bed, into the chilled air, and got dressed. Downstairs, he stopped off in the bathroom before heading to the kitchen. It was packed full with the others eating and talking. They joked around while he drank the hot coffee Stone handed him. Bitter, but at least it was hot. On the front lines, he'd dealt with infinitely worse. Much better than the few days here and there he'd gone without.

Remonet's chair scraped against the floor as he pushed to standing. Strolling up to Sully, he pulled a scrap of paper from the pocket of his faded blue jacket and held it out in between his fore and middle fingers. "Here," he said, "Take it."

Sully plucked the sheet and examined both sides. It was a blank square of slightly crumpled once white paper. "Uhh…What is it?"

Remonet sent him a playful grin, the corners of his warm eyes crinkling as he leaned back a bit, crossing his arms. "Your ticket out of trouble, if you need it."

Eyebrows raising, Sully glanced down and gave it a closer look, flipping it over again. "It's just a piece of paper."

"Is it?" Remonet asked, smile broadening.

"Isn't it?"

There were some chuckles from the others and Stone cleared his throat. "Stop teasing and explain, hmm?"

Amusement sparkled from Remonet, and it was contagious. Sully momentarily forgot about the sense of impending doom that Elliot was casting over everything. "It's magic," Remonet said. "My skill—"

"One of many," Charbonneau joked, fond sarcasm lacing his words and Remonet chuckled.

"Ferme-la. My skill is infusing things with magic. Paper is an easy target; it has no internal workings to worry about messing with. I once fused magic with a pocket watch to—not important—let's just say it didn't tell time proper after. Anyway, this one? It'll freeze someone for a while. Make them real suggestible."

"Suggestible?"

"Mhm. You tell them what to do, they'll listen. Emergencies only, and don't trust it to last hours or anything, but it can get you out of a jam. All you gotta do to activate it is be holding the paper when you say sassafras. Ideally pressing the paper against the person you want to incapacitate to direct the flow."

"Sassa—"

"Fras, yeah. Don't waste it now."

Oh. Talk about going off early. "Why that word?"

"Are you gonna go around saying it for no reason?" Remonet asked, thick brows raised high.

Sully's lips twitched reluctantly up. "Guess not."

"But you'll remember it. It's an oddly unforgettable word. Fun to say. Also, it just plain makes me laugh," Remonet said, grinning again. "Having folks run around in a fraught situation yelling sassafras. You should hear that one with his accent." Remonet jabbed a thumb in Charbonneau's direction. In return Charbonneau muttered something in French that was probably uncharitable judging by his tone.

Sully smothered his own laugh. Stuffing the paper in his pocket, offering his hand to Remonet's warm, confident grip. "Thank you. I appreciate it."

Remonet inclined his head in acknowledgement and sat back down.

After Sully finished his coffee, he washed out the cup and wiped it dry. Then Stone ushered him outside.

The second they were through the doors, Sully felt Stone's

trepidation rising. He barely held back an irritated sigh as they mounted their vehicles.

"Just follow me," Stone said.

Obviously.

Sully nodded. He adjusted his warm hat, put on the goggles and the leather facemask to keep from getting too wind-chapped, and jammed his foot down on the kickstarter.

A THICKET OF BARE beeches and oaks lined the right side of the field they stopped in to refuel and eat breakfast. Some of the smaller trees still clung to their tightly furled brown leaves, and they rustled in the chill breeze. Sully shook his hands to warm them up after the tight grip he'd had on the handlebars. Around him the slowly sloping hills stretched to the horizon, dusted in a light layer of patchy snow, dried grass peeking through.

The silence made him almost as uncomfortable as the churning mix of forlorn emotion Stone was trying to keep him from noticing. He wasn't used to the lack of noise yet. Or the lack of chaos. The only sound out here was the occasional crow cawing three or four times in rapid succession which made the stark quiet all the more noticeable.

Sully's fingers were cold, but no colder than he'd gotten used to them being in the trenches. He picked at the bread Stone had handed him and chewed a mouthful. In his pocket was the apple he was saving for after whatever unfortunate conversation they were about to have, when he could hopefully enjoy the rare treat. It was slightly wrinkled and worse for the wear, but still better fare than anything he'd gotten with the British.

"Spit it out," he finally demanded, breath clouding in front of him. Stone's attention snapped up from the tree he'd been staring a hole through, blue eyes wide. He didn't look like the tough commanding officer he was supposed to be, but like a little kid who knew he was about to get in a world of trouble. "Whatever it is you're working up to, just say it. And quit trying to hide how you're feeling. It's not working and it's giving me a damn headache."

"I..." Stone hesitated, dropping his gaze, worrying his bottom lip.

Fuck. Was that it?

"Is it because you know what I can sense? Is that why you're so on edge?" Sully waved a hand, anger intensifying at an alarming rate. Years' worth of insecurities, the fear he could never let people know what he felt rose up, thundering furiously in his chest before making a throbbing, angry home next to the exhaustion. "Here's some news, I don't want to feel what you do any more than you want me to. But neither of us gets a choice in it. I'm not *trying* to sense what you're feeling, just do. So sorry if that bothers you, but you can fuck off if you think—"

Stone held his hands up in surrender. "Warren—Sullivan, stop! You're wrong. It's nothing *you've* done. It wasn't you at all."

Sully's heart pounded as he watched Stone's eyes shut for a moment. A sigh escaped him in a visible wisp of fog.

Why does he have to look so good all the time? How is that fair?

"Then what the hell's going on? 'Cause you're hiding something, I know you are. So just tell me, Stone."

"You're not going to like it," he said, finally looking at Sully again, those damn pretty eyes so contrite, a whisper of fear in the air. Fear of what? Fear of how Sully might react? His stomach cramped, not a good sign. And not something he enjoyed feeling from Ellio—Stone.

"I already don't like it." Sully crossed his arms, defensive, frustrated. "And I like it less every goddamn minute you're not explaining."

"Right. Er..." Stone took a deep breath and blew it out, his head tilting slightly to the side. "Have you been dreaming of me, at all, over the past few months?"

How in the hell does he know?

Sully's face burned. His heart tripped over itself. "Awfully big opinion of yourself, you've got."

The smile Elliot gave him was wry and a little sad. "That's not an answer. And judging by the color of your face, I can tell you recall them to some degree."

The heat flooding his face surged again. His chest tightened uncomfortably. "It doesn't mean anything. It's only dreams."

"They're really not," Stone said, his voice gentle like he thought Sully needed the information delivered carefully or he'd break. Like he thought Sully was so weak he couldn't take it if he just came out and said whatever the hell he was trying to. "Or rather, they are dreams, but they're also real. I was there. In your mind. I'm a dreamwalker. That's my other skill, the one I told you was a secret."

The truth of Stone's words hit him like a ton of bricks. He almost stumbled under the force of Stone's emotions, the ones silently begging Sully to forgive him. All that did was make his anger burn hotter. "In my head. You were in my head? For months?"

Stone bit his lip, a desolate gaze imploring Sully to listen, to understand, but this was over the edge. This was someone in his head. The one place you'd expect complete privacy especially when nothing else was private anymore. When the degradation and humiliation of cramped, foul, trenches were all you had, when the only things you could control about your situation were the ones inside of you, that space was even more sacrosanct. How could Elliot not know? How could he not understand?

Wrapping his arms around his middle, Stone struggled, and Sully felt him fighting for composure. "I didn't plan it but you—"

"Oh, this is my fault somehow?" Scoffing, Sully took a few steps backward to put more distance between them.

Stone followed a step, then stopped abruptly. "No, of course not, but if you just let me explain."

Contempt and violent angry impulses shoved out reason. God, this was worse than anything he imagined. "Nah, I don't think I will. No wonder I'm so confused around you! I can't think straight about this. I can't." He clenched his trembling fists at his sides, fingernails biting into his palms. His mind raced ahead in wild leaps and bounds. "Is that why I can't sleep? Jesus wept, Elliot."

Shaking his head, Stone started toward him again, one hand outstretched, reaching for understanding, but Sully didn't want to understand. "No. I was helping—"

"It sure as hell doesn't feel helpful right now. Stop. Just save it." Sully clamped his mouth shut. Exhaled sharply through his nose. He couldn't control the direction of his thoughts, or his feelings. The twisted up, knotted mess of them, so tangled he might never find a way to unpick it. And in the middle of it all, the ones screaming at him to listen, to forgive. Worst of all, he couldn't tell if those were Stone's or his. "I need to think. Away from you and everything you're feeling. Before I say something we can't come back from. Just do me a favor?"

"Anything," Stone agreed instantly, his raw expression knives stabbing into Sully's chest. Or maybe that was the mass of agonized, apologetic, misery he was radiating.

That's not fair either. It's not fair to put that on me.

"Stay the hell out of my head from now on. It's mucked up enough in there from everything I been through without being wrapped all around your fucking finger." He cut himself off before the rest of the vitriol building up in the back of his throat spilled out. He needed to stop this, mitigate it, control it. Didn't know if he could.

"I—" At Sully's hard expression, Stone stopped short. He nodded, a stilted, jerking motion.

"We done here?"

Stone's lips parted and closed. He swallowed with a heavy bob of his throat, and Sully watched him try to tuck all the vulnerable bits of himself away. He could feel him trying to reel in his emotions and didn't have the energy to yell at him again and remind him it was a useless, annoying fucking gesture. "I suppose so."

"Good."

CHAPTER TWENTY-ONE

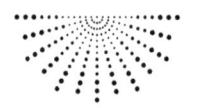

THE BRIEF GLIMPSE OF sunlight on the drive back to the house was long faded by afternoon. Elliot was—there was no other word for it—brooding in the dim kitchen while the others had Warren outside. They were putting him through training Elliot should have been supervising. Warren would perform better if Elliot let him have space today. Watching might aggravate him again and there were enough curious eyes on them after they returned in foul moods.

Elliot rubbed his finger along a deep gouge in the table. How was he so terrible at this? First Charbonneau, then Warren. Maybe it wasn't a matter of finding the proper words. Some things couldn't be softened with language no matter how pretty the trappings. He missed books. In books, people were easy to understand. Their motivations and personalities dictated their actions and reactions. You could always see where they went wrong and how you'd have done it differently.

Real people were harder. They didn't always make sense.

Things were happening in their heads and hearts you weren't privy to. Never could be. Real people were chaotic, prone to fits of passion they released or concealed.

He'd known Warren would take it badly. Who wouldn't? But he'd hoped he could explain it in a way that wouldn't leave them so at odds. He hadn't anticipated how much it would hurt Warren. How deeply violated he would feel. How low Elliot would feel in response. What could he have done differently? Surely walking away from someone so desperately in need of help would have been the greater sin?

His imaginings were interrupted when the kitchen door swung open with a blast of frigid air. He didn't have to look to recognize those stomping feet, or the door banging shut with just enough force to get his notice.

"Right, then," Bellona said, marching over to the seat across from him and dropping into it. "Now that they're all busy with your boy, what happened this morning?"

Elliot's face grew rapidly hot. "He is very much not mine. Would you keep your voice down?"

"I thought the two of you were sneaking off for a little fun, but you both came back wound up tighter than a pocket watch. Something happened and he's grumpy, and you're wallowing, and I don't mean to pry, but I would really like to know what kind of situation we're in for."

He wished he didn't need to explain this. It was awkward and humiliating enough. "I told him about the dreams."

"I did warn you it was pertinent information he ought to have been provided with. And that he might not take the concealment well," she pointed out, though she didn't sound disapproving, only slightly exasperated.

"Of course you did, and I dismissed your advice because he

might have said no to coming," Elliot replied. He swiped angrily at his jaw, knowing he shouldn't have kept the information from Warren, knowing he would have made the same choice again whether or not Warren ever forgave him.

"That would have been his right."

"He would've *died,* Bell. Used as cannon fodder when he's so much more than that. You don't understand. He was weaker every time we met. The things he saw, the things *I* saw through him—I don't know how he survived. Some of it was exaggerated, granted, dreams are never entirely accurate, but much of it wasn't and I couldn't let it kill him when I could save him."

Bellona massaged her forehead, her dark blue eyes slipping shut. "You can't make people accept saving. And you don't know he would have died, you worried he might. Elliot, he still could. Here, with us, he still could. You know that."

"But the odds—"

"Blast the odds. He still could, and you cannot allow every decision you make to be influenced by this need of yours to keep him safe. It's not your decision to make. It never was. I know you understand that you can't go into a person's mind as you please, but with him you overlooked it because you care so deeply. You cannot continue to use that excuse. He's a member of this team and you must treat him like any other man, capable of deciding for himself what he wishes. Fail to do so, and you will end up losing him in every single way."

What if I already have?

"I think I've lost him anyway."

Bellona grimaced, and tilted her head to the side in acknowledgement of the possibility. He was glad she wasn't the type to offer meaningless platitudes. "Buck up. At least he's still alive. And there's always the chance you might not have put him off you forever. Some people find your charms appealing I'm sure."

It seemed the dressing down was over. A sardonic smile twisted Elliot's lips. "I'll have you know my charms have always been highly in demand."

"Of course they were." She kept an impressive straight face.

Elliot sent her a mock offended glare. "They were—they still are! Look you!"

Laughing Bellona pushed up from the chair. "I'd better get back there and make sure they haven't maimed your boy too badly."

She was walking to the door when Elliot spluttered, "I told you he's not—"

"Sorry, Captain, can't hear you," she called over her shoulder, flashing him an impish grin as she closed the door behind herself.

Once more he was left to brood. Once more he replayed the confrontation with Warren in his head and struggled to determine how he could've contained Warren's reaction. And when he was done with that, self-loathing at a record high, he attempted, unsuccessfully, to determine a path through this mess. Warren had ordered him out of his dreams, so he couldn't interfere, no matter how much his chest ached at the thought of what those unchecked nightmares were doing or how restlessly Warren slept. It was no longer his place to provide relief. It never was. And that was the problem.

But it could be if he could explain things properly. When Warren was ready to listen. Right now he wasn't receptive. If Elliot pushed, he might never be. No. He had to be patient. He needed to give him the distance he asked for. At least as much as he could while they shared a bed. And while he had to aid in Warren's training.

The real test would come when they saw how he took orders from a man he currently despised.

Something in Elliot's chest twisted painfully. His heart, he thought dismally.

∼

WARM DAMP BREATHS TICKLING the back of Elliot's neck slowly ferried him closer to consciousness. The muscular body pressed up against him, and the solid weight of an arm draped low over his waist, was pleasant. He wanted to luxuriate in the feeling. He wanted to float half-alert and sleepy and pretend he deserved this. Could have it.

What wouldn't he give to wake up like this every morning? It was a bittersweet sensation, and he couldn't linger no matter how wonderful it felt or how good Warren smelled.

Elliot had to extract himself. He didn't want to embarrass Warren. Or make their situation any worse or any more painful. Letting out a slow breath, he began to rise, stopped by the arm around his waist tightening.

"Stay," Warren mumbled, voice thick with sleep and tingling along Elliot's skin, settling somewhere under his ribcage near the battering pulse of his heart.

He didn't know what he was asking. He was probably mostly asleep, simply comfortable.

"I can't," Elliot whispered, chest constricting. "You're supposed to be angry with me."

Warren didn't move. His chest rose and fell against Elliot's back. "Still am. Stay."

Aching with want and certain it was an atrocious idea to agree,

Elliot squeezed his eyes shut. Fought his own longing. "You won't thank me later."

"Probably not. Stay anyway." Warren let out a soft sigh Elliot felt to the tips of his toes, his whole body warming with it. It would be so easy to sink into this. To pretend everything was all right, if only for a short time.

He shouldn't. Really, really shouldn't. He wasn't allowed to enjoy something this tender with the bad blood between them. There would be consequences. And hadn't ignoring the consequences of his actions gotten them into this predicament in the first place? Warren hadn't forgiven him yet, possibly never would.

But Elliot meant it when he told Warren he'd do anything for him. Meant it without reservation, without question for his own comfort, and this was something he could do, however small. His selfish impulse to pull away and save himself from hurting worse was all the more reason to do as Warren asked. Be unselfish for once.

So he relaxed his body, closed his eyes, and let himself be held until Warren's breaths evened out again into the softest snores. He ignored the firm ridge pressed against his backside, and after he'd sufficiently tortured himself with things he couldn't—might never again—have, Elliot slipped from Warren's slack grasp. Silently, he retrieved his uniform and dressed in the chill dawn air.

He couldn't help a glance back at Warren whose dark hair stuck up every which way, long sooty lashes resting softly against his smooth skin, still clinging to the last breaths of a summer tan. He was heartbreaking and beautiful and soft with his face peaceful for once.

If Warren got some undisturbed sleep for his sacrifice, it was worth it. Truly the least Elliot could do. When the persistent raw aching in his chest worsened, he forced himself to leave the room, boots in hand so he wouldn't wake Warren as he walked out.

CHAPTER TWENTY-TWO

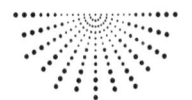

SULLY SAT ON THE bed with his back propped against the wall. A hole in his sock came to his attention when a draft made him shiver. He'd need to mend it when he found the energy. His uniform wasn't doing the bedding any favors. He'd been sparring with Hoffman. Body bruised, exhaustion weighed down every part of him.

The promise of warmth tempted him to crawl beneath the blanket for a nap. If only he could muster the ability to make it that far.

Like I'd do anything but lay here watching the sun move across the sky out the fucking window anyway. I couldn't be more pathetic. That'd be impossible.

In the days since Stone had told him about dreamwalking, Sully refused to discuss it and Stone hadn't pushed him. Neither mentioned the fact that they both lay awake at night, staring at opposite walls while Stone tried not to let Sully feel swelling tides of longing, guilt, and too many confusing, mixed up things for

Sully's mind to sort into neat categories. Meanwhile Sully's growing sense of abandonment confused him. He was the one who told Stone to stay away. He was the one who didn't want his head messed with. So why was he aching like he was losing something important? Like someone died and left him to fend for himself all over again?

Each morning Sully found himself wrapped around Stone, unwilling to let go. He wasn't sure which was worse, when the feelings intensified because of it or when Stone tried and failed to hold them back. Either way it hurt, and it shouldn't. It shouldn't.

Sully couldn't stop revisiting how he'd exploded at Stone twice now. He hated losing his temper. It made him feel immature and irrational. Twenty-four was plenty old enough to know better than to yell and leap to the worst possible explanations, but he couldn't contain the startling strength of emotion Stone brought out in him. After a lifetime of practice separating his feelings from those around him, he was an expert at it. So how come whenever he got too close to Stone, everything he knew how to do went to shite?

And now there was another layer confusing him further. Because the harder he tried to remember the dreams Stone told him were real, the more they were drifting to the surface for him to examine in the painful bright light of day. He could recall his own humiliating desperation and need. Elliot holding him close and murmuring nonsense after he relived the Eastland disaster.

The clean, fresh scent of Elliot where Sully had tucked his face into Elliot's neck, familiar and comforting. The same one he kept waking up far too close to in the mornings. Warm, sure hands moving over his back in soothing circles.

"Just catch your breath, it's over."

Every memory dredged up came with a throbbing pang in his chest, a lonesome craving, a wretched desire to throw himself in those sturdy arms again and let out all of the pent-up fear and horror of the last months. To be weak in the worst way, and he couldn't let himself. Not if he was going to get through this without breaking apart.

His own feelings needed sorting out. If he let himself get sucked into the tempest of Elliot's he might not find a way out again. Wasn't even sure he'd want to. The tantalizing prospect of all those good feelings lurking on the other side of the bad dangled like a carrot, drawing him closer to letting go of his resentment. But stubborn pride kept him rooted firmly where he was.

"You're a mess, Sullivan."

His head was too heavy for his neck, so he dropped it back against the wall and stared out the tiny window at the expanse of snow dusting the trees and hills. Got lost in endless white, and it was almost like sleeping. Only it wasn't. At all.

Fingers rapped against the closed door. Sully's heart jumped into his throat. *Try to be more pitiful, I dare you.* "You can come in."

The door creaked open, and Bell appeared. Sully's shoulders sagged. Of course it wasn't Stone wanting to speak with him in private. Why the hell would he hope it was?

"So," she said, entering and shutting the door behind her. "Stone would have my head for this, but I thought you might need a friend."

Sully's mind instantly threw up an image of the last friend he'd had, blood seeping from his shoulder, lips flattened in a pained line. His throat burned. He ought to write to Allison to check in on him. "You wouldn't say that if you knew what happened to the last person who called me their friend."

She shrugged and sat on the foot of the bed, dark blue eyes

watching him intently. Sully raised his brows but didn't comment. "Did you kill him?"

"What? No, of course not," Sully protested, crossing his arms defensively.

"Hurt him?"

Might as well have. "No, but it was my fault."

Her lips curved in a lopsided, sort of sad smile. "Then I won't waste my time worrying. I'm not sure if it's escaped your notice, but I don't frighten particularly easily." Sully didn't know what to say. That hadn't escaped his notice. He'd never met another woman in the middle of a battlefield, and he remembered how calm she'd been. You couldn't get much braver. "Besides, the tension in this house is becoming absolutely unbearable. And we've all got a job to do around here. So, cough it up. Tell me the issue, let's have it."

Sully's muscles tensed. "It's not that I don't appreciate what you're trying to do—"

"If it helps I do know your history together, and I don't care in the slightest about your preferences." Bell emitted earnestness, it practically glowed off her.

A buzzing started in his ears, chest tightening. Stone told her?

"If you're working yourself into an uproar, you should know he didn't have to tell me. I guessed as much. And for goodness sake, don't be so shocked. It's not as though either of you are terribly subtle about the way you stare at one another. All puppy eyes and sad faces when you think you're unobserved."

"It's—" God, were they that obvious? *Stop fucking looking at Stone unless necessary.*

"Complicated? Yes, agreed. And you're attempting to find your footing here, so there's added stress on top of the rest. That can't possibly be pleasant." Her brows pinched in perfect sympathy.

"Yeah, well." Sully stared back out the window, clenching his jaw. He didn't even want to have this conversation with Stone, let alone his apparent confidant. He might be stuck feeling everyone's feelings, but he never liked to talk about his own. "I'll be fine."

There was a long pause, and then Bell asked, "Do you trust him?"

Of course he did. In a heartbeat. "What?"

"It's a simple question, but terribly important. If you can't trust him, how will you respond to his orders in the field? Your trust was breached, no matter the intent. It's no small thing to overcome. However, if we're going to be an effective team, you've got to move beyond this. I don't suppose the two of you could simply...talk?"

Sully rolled his eyes, and she lifted the corner of her lips in a faint smile.

"I'll manage. Trusting him as my commanding officer is different. It won't be a problem. I can take orders fine. Took them from men I liked even less. Is that all you wanted?"

Bell released a resigned sigh and stood, tucking a wisp of black hair behind her ear. "It's not, but I can tell when a man's adamantly refusing to reflect on his emotions and no amount of insightful prodding will aid."

Sully repressed a smile at that. Edie and Anne would love her.

∽

LEANING AGAINST THE COLD exterior wall of the house, Elliot watched as Charbonneau and Warren sparred. They were locked in an intense struggle. Charbonneau's skill gave him the advantage of speed and strength over Warren, but that only went so far against an opponent who could confuse you into thinking he was somewhere else.

Mail had been delivered that morning along with an urgent message from Général Courtemanche. They had two days before Warren would be tested by fire. It wasn't enough. He hadn't even gotten two weeks to train with them.

There was far more danger to him at the front. He'll manage. There's no other option.

Elliot sealed his lips around a cigarette and dug through his pocket for the metal tin containing his matches. He needed the boost; it felt like he hadn't slept in months. Striking the match, he held the flame to the end as he inhaled, drawing smoke smoothly into his lungs. Dropping the match into the snow, he watched it rapidly extinguish with a sizzle before he lifted his gaze to the combatants once more.

Charbonneau lunged for Warren and rolled in the snow to recover when he didn't meet the expected impact.

The crunch of boots in the snow alerted Elliot to Bellona's approach. "He's holding up against Charbonneau," she said, stopping at his side and folding her arms as she watched them.

Elliot hummed his agreement and took in another lungful of smoke. He blew it out slowly.

"You both look like you haven't slept a wink in ages," she observed, concern under the light tone of her voice.

Flicking the ash from the glowing tip of his cigarette, Elliot sighed. "He sleeps. Eventually. He just—it's not restful."

"And what's your excuse?" she asked, turning to face him.

Elliot avoided her gaze. "Leaving him there night after night is not exactly pleasant. I go to one of my sisters and feel like shit for abandoning him to it, though he told me to." He paused, not wanting to admit the rest. "And I miss him. I made his dreams better because he needed me to, but I'm not so daft that it escaped my notice they were a haven for me as well. That I let myself believe I was safe there. And that although I knew it was only a part of him, not the complete person I..."

Elliot shook his head and stared up at the cloudy gray sky. The chill of the winter air seeped beneath the woolen layers of his jacket and uniform. *I loved him,* he couldn't say. *I knew better and I fell for him anyway.*

He couldn't help it. Warren made falling so effortless. And he knew he didn't know everything about Warren, not awake at least, but Elliot thought he'd love him even more when he got to. How was he supposed to stop himself? He'd always been prone to fast and deep passions, but none had persisted quite like this.

Bellona leaned against his side, offering silent support. "Couldn't you tell him some of that? Or explain how it started? Or talk to him about it at all?"

Exasperated, Elliot took another draw of smoke, then dropped the remains into the snow. "I can't. Look at how poorly the last two times have gone. He specifically told me he needs to think without my interference. I can't force him to listen before he's prepared. It wouldn't be fair."

Bellona muttered something under her breath, but all he caught was a disgusted sounding, "Men."

He couldn't disagree, but raised a brow at her anyway, and she widened her eyes innocently.

"I finished reading the documents Courtemanche sent," Elliot said, grasping for something less personal to discuss.

"Do tell."

"They examined the vials we recovered. Chlorine gas laced with magic. The exact nature of it was impossible to divine without testing."

"So they tested it?" Bellona guessed.

Elliot wrinkled his nose in revulsion at the detailed recollection he'd read. He leaned back against the cold stone. "Mm. On mice. Killed them, of course."

Bellona scowled. "Of course."

He waited a beat, then shared the profoundly disturbing part. "Moments later they appeared to revive."

Shocked, she quickly tensed. "They—"

"Revived, yes. Some of the skilled scientists described them as 'wrong' though they couldn't explain how, solely that the magic had an effect. They placed the momentarily deceased mice in cages with unaffected mice and it was a bloodbath. They tore the others to shreds. And when they tried to end the experiment, the infected mice proved extremely difficult to terminate."

"Wonderful."

"Oh, it gets worse. In the intervening days, Courtemanche has received intelligence which suggests the Germans have moved this research to a new location. One we haven't compromised, where they're carrying out experiments of this gas on captured French citizens. The information is vague, but it suggests if the tests are successful, they'll begin stockpiling. Our source claims they're preparing to perpetrate larger scale testing."

"How on earth have they even crafted something like this?" she asked, resting her hands on her hips. "How do we counter it?"

"That's part of what we're to discover. We've been tasked to covertly enter the new location and attempt to retrieve any formula specifications or indications of where it might be deployed, unnoticed. Any other information we retrieve could prove useful, so we'll take whatever we can get our hands on. We've been ordered not to engage unless absolutely necessary."

Bellona stared at him, baffled. "We're not going to shut them down? Blow it up on the way out?"

Elliot gave a quick shake of his head. Whether he agreed with HQ's assessment or not, it wasn't his decision. "According to Courtemanche for the time being, we're too valuable to risk a confrontation. The resistance we could encounter might prove too large to overcome and we must return with that information. It's unlikely this is the only site they're experimenting at, and we are rather less sure of what explosives might do in this situation than they would prefer us to be."

"That holds water." Bellona's small, upturned nose wrinkled, and her lips pursed. "I still don't like it."

"Nor I."

After a short pause Bellona asked, "This sounds like necromantic magic, doesn't it? Do you think Albrecht is involved?"

It had occurred to him. He almost hoped she was. That they'd have an excuse to go after the woman who'd led to Swift's demise. Anger and guilt bubbled in his stomach. "I suppose we'll find out soon enough."

There was a triumphant noise from the field, and they both glanced over to see Hoffman patting Charbonneau on the back, Sully glowering. "Your boy lost."

Elliot expelled a weary breath. "You really oughtn't call him that. Considering it's untrue and should anyone overhear—"

"They would simply think I was teasing you about your new recruit losing. Though I realize I shouldn't have poked at a sore spot, for that I do apologize."

Nodding acceptance, Elliot rubbed his gloved hands over his arms in a vain attempt to warm up. "We'll need to brief the others and devise a plan. We've got to move in two days when the preparations on the other side of the line are in place."

Bellona frowned at Sully, who was now laughing at something Charbonneau said. "I thought we'd have longer to get him ready. He hasn't even learned to shoot with a pistol yet. At least he's competent with a motorcycle, but anything requiring fancy driving?" She inclined her head, suggesting doubt.

He concurred. "There's no choice. We cannot leave him behind when his skillset is so perfectly suited to a covert mission. HQ would be breathing down our necks about what he's here for then. We've the rest of today and one more full day. We'll determine the essentials to teach him in the time allotted. Trust me, I hate the idea as much as you do. It's killing me to put him at risk like this, but you were right. I've got to treat him like anyone else in this unit. It'll have to suffice."

Bellona huffed as she rested her weight against her shoulder pressed to the stone wall. "Oh, now you've said it that way, it still sounds bonkers."

"Helpful."

"Am I not always?" Bellona took one look at Elliot's face and relented. "We'll teach him everything we possibly can and keep watch over him as much as we're able, of course we will. It won't go the same this time."

Elliot's chest froze. For a moment he couldn't breathe. Releasing air in a slow breath through his nose, he nervously rubbed his palms against his pant legs. "It can't."

Bellona clapped a palm to his bicep in solidarity. "It won't."

CHAPTER TWENTY-THREE

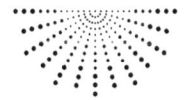

"SQUEEZE IT SLOWER," STONE suggested from behind Sully's right shoulder, words heating low in his gut, distracting him from the biting cold. He was talking about the trigger of the pistol. Not that Sully's cock much cared, it perked up anyhow. The frustration of the poor shots he'd been making suddenly less pressing.

He followed Stone's instructions, tightened his overlapping grip on the handle, lined up the sights and slowly squeezed. The pop of the pistol firing and the empty cartridge ejecting hardly penetrated his concentration; he missed the wooden target again. "Fuck."

Firing accurately with a pistol was so much harder than with the rifle he was used to. With that he was an excellent shot. Learning to shoot the rifle had taken practice too, but the hope his experience would translate to an ease with pistols was profoundly mistaken.

"It takes time," Stone said, sympathetically. Which made it so much worse. "You should have seen how awful I was."

"Like you've ever been less than perfect at anything in your whole entire life," Sully muttered, then squeezed the trigger twice in a row before Stone could respond. One dinged the edge of the target, splinters shattering outward. Oh. Was he actually getting better?

"Try widening your stance, and straighten up, you're leaning slightly back." Stone's voice was cool and calm.

Sully corrected himself, fired again, cursed again. The slide stayed back as he needed a fresh magazine. Silently, Stone handed him a new one and took the one he ejected, their fingers brushing. Even through gloves, Sully couldn't pretend he didn't feel a tingling flush of warmth travel up his arm at the contact.

"Keep going. I brought plenty for practice." Stone didn't sound the least bit affected, but Sully knew better. An enticing electricity crackled between them. Sully couldn't decide if he loved or hated it.

In twenty minutes Sully hit the target twice more and winged it once. Grinning, Stone cuffed him on the shoulder after the last shot struck home. He seemed so happy and carefree, Sully's chest clenched. If it wasn't for the olive drab uniform and service cap perched on his head, he'd look exactly like he had that night on La Salle with his emotions all there on his face for anyone to see. Shining like a beacon of light and hope that Sully had been helplessly drawn to. He still was. Inescapably.

Then Stone seemed to remember himself. His smile dimmed, and the joyful bubbling in the air around them quieted, though it didn't vanish entirely. "Excellent work. See, you are improving."

Sully lifted a critical brow. His arms were tired from holding them out in front of him and absorbing the recoil, his fingers beginning to cramp with cold and tension. He was an abysmal shot so Stone's cheery optimism grated. "Wouldn't call that improvement. Luck more than anything, I bet."

"I beg to disagree. With some more practice you'll be in excellent shape. That's enough for today, however. Much more and you'll be too sore. We need you in top form tomorrow."

Sully grunted, flicked the safety on his pistol and slid it into the holster at his waist. He missed the weight of his rifle. It was familiar, and he was used to reaching for it in a crisis. Knew if he had it, he could be counted on to make the shot. He also knew it was impractical for their mission. Besides, it was unlikely he'd be using a firearm if all went according to plan. And if it came down to it, he'd just have to hope he would be close enough not to miss.

"Come on." Stone nodded back down the path they'd trudged down, away from the house, earlier. The snow and crispy grass beneath crunched under their boots. "We'll go over the mission once more before supper, and then everyone can do as they wish for the evening. Some time to relax should do you good. We've kept you rather busy the last two days."

"Yeah, okay," Sully grumbled, lacing his fingers together and stretching them out in front of him to relieve some of the discomfort as they walked. He needed to respond to the letter he'd gotten from Anne. She gushed about a boy Edie had introduced her to. His overprotective first reaction was to warn her to be careful and behave, but saying so would have the opposite effect. Anne was nothing if not contradictory. So he'd ask questions and try not to worry overmuch. Ha.

Maybe he should write Edie a letter begging her to keep an eye on things.

"Do you feel prepared?" Stone asked as they crested the slope behind the house.

"Hmm?"

"For tomorrow. Is there anything you think you need that we haven't addressed?"

Sully blinked twice in rapid succession. Commanding officers didn't ask him what he needed. He was used to being told to make do. Actually, he was used to not asking for things at all because he wouldn't receive them anyway.

Was there anything he needed?

"I...uh..."

Elliot stopped and faced him, so Sully stopped too. There was a determination in Elliot's mood that he couldn't interpret. "I realize you're still angry with me, that's fine. I can live with it as long as you know you're still able to ask me for anything you require. You cannot do your job if you do not have the things you need, so if there's anything please ask."

Was Sully still angry? He didn't think so. His anger never lasted long. It burned hot and fizzled out quickly, leaving him full of regret more often than not. He was tired, volatile. At night, half-remembered nightmares and memories blended together in gory combination, but he couldn't ask for help with that. Couldn't make himself admit he was wrong, that he needed Elliot to make his bad dreams go away. Little more than a kid needing to be coddled. He could handle his own mind. Could power through the exhaustion. He'd done it for months.

Ignoring the tiny voice in his head that pointed out he'd only been able to do so because of the respites Stone provided, Sully shook his head. "Nah, there's nothing."

He only despised himself a little for the concern Stone tried so hard to conceal.

SWEAT ROLLED DOWN SULLY'S spine, sticking his dirty shirt to his back. He wanted to peel off the too-small coat, but it wasn't worth the hassle. Instead, he wedged a finger into his collar and loosened his tie.

"Now don't do that, Warren. You're almost respectable," Ma said, her bright green eyes shining down at him. He could almost believe she was happy if he didn't feel the grief and depression clinging to her and souring the air around them. Even over the noise and fleeting sensation of passing emotions from the crowd, her pain was so crisp.

The train was huge, dark and daunting. Something stuck in Sully's throat. He didn't want to go. Ma stopped just shy of the doors and checked around for him. "Come on, then."

Biting his lip, Sully shuffled forward sullenly. His stomach tied itself in knots, a cold shiver travelling from the base of his skull down his spine as he hesitated.

Ma's warm eyes sparkled in the sunlight. "Don't look like that, sweet. It'll be a grand adventure, you wait! You'll get to meet your Uncle Thomas. There's a new baby cousin for you to help with. Only think of all the times you pestered me for a brother or sister. Now you'll have one. I bet she's lovely and you'll get along and be so happy."

Frowning, Sully examined her face, saw something he didn't know how to explain in her expression. "You'll be there soon, won't you? So we can be together again?"

Ma cupped his cheeks and smiled so soft. Sully's stomach cramped, his chest aching. "Soon as I can, sweet. We'll be together again one day."

A whistle sounded and he adjusted the cheap pack on his shoulder. A few changes of clothes for him and one of the books of stories Ma used to read him tucked in the bottom for the baby. "Promise?"

Something flickered in her eyes, and the ache in his chest grew exponentially. "'Course I do. You've got to go now, or you'll miss it. Please go, Warren."

Sully didn't want to, something was wrong. She dropped her hands and jerked her chin toward the train. "Thomas will be waiting for you. Go on now."

Her most authoritative voice worked on him, always had. "Okay."

Ma hugged him and whispered she loved him, told him to be good, and Sully started to step onto the train. His foot braced on the metal step to heave himself up—

Everything froze, time skipped.

He was standing back on the platform. Ma was soaking wet, dark hair dangling to her shoulders in sopping clumps, blood climbing up her pale green sleeves, trickling from the corner of her white lips. Sully couldn't breathe. He wanted to scream.

"You left me," she rasped, an expression he never saw her make before twisted her beautiful, kind face.

"You made me," Sully gasped, backing up, tripping over the step and hardly catching himself.

She took a trembling step forward, bare feet leaving a puddle of water in her wake. "You should've stayed. Could've saved me. I needed you."

Sully blanched, throat burning with acid.

"You let me die, Warren." She took another unsteady step toward him.

Sully held his hands up in defense, sidestepping the metal, trying to get away. "No! I'm *sorry*. I didn't mean to. I didn't know."

"Liar!" she screamed, voice cutting through him like glass,

shards tearing into his flesh. "How could you go? You felt what I was going to do."

Sully's heart lurched. "I didn't know, Ma! I swear I didn't. You were grieving, we both were. Da...I didn't *know*. I was eight! How could I have?"

"You knew enough." She closed in on him with another shaky jerk of twisted legs. "You felt my pain, you always could. Always tried to fix it. Always made it worse, didn't you?"

Chin trembling, Sully scrubbed at the tear tracks on his face. Terror and sorrow crashed over him in pulverizing waves, almost pulling his feet out from under him. "I'm sorry." His voice cracked. "I'm sorry. I tried."

She got small and quiet. "I was alone. No one cared, not even you, my own boy."

Gasping in a choked breath, he tried to explain, to make her understand. "You were always sad. Even before Da died. Fluctuating, up and down like a Ferris wheel and you left my head spinning. I couldn't *balance* myself. I was just a kid. Didn't know I was blocking you out. Didn't know I was only getting part of it."

Her lip curled, eyes fixing hatefully on him. "It was your fault."

"I know," Sully admitted in a pained voice, emotion scratching in his throat. He swallowed hard. "I know it was, and I'm sorry. I'm so sorry."

Everything was wrong. Someone was supposed to be here, helping him. *Elliot*. Where the hell was Elliot? Sully needed him. Needed him so much and he didn't understand why he wasn't here. Why he wasn't stopping this.

Please, please, please. Don't leave me here. Don't make me do this alone. Elliot, please!

Cold, clammy hands cupped his cheeks, and Sully shuddered,

shutting his eyes so he didn't have to see. Every muscle in his body locked up tight. His stomach dropped.

"Not sorry enough," she whispered in his ear, slimy hair dragging over the side of his face.

Sully jerked upright in bed on a ragged gasp, shaking violently. Elliot startled next to him, and there was the whisper of a touch on his arm. Stumbling out of bed, Sully bolted from the room.

CHAPTER TWENTY-FOUR

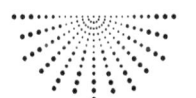

FOOTSTEPS POUNDED DOWN THE stairs and Elliot exhaled loudly as he got up. The cobwebs of sleep clung to his mind for the briefest moment. Rubbing at his eyes with one hand, he groped for a match with the other. Christ, he missed electricity.

Lighting the candle as he rose, Elliot cursed when his bare feet hit the cold floor. He quickly shoved into his boots and grabbed a robe to throw on for added warmth over his underwear and long-sleeved white shirt. He grabbed the candle and rushed out the door only to be met with four curious faces. Of course the noise had woken every last one of them.

"Go back to bed. We've a mission tomorrow. It's nothing to be concerned with."

Hoffman shrugged, Remonet nodded, and they disappeared back into their room. Charbonneau evaluated him longer before he grunted something indecipherable and did the same. Bellona rose her brows and crossed her arms.

"He'll be fine, I'll make sure of it," Elliot whispered. "Get some sleep."

Sighing, she relented. The steep, narrow stairs were a deathtrap he carefully descended, always clumsy when he'd just woken. It was a marvel Warren hadn't fallen in the dark.

The sound of retching reached his ears as soon as he arrived at the landing. Hopefully Warren had at least made it to the toilet or the sink.

Elliot followed the gasps and curses between heaving to the bathroom. The door was left ajar in Warren's haste, and their eyes met briefly in the candlelight. Warren's hair stuck damply to his forehead. His skin was unusually pale, forehead and upper lip beading with sweat. His face contorted and he turned back to the toilet he was kneeling in front of, once more emptying the contents of his stomach.

After, Warren drew in a shaky breath, trembling. He collapsed, wide-eyed, back against the wall and struggled to catch his breath.

"Finished?" Elliot asked.

The floor must have been ice beneath the bare skin of his legs and the thin cream material of his shorts.

"Think so," Warren mumbled, eyes shut against the light.

"Would you like me to get you some water? Or is there anything else I can do?"

Warren kept his eyes closed, swallowing twice before he managed a husky, "Water, please."

"Right, I'll only be a moment, will you be all right in the dark?"

Warren nodded faintly and didn't try to speak again. Elliot didn't blame him.

Upstairs, he grabbed the first clothing he set eyes on, his navy fisherman's sweater and Warren's uniform trousers. Tucking them under one arm, he went back down, then lit the kerosene lamp in the kitchen so they could have light to talk by later. He fetched a glass of water and returned to the bathroom.

"Thanks," Warren mumbled as he accepted the glass. He swished some water around his mouth, leaned over the toilet and spat before resuming his position against the wall. Color slowly returned to his face as he avoided Elliot's scrutinizing gaze. He sipped the water, then set it beside himself. "I'm okay, just…" he glanced quickly at Elliot and away. "Bad dream."

Elliot's throat tightened. "You must be frozen, take these."

Warren accepted the bundle of clothing, his gaze still averted.

"Yeah, thanks for that too. Look, I need to clean up. Wouldja mind stepping out?" he asked, voice flat and emotionless.

Elliot waffled. Leaving Warren on his own went against his better instincts, but if the situation was reversed, he'd also want privacy. "Of course. I'll wait in the kitchen. You keep the candle," he said, setting it on the floor near the door. "I've got a lamp on in the kitchen."

"Don't need to wait up for me." Warren levered himself up unsteadily. He sent Elliot a strained smile. Utterly false, utterly unacceptable. It was high time they talked. "I'll be fine."

"I've no doubt you would, and yet I insist. Take your time."

Elliot left before Warren could protest further. Returning to the kitchen, he sat in a chair that faced the washroom and gathered his thoughts. How could he approach this tactfully without prodding at Warren's wounds? It was clear the trauma of frontline warfare along with the lack of sleep was exacerbating Warren's preexisting nightmares. His condition would only degrade if they didn't come up with a solution to give him some relief. The sooner the better. Elliot needed to find a way to push without shoving Warren directly over the edge.

Why must that be so difficult to accomplish?

The correct approach continued to elude him when Warren slipped silently into the kitchen and slumped down in the chair opposite Elliot. Folding his arms on the table, Warren rested his cheek on them and shut his eyes. Long dark lashes fanned his high cheekbones. The flickering firelight bounced shadows across his face and made his thick dark hair pitch black. A few strands he normally brushed back curled over his smooth forehead, concealing his slight widow's peak. The shadow of stubble dusting his wide jaw was the only sign of his age.

Elliot could watch him like this forever. He appeared so young. He *was* so young. Twenty-four was hardly old enough to carry all of the suffering he'd been dealt. If he could take some for Warren, he would in a heartbeat.

I wish he would let me help. I wish he'd understand accepting he needs it doesn't make him inadequate.

The slow, steady rise and fall of Warren's back and shoulders made Elliot wonder if he was trying to fall asleep right there. "How are you feeling?"

Warren didn't move, but his lashes fluttered. "Not gonna be sick again, anyway."

"Was it—"

"Just a bad dream. You probably saw them all," Warren mumbled, dispassionate voice low and raspy. Like if he didn't sound bothered it couldn't hurt him.

"I wouldn't say that. Your subconscious was very creative," Elliot said, and instantly kicked himself.

Warren opened one eye, searching for something. Whatever it was, Elliot hoped he found it. "The one about my ma?"

Elliot shook his head; he'd never walked into a nightmare about her. They'd only briefly talked about his mother. Both of Warren's parents had passed unexpectedly within a year of one another when he was eight. He'd gone to live with his Aunt Margaret, Uncle Thomas, and baby Anne. And he'd been happy there, he claimed, until fate intervened to steal them away too. It was so blasted unfair. People Warren loved kept being ripped from him.

In contrast, Elliot had only ever lost one, to a long-acting illness. It wasn't pretty or painless, but at least he'd gotten to say goodbye to his mother. Warren had never had that opportunity. Not with either set of parents who raised him. "Will it help to tell me?"

Warren burrowed his cheek deeper in the crevice his arms created, hiding half his face. His one visible eye shut again, lashes drifting to settle like a smudge on his cheek. "Don't know. Never told anyone before. I don't exactly remember how the dream goes. Just know what it was about. It's hard for me. To talk about her."

Nervously licking his bottom lip, and then pressing them together, Elliot treaded softly. "You could try. I won't judge you, simply listen. I do it for the others when they need to unburden."

Warren didn't respond for long enough Elliot worried he really had fallen asleep. Then he cleared his throat. "Did I ever tell you I lived in New York?"

Reluctant, not wanting to ruin whatever spell had cast a truce between them, Elliot admitted, "You were an adorable newsie."

A faint smile graced Warren's face. "Right. You saw that fight."

Just a moment? He remembered? Since when? Elliot's pulse rabbited, but he didn't draw attention to it. He tried to keep his emotions from screaming his confused elation at Warren. "You were scrappy. I was impressed."

"Mm. I was eight when Ma sent me to live with Uncle Thomas. She told me she'd follow. Dropped me off at the station, but she felt…so much sadder than she should've. I didn't think enough of it. It worried me, but she'd always been different from most people. Her moods whipped up and down. Everyone fluctuates and changes, but there's usually a reason, or something that does it. Hers was like a switch flipped."

"Ahh."

"She was a good mother," Warren said, opening his eyes once more, staring into Elliot's like he urgently required him to understand that essential fact. "She knew I was skilled, and she never made me feel wrong about it. Uncle Thomas was too."

"I believe you." It seemed important to say. And Warren's reaction confirmed Elliot's gut feeling.

His eyes widened, dark and fathomless in the poor lighting, and it was so reminiscent of that night outside of the Hotel LaSalle. When it was all so simple, but Elliot's heart pounded against his ribcage anyway, something glowing in his chest like the fire catching and growing hotter. More intense after all this time.

I was always destined to fall for him. Even then I felt it starting.

Warren broke their stare and brushed the hair away from his forehead, fingers sinking into the thick strands. "Yeah. It's hard to explain, but she's how I knew I could tune out pain and anguish. I'd unconsciously been doing it for years with her. And that day I didn't notice how awful she felt or how much she needed me to stay." Warren squeezed his eyes shut again, his agony laid bare. Elliot ached to reach out. "I got on the train. She told me to. She promised she'd be there with us soon as she could afford another ticket."

Warren lapsed into silence, staring at the dancing flame in the lamp, eyes damp. Elliot watched him exhale slowly through his nose, straightening up to lean back in the chair.

"What happened?" Elliot gently prompted when no more appeared to be forthcoming.

"We saw it in the papers before I got the letter she wrote me. *Woman leaps from Brooklyn Bridge,*" Warren spoke woodenly. No sign of his earlier anguish, as if he'd reached his limit and the only way to finish the story was to deliver it devoid of emotion. "And I had this sick twist in my stomach, even though they didn't have a picture or a name. Sometimes I dream she tells me it was my fault." He paused and sent Elliot a smile tinged with sorrow rather than amusement. "It's funny after all the stuff I've seen, that's still the one that scares me most."

"In the letter did she say—"

"That she blamed me? No, not at all. She actually begged me not to blame myself. It didn't matter. I did. I do," Warren admitted. "I should've known, should've stayed. Maybe I could've talked her out of it."

"I'm so sorry, Warren. I'm sure you've already discarded all the reasons it isn't, so I won't repeat them. Is there anything I can say?"

Warren shook his head. "Nah. Elliot, I'm tired."

Should he offer to help with that? To keep away nightmares, if only for the rest of the night? He couldn't. Warren had trusted him with that memory. It wasn't fair to trade on that trust while he was emotionally vulnerable. What if he detonated the progress they just made?

"Of course. We ought to get some more sleep while we can. Mission tomorrow, you know," Elliot said, raising his arms over his head and stretching his back with a satisfying arch. He felt Warren's eyes burning into him, and a flush stained his cheeks.

Do not under any circumstances, read into that.

With a slow nod, Warren rose to his feet.

In the dark, facing opposite directions beneath the covers as had become their custom, Elliot couldn't stop wondering if he ought to have offered more. Maybe tomorrow, after the mission he could try to broach the topic again. Make Warren see it was mutually beneficial, not a sign of weakness. It didn't make Warren weak if it wasn't only him. If it was them together and they both required it.

Tomorrow.

Behind him Warren adjusted the blankets and shifted slightly. "Thanks. Y'know, for listening."

A warm sensation suffused Elliot's chest. Hope. "Of course."

CHAPTER TWENTY-FIVE

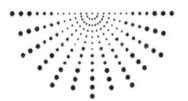

THE VEHICLES WERE PRECISELY where their contact had promised they would be. Sully had never ridden in this kind of a car, a glossy black open-top that looked similar—maybe was exactly the same for all he knew—as the ones their higher-ranking officers were driven around in. Other than the motorcycles, which were still a novelty, he'd only been in transport trucks, jostled around in back with too many other men who were loud with chaotic emotion and inane chatter.

This drive was quiet and tense. Sully felt the others settling into calm alertness, and he was reminded this was somewhat routine for them. That crossing the land he and fellow soldiers fought, sacrificed, and died bloody to gain a few feet of was easy for them. They had to time Bellona's transports carefully, but with either he or Hoffman along, the Germans never even noticed them. It was unsettling.

Alone in the backseat of the car, he spread out. Watched Elliot's pale hair whip in the wind. The road in front of them was poorly illuminated by headlamps, and everything else by the sliver of silver moon in the sky. Elliot's black jacket was an ink stain below the night-bleached wisps of his hair. Sully was fascinated by the visual.

The crisp air bit his cheeks and slithered down his collar. The civilian clothing he wore did about as much to keep him warm as his uniform, which meant not nearly enough. At least he'd grabbed a warm hat that kept his ears from freezing clean off.

Wearing something that wasn't a barely presentable uniform felt strange now. He'd been kept in the front lines so often he'd never had the chance to wear anything else. Laundering one uniform each time he was given the briefest respite. Other soldiers rotated out much more frequently and spent longer away. Not the skilled. They were too few to spare. Giving them time away from the fighting meant heavier losses. Might be the difference between winning a battle or retreating.

Would wearing something like this ever feel normal again? Would he live long enough to find out?

Sully pinched the tightly-knit navy sleeve of the heavy sweater he wore over his shirt and rolled it between his gloved fingers. It was Elliot's. The same one he'd given Sully to wear last night. Last night when he spilled his guts and almost begged Elliot to stop the nightmares. So exhausted he clung to his pride by the thinnest thread.

These distracting thoughts weren't helpful. He needed to rest the best he could until they arrived, and his skills were needed. The brief time they spent crossing the lines left him drained physically, emotionally, and magically.

Closing his eyes, he thought of his life before all of this. How he felt the day Edie had offered him a job at her agency. Her keen eyes had sparkled. "What's a smart, intuitive guy like you doin' workin' in a dump like this?"

He hadn't minded tending bar in the lackluster club he'd been employed at, but it hadn't been interesting either. Back then, he'd been surviving. Keeping a roof over Anne's head. Not thinking about what he wanted to do. Nothing beyond getting enough money mattered.

"D'you like solving puzzles? The cases we get ain't your usual run of the mill cheaters and deadbeats." She'd leaned close, that smile twisting her painted lips, the one that made most men ache to know her secrets. If they were interested in pretty women, anyway. "We investigate things…a little more magical."

The hint of knowing made his heart pound, and a flicker of fear lick his spine, but the pay was better than he made at the bar, and after she tipped her own hand, he was intrigued. Everything fell into place fast. Before he knew it he was a staple at Edie Isles Detective Agency. A natural, Edie called him. She'd pegged him as skilled from the start, part and parcel of her own skills, and when he'd finally, cautiously admitted exactly what he could do she'd been tickled. "Our own little lie sniffing barometer."

When the car slowed, Sully jolted and cracked his eyes open. They drove onto a small hardly noticeable turn off, puttered a few feet into the woods and rolled to a stop. Shortly after, the second car with Charbonneau, Hoffman, and Remonet parked behind them.

This is it. Time to prove I can handle this. Time to prove Stone didn't make a mistake choosing me.

They climbed out, and Sully made sure to retrieve the haversack to stuff full of whatever documents he could lay hands on. It wasn't like most of them could read the damn things to tell if they were important or not. Elliot was the only one of them with passable skill at speaking and reading German. There wouldn't be time for him to check over everyone's shoulders. Not if they wanted to be quick and efficient, and they had to be if they weren't going to get caught.

Transporting them all from the cars to the shadows of the building they were targeting took precious time. It was a safe way to make sure their vehicles weren't discovered.

The moon was high in the sky as they arrived at their destination. The complex sprawled inside of the barbed wire fences. Two wide square barracks to the east housed soldiers who either guarded or worked at the facility. In the center lay another large concrete building that contained offices and laboratories. They had only received the scantest information about what could be waiting for them inside. There was no indication if the project they were pursuing information on was the only experiment being conducted here. For all they knew they might return with information on others or discover fresh horrors inside.

What they did have was detailed intelligence on the timing of security. Their movements now were planned to the last second. Edging carefully and quietly through the cover of darkness, Sully focused on deepening the shade to blot them from view if anyone happened to look their way.

Near the rear of the building, they found a window where the lights were off and after a quick glance to be sure it was as empty as it appeared, Bellona cupped her hands to the icy glass and peered inside more intently. One moment she was standing there, the next she vanished and appeared on the other side of the glass, winking at them. Tilting her head to the side, she listened—checking for any sign she'd been overheard—then slowly she unlatched the window and silently opened it.

Charbonneau interlaced his fingers into a makeshift step and helped each of them up through the window before he jumped up and seamlessly hauled himself in behind them.

Exactly as discussed, Sully was the one to crack open the door, simultaneously projecting that nothing was happening. Once he stepped out into the dimly lit hall, he made sure it was clear before waving the others out. Bellona remained behind to search the office. After she would continue down this hallway to the other four offices. Meanwhile Charbonneau, Hoffman, and Remonet took the long hall to the left. Sully and Elliot moved to the right.

The sterile white halls appeared deserted. Still, Sully stretched his concentration thin on muffling their footsteps. He strode quickly toward the end of the long hall, where there was a doorway on either side. Elliot inclined his head right, indicating Sully take that room. Nodding his understanding, Sully reached for the door handle.

The pistol he could hardly shoot straight weighed heavily where it remained tucked in the holster on his belt. He wished he had his rifle. Not that it would do him any good. The sound would bring soldiers in the nearby barracks running. Illusions and the hope he noticed any change in the anticipatory tension of the moods around him were all he had to rely on.

Pushing open the door, Sully crept into a deserted laboratory. Diffused light from the hallway shone in, lighting up desks covered in scientific instruments. Glass tubes and jars with mysterious liquids of varying color caught his eye. Sully didn't dawdle to stare. On the left wall stretched an elaborate system of rubber tubing and shiny glass globes, currently devoid of any substance. It gleamed ominously as he moved forward.

Deadly quiet strung tight as he approached the back of the room, along which several tall metal filing cabinets stood. Split between attending to the illusions he was weaving, his destination, and keeping himself alert for anyone entering behind him, it was no wonder he didn't notice until he was standing right next to it. Sully's heart launched into his throat at a soft rustle, low and to his left. He staggered back, hand rubbing the center of his heaving chest.

In a cage no higher than Sully's thigh was a small sleeping girl. The top of her dark brown hair pressed against wire mesh, her knees bent because the enclosure wasn't long enough for her to lie comfortably. She was covered in a thin blanket and slept on the hard floor. Sully's heart broke with a pang that stopped his breath. Whatever this little girl was dreaming of, it was keeping at bay the harsh horror of reality—the only emotions he sensed from her were peaceful.

What the hell is she doing here? How the hell could anyone put a little kid in a fucking cage?

He glanced around at the equipment, and knew with a sick certainty what they would do if he left her there. This wasn't part of the mission. They hadn't planned to rescue anyone. But Sully couldn't in good conscience leave an innocent girl to this fate.

She's just a kid. Anyone would make the same damn choice, and if they wouldn't, then fuck them too. She's coming with us. Soon as I get what I came for, I'll get her out of there.

He set about collecting as many documents as he could from the filing cabinets. Too many to take them all, so he grabbed a few files from each drawer and hoped they yielded helpful information. Once his haversack was full, he stuffed loose papers into the pockets of his pants.

And finally, he knelt down in front of the cage. Was there any way to help her without frightening her worse? Sully yawned and rubbed a hand over his mouth, called up energy reserves to focus.

The illusions he had stretched all over the building were leeching everything he had.

Glancing over his shoulder, he checked to make sure the coast was clear and once he confirmed it was, he dropped the visual concealing him and shifted his dwindling ability to muffle any noise talking would make. "Little girl?"

No response. He could see her back rising and falling with steady breaths. Scaring her was the last thing he wanted to do, but he needed her awake.

"Hey, little girl," Sully said, louder. This time her head shot up, smashing against the wire as she instinctively tried to get away from him. Her terror smacked Sully in the face and clutched at his chest. He held up his hands in a placating gesture he hoped was universal. "Shhh, shh, shh. I'm here to help. Don't be scared. It's okay. It's okay."

Her breaths were coming in sharp gasps and she stared at him with huge fearful uncomprehending eyes. Maybe she didn't speak English. Was she German? French? He didn't know any German, but he knew a few French words he'd picked up in the trenches, including, "Anglais?"

The girl's paper white lips parted, like she was going to speak to him, then she gave a quick shake of her head, and clasped the small gray blanket she had tighter around her slight body. The tiny thing couldn't have been more than six or seven and she was half-starved. Fresh rage kindled in Sully's gut, but he kept his face friendly. "French—France?"

She nodded. Sully wished fervently that Elliot had chosen this room instead. He'd be able to speak to her.

I'm fucking useless here. Shite.

Stop panicking, it's not helping. Try harder damn it.

"American," Sully said, pointing at himself. *Even if she knows the goddamn word will she know it means I'm not here to hurt her?*

The girl's brows pressed together, and she didn't relax, not exactly, but Sully felt her fear lessen just a fraction. Maybe she did understand to a degree.

"I'm going to help you, okay? Daide?" He probably butchered that one, but he thought it might mean help. He'd heard injured French soldiers yelling it anyway. Her head titled, confused. Shite.

Sully tried to pronounce it more carefully and a cautious hope blossomed in her.

"Aide?" She followed up with an excited flurry of French Sully couldn't hope to interpret.

"Aide," he confirmed, sure now he'd gotten it right. Sully looked for something to break the padlock on the cage.

There, wrenches!

He wedged them into the shackle, using the leverage it created to force the lock open. It took three adjustments, but the shackle finally popped free. He scrambled to get it off, tossed the lock onto the floor and stepped back as he opened the wire door, giving her room to climb out.

The girl crawled onto the cold floor and stood on bare feet. Her courage surged, relief dizzying him along with her. Since she had no shoes, he'd have to carry her outside. That blanket wouldn't keep her warm enough either. Maybe he could wrap her in his sweater. He could take the risk of exposure in his long underwear. It wouldn't be pleasant, but he'd survive.

"All right," he said, giving her an encouraging smile. "Now we need to be quiet, can you do that?" Sully mimed be quiet with a finger pressed to his lips.

Nodding, the girl repeated the motion and offered him a shy smile of her own in return.

Cold metal pressed the back of Sully's head.

Fucking hell.

Of all the boneheaded, downright careless things he could've done, he'd dropped his guard. It was suddenly, abundantly clear just how fucking risky that was. Just how massive a mistake that was.

"You move, I shoot," said a deep, heavily accented voice behind him. The slight color in the girl's face drained. Her eyes welled with disappointed tears. Sully cussed mentally as he scrambled to come up with a plan.

He was far too drained to sustain a physical illusion and if he threw up a visual one and moved, his friend here would feel it. Sully's brains would spatter the wall before he so much as blinked. He could tell the girl to run, get his head blown off, thereby alert the others to flee, and at least give her a chance at escape, but would she understand him?

What the hell is French for run? Run-é?

Sully almost let out a hysterical laugh at himself. He was so fucked.

Cold determination and burning hot possessive rage edged into his awareness. A sense of relief swept through him, so intense it weakened his knees.

Elliot.

He caught the girl's eye and winked at her, concealing the sound of Elliot's approaching footsteps. Sully pressed his lips together to stifle an elated laugh when he heard the German grunt what must've been a curse.

"How precisely did you put it?" Elliot asked, voice deceptively casual for the intensity of his emotions. "Oh, right. You move, I shoot. You shoot him, I shoot you. But I will not make it clean, and I promise you it will hurt for a very long time before you finally expire in agony." He switched to German, Sully assumed repeating the message, though he wasn't entirely sure.

It shouldn't make something flutter in Sully's chest, hearing Elliot threaten to kill someone for him. There went his heart doing it anyway.

"Good timing." Sully was surprised his voice was steady and came out normal.

"Always. Now, lower your weapon." There was a cocky smirk in Elliot's words. Sully felt the German's reluctance and fear as the barrel moved away from Sully's scalp. A second wave of relief flooded Sully now that the immediate risk of death by a finger twitching on the trigger was averted. "Sullivan, relieve him of that Luger, if you would be so kind."

Turning, Sully complied and slipped it from the German's unwilling grip. He was livid, churning with rash emotion. Sully had to work hard to keep his gaze focused on the threat he posed instead of flying to Elliot's face.

Then without saying a word, Elliot's hand clamped over the soldier's mouth. In the same second, the German went whiter than a ghost, muscles rigid. His eyes rolled back into his skull, and he collapsed onto the ground in a dead faint. Sully's brows rose. Face tightening, Elliot looked away.

"The pistol would have made far too much noise, and we haven't the time." Elliot tucked his gun back into his holster, eyes darting over Sully's form as if searching for any previously unseen injuries. "I'd ask what the devil you were doing getting yourself captured except we haven't the time for that eith—" The rest of his sentence fizzled out as Sully stepped slightly to the side, revealing the girl in her worn, ragged dress, and dirty blanket.

Elliot's mouth went slack, momentarily speechless. "What the—?"

Sully grinned at him, a flash of impertinent triumph. "What happened to not having time, Captain? Girl, kept in cage, saving. She's French and I don't speak it, so if you could relay that we're going to rescue her, she'd be a lot less terrified that we're about to do her in too. Then we can all get the hell out of here before someone comes searching for him."

Muttering something under his breath, Elliot knelt in front of the girl. He spoke in a soothing, lilting voice. Sully tried not to notice how sweet he was with her. Not to mention how attractive his French accent was. Didn't need more reasons to harbor inappropriate and perplexing passions for Elliot Stone.

Her eyes watered, and she looked between them, wavering, before she threw herself into Elliot's arms, whispering what Sully figured were words of gratitude.

Elliot peeled his jacket off, murmuring as he wrapped it around her shoulders, and scooped the girl up. "We have to hurry. How are you holding up?"

"Peachy," Sully replied, ignoring how awfully close to not peachy he'd been. How close to the surface his emotions were roiling as a result. "I'll check the hall and give you the okay."

CHAPTER TWENTY-SIX

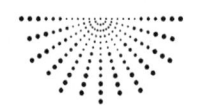

ELLIOT KEPT HIS RISING temper in check throughout their escape. A seething mass of fear and fury curled in his gut like a fist clenching on the long drive to the abandoned farm where they would recuperate, replenishing the energy stores they required to covertly cross the line to safety.

He might not have Warren's skill at reading emotions, but he felt Warren watching him, waiting for the inevitable explosion. And it was inevitable. Somehow that made him burn hotter. He despised losing control of his anger like this.

His thoughts returned again and again to the moment he walked into that laboratory and saw a Luger to Warren's head and heard the German bastard threaten him.

If I'd been moments later...

If Warren had done something foolhardy...

If he hadn't the energy to hide my approach...

None of it should have occurred. Warren should never have let himself be seen. His skill was supposed to keep him safe, for Christ's sake.

The fact he hadn't been able to protect himself was evidence of exactly what Elliot suspected: he wasn't sleeping enough to be in top form magically or physically. If he kept on the way he was, he would wind up dead for it. Elliot's mind recoiled from the possibility. His chest burned and tightened, and he clenched his fists on the wheel until his knuckles ached with the strain.

They abandoned the cars to the rear of the farm, where their contact would pick them up again tomorrow. Faster vehicles, more suited to avoiding daytime notice would be used to get closer to the front.

Behind Elliot, Charbonneau carried Emilienne, the little girl Warren almost lost his life for. As they crunched over crisp, frosted grass he spoke quietly to her. Once, Elliot was certain he heard a tiny giggle. He wasn't surprised to find Charbonneau was good with children. He had two young girls, currently residing with his sister and her husband until he returned.

It was one of the reasons he'd been so unforgivably slow regarding the depth of his relationship with Ollie. He was a widower though, and Elliot knew intimately that some people who preferred men married anyway. Or he might not prefer a single type of person at all. Elliot was flexible himself; it oughtn't be a surprise to encounter others with similar inclinations.

By the time they trudged up to the crest of the hill that led to the farm, Elliot's temper had banked only a little. The tether of his control nigh to snapping.

"Hoffman," he said softly, halting the others. "Would you?"

"Yes, sir." Hoffman crept forward, checking the coast was as clear as it appeared in a practiced routine.

"I don't sense anyone. I could help scout," Warren offered, face flushing slightly at the malevolent glare Elliot sent him.

You've got little enough energy left, you won't waste it pointlessly over this, he didn't growl. "Hoffman will do fine. If I wanted you to help him, I would have asked."

Squaring his shoulders in the face of whatever violent outburst he felt beneath the surface of calm Elliot projected, Warren tried again. "Okay, well, I'll set up an illusion then, to conceal a fire and any trail we might have left if they try to pursue us." Something in his voice dared Elliot to decline.

No. The fight brewing between them absolutely could not take place with Charbonneau, Remonet, Bellona, and little Emilienne witnessing it. Elliot clenched his jaw, because there was no justifiable reason to refuse the offer without inciting precisely that. "Wonderful."

At Hoffman's whistle they marched forward down the slope to the farmhouse. Its cold stone exterior and wooden shutters a welcome respite for everyone else while Elliot stewed.

Sleeping assignments were quickly dealt with. Bellona and Emilienne sharing one room. The other should have gone to Elliot, but if Warren wouldn't be sleeping until morning, Elliot didn't intend to either. Instead, he offered his room to Charbonneau and Remonet. Hoffman took first watch, setting up in the kitchen near the wood stove he planned to light.

Charbonneau took a moment to reveal what Emilienne had spoken of on their journey. She'd been captured with a group of villagers, including her parents. One by one, they'd been taken from a prison near the barracks and brought to the lab. What had happened to them once they were taken remained a mystery. She'd only been brought to the cage that night, and she didn't speak German. Elliot suspected they were using the villagers as test subjects, and it made him sick to think of what could have happened to the poor girl. It was bad enough her parents were probably dead. If there was one small mercy, it was that Sully had found her. Too bad Sully had almost gotten himself killed in the process.

Once Charbonneau retreated to rest like the others, Elliot turned to Warren and gave him a flat stare that defied rebuke. "Might I speak to you outside, Corporal Sullivan?" He kept his tone polite, however it was clear he wasn't making a request.

Warren flinched, then forced himself to relax, nodding. "Yeah, sure."

They stepped out into the dark icy night, Elliot's flashlight illuminating the sparkling frost as Warren tailed him to the barn. It seemed sturdy enough, if somewhat worse for the wear.

With every step, Elliot felt less in command of the emotions he'd been holding at bay, temper spiking dangerously. He should've pushed. He should've offered last night. Unbearable fury with himself and Warren rose in a sweeping tide of recrimination.

Warren's lack of energy affected every member in their unit. If he couldn't be trusted to maintain his illusions, he put all of them at risk. Elliot wasn't only responsible for Warren. He was responsible for all of them. And he was terrified.

It was time to have it out. They needed to resolve this. By whatever means.

He almost died. For what? I know he's proud, I know he's stubborn, but it cannot happen again. It absolutely cannot.

Elliot pulled open the heavy wood door, rusty hinges resisting his efforts briefly before giving with a dreadful squeak. He motioned for Warren to enter first. It was hardly warmer inside than out, but at least the wind was blocked by the solid wooden walls aside from the occasional whistle through a crack.

The silence was fraught as Elliot set the flashlight on a ledge and crossed his arms. He turned to face Warren a few steps away. Neither of them spoke. Warren warily watched, waiting.

"How did he get close enough to you?" Elliot asked, voice sharp.

Warren's face colored as he winced. "I—it was—"

"How did he see you? How did he sneak up on you, Warren?"

A defiant tilt to Warren's chin all but telegraphed the lie he was about to tell. "My full attention was on the girl, getting her out."

Not an outright lie but not the whole truth either. Anyone who hadn't spent time learning all the ways Warren would avoid this sort of admission might not recognize the omission. Anyone who wasn't Elliot.

"Right, and so that made you lose the ability to conceal yourself, did it? Made you fail to notice something amiss behind you? You didn't *feel* him approaching because you were otherwise occupied? I wasn't aware you were so easy to distract. Distractible people don't make it long on the battlefield, from what I've heard. It's quite the miracle you've come this far unscathed then, isn't it?"

Warren faltered, his cheeks going deeper red, his brows thick black slashes above dark, mutinous eyes. "That's not fair. I was—"

"For Christ's sake, Warren. You're exhausted, why can't you simply admit it? I know you've hardly been sleeping; I lie right next to you in that fucking bed. Christ. You've allowed yourself to be worn down until you are forced to take risks conserving your energy. You're rationing it. Picking and choosing when you genuinely require it. Only your judgment is compromised there too, because as I said, *you are fucking exhausted.*"

Warren glowered at him, hackles rising. "What do you expect me to do about it? I'm doing all I can," he growled, flinging his arms out. "I can't sleep and when I do, I guess you already know what's waiting for me there, don't you?"

Elliot's temper finally erupted in a massive burst. He crowded forward into Warren's space, his pulse a rushing sledgehammer in his skull. "Why must you be so damned stubborn? You were nearly killed, Warren! I could have watched your head be blown to pieces. If I'd been a moment later, we might not be having this discussion. Because you can't simply ask for what you need. Why can you not allow me to help?"

Rage strained and twisted Warren's features. "Because," he shouted, meeting Elliot's aggressive posture with his own, shoving forward so they were chest to chest and glaring daggers at one another. "Because I hate feeling weak. I hate it. I don't want to need you to fix my head so I can sleep. I ought to be able to handle my own mind. And I can't. D'you have any idea how pathetic that feels? And then you want me to *ask* you to fix it? After I already told you to fuck off?" Warren barked out a harsh laugh. "Didja really think I would do that?"

"Yes," Elliot exclaimed, frustration like ragged fingernails clawing down his spine. "That's precisely what I want! And you are not weak for needing it, nor for asking. I have *never* thought you were. Not once. Not ever. I know you, Warren. I know the core of you, and there is nothing but strength and bravery and everything good in this world there. Everything worth fighting for. You're not weak."

Warren's fingers curled tightly in the lapels of Elliot's coat. To drag him closer or shove him away? The emotions flitting across his face sent a thousand mixed signals. Maybe Warren wasn't sure what he wanted either.

"But I am," he said, voice near to breaking, rough with anguish. Wrenching Elliot's heart. "Because it's more than needing you to chase away my nightmares. It's *you*. I miss you so much more than I should. Every time I start to remember you in my dreams, it's like a wound opens in my chest and I can't stem the bleeding fast enough, it soaks into my bones, and it makes me..." Warren paused, staring into Elliot's eyes, breaths fast and shallow against Elliot's chest, heartbeat racing. "It makes me feel too much. Makes me want too much. Things I can't possibly have. Things I can't ask for."

Elliot's own breathing faltered, adrenaline and something much more meaningful rushing in his veins, intoxicating him. "Ask me," he insisted, wanting to reach up and touch Warren's jaw, to offer physical comfort. "If you want something, you have to tell me."

The struggle playing out in front of him, plain as day on Warren's expressive features, almost shattered his resolve, but he couldn't give in, not now. Warren needed to say so. It was imperative he learned to admit when he needed help, when he wanted something. Accepting it had to be his choice alone, Elliot brought him as far as he could, as close to the realization that anything Warren asked of him would be granted.

Trust me. Please just trust me.

"I..." His glimmering eyes begged Elliot to supply the words, and when he didn't Warren dropped his gaze to Elliot's chin. Silence stretched and went on. Emotions shifted across Warren's face. Elliot could see him battling himself every step of the way, laboring for every inch of ground. Finally, Warren's shoulders sagged as if the fight had gone completely out of him.

Warren sucked in a slow breath, and softly said, "I need your help. At night. To sleep. And..." He looked back up, the challenge in him reigniting, as if getting that first admission out broke through a wall and now he couldn't stop. "And I want *you*," he said, fierce for all it was whisper quiet, pushing up on his toes, jerking down on Elliot's lapels. Their mouths crashed together in a hard kiss far too long coming.

All of the anger festering in Elliot's chest flamed into desire, longing so bright his entire body throbbed with it. He sank his gloved fingers in Warren's thick hair. Held him close as Warren's lips parted, tongue delving into Elliot's mouth, flickering against his. Groaning, Elliot matched Warren's desperation.

Finally. Christ.

Need for air broke them apart. Gasping, their eyes locked, and then Warren was on him again. His mouth pressed frantic kisses along Elliot's cold jaw, stopping to suck beneath his ear, spangling surprised pleasure through him in a flowing pulse. The damp trail he left cooled quickly. The contrast to his hot mouth made Elliot shiver and pant.

He slid his fingers along the breadth of Warren's muscled shoulders, gripped at his biceps. Pressed himself forward and shoved his growing arousal against Warren's hip, showed him how good it was. He felt as much as heard the moan Warren let loose against his skin with an answering roll of his own hips. The visceral satisfaction of Warren rutting against him stoked a primal possessive flush of lust. Elliot wanted him so badly.

He's so...I'm so...

"I missed you," he blurted as Warren fumbled hands between them to get at the fastening of Elliot's trousers. "This of course, but I missed *you*."

"Me too," Warren agreed, not slowing for a moment. "These fucking gloves," he muttered when his fingers slipped on the buttons. There was a rustle. Then the soft sound of material hitting the dusty ground at Elliot's feet. He didn't look, because Warren captured his mouth again, and a moment later his icy hand closed around Elliot's hot hard cock—startling and arousing—and Elliot bit down on Warren's lip, moaning. A high, tight sound he couldn't hold back.

The sensation was so tantalizing, so wonderfully exquisite he almost forgot his manners. Jerking his mouth free of Warren's, he clamped his teeth down on the leather of his own glove and pulled it off, letting it drop to the ground too.

Soon they were stroking one another, the cold air half-forgotten as they thundered toward inevitable climax.

I love you. Christ, Warren, I love you. I love you.

He didn't say it yet, couldn't. But he hoped Warren felt it in each tender caress and kiss.

Every gasp Warren made, every desperate sound, every needy jolt of his blood-warm straining cock in Elliot's palm was a vibrant reminder that he was here, alive. Warren's grip went a little slack. In response Elliot squeezed his own fingers tighter, sped his movements. Reveled in the way Warren dropped his head forward, resting heavily on Elliot's shoulder. His free hand grasped the back of Elliot's coat and held on for dear life, breaths hitching.

"I want you," Elliot whispered heatedly into Warren's hair. "So badly, you can't possibly comprehend."

"I do," Warren panted, shuddering, letting out a soft groan. "Want you—God, Elliot—I want you more."

"Someday we'll have nothing but time," Elliot told him, words rough and wicked. Indulging in a fantasy he had often. "No need to rush, no danger waiting for us, nothing but time to explore and touch and feel, and I'll take you so slowly, so thoroughly that you'll never forget I was there. I'll own a part of you. Mine forever."

Warren moaned, desperate, the sound making Elliot throb painfully in Warren's loose grip. "Already won't. You already do."

Christ. Dizzy pleasure at those words slammed into Elliot. He wanted to see Warren fall apart. "At the bar when we met, do you remember how I—"

"Ah. God, yes, please." Elliot felt Warren swelling in his hand, so close already, and he focused, passing a wave of euphoria into him. Warren stiffened instantly, his breaths stopping. Elliot barely cupped his gloved hand in time to catch it when Warren spent with a shaking gasp, clinging and trembling, pulsing again and again in Elliot's palm. He wrung out the last drops of Warren's pleasure and tucked him away, out of the cold.

Warren sagged against him, the rough wool of his sweater dragging over Elliot's sorely neglected cock, sensation shivering through him. Ignoring his own need in favor of holding onto Warren as he gradually recovered, Elliot enjoyed the solid weight of him. The heat between them kept him warm enough.

"Fuck," Warren murmured, long moments later, voice smokey. Elliot's cock reacted to it by swelling. There was a chuckle in Warren's voice as he finally seemed to notice he was still holding a very engorged cock. He gave it a gentle squeeze. Elliot inhaled sharply. "Hmm. We ought to take care of this, huh?"

"Oh. If you don't mind," he said, only the slightest bit breathlessly. A true feat.

"Fast or slow?" Warren asked, pumping him once, Elliot's hips surging forward to meet the stroke. It felt so good he whimpered and struggled not to beg.

"Fast, Christ. It's freezing out here. I'll be lucky not to get frostbite at this rate."

Warren laughed then, a bubbly, marvelous sound, nuzzling the skin above Elliot's collar. "Bet I can make you forget all about the pesky cold," he wagered.

And he did.

CHAPTER TWENTY-SEVEN

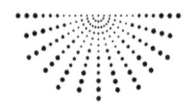

December 13, 1917
Fienvillers, France

SULLY LAY IN THE dark, facing the wall, eyes tracing the large cream roses and vines that climbed the vertically striped blue wallpaper. He could hardly make them out in the faint moonlight. They were faded with age, the difference between the dark blue and light blue stripes nearly identical. Slim silver lines between each stripe were the only way to tell them apart where the sun had mostly bleached the color.

Behind him, Elliot silently faced the opposite direction. The events of the night before in the barn were still fresh in Sully's mind; he couldn't stop thinking about it. After, they'd cleaned up and retreated to the relative warmth of the farmhouse, where they'd spent the night in the parlor quietly talking while Sully maintained the whisper thin illusion around the house.

In the light of dawn, Elliot had coaxed him into dozing, so he'd have enough energy to help them cross the line that afternoon. He felt like he hardly closed his eyes when Elliot shook him awake. They brought Emilienne, kitted out in clothing pilfered from each of them to keep her warm on the ride. Back on their side, Charbonneau made arrangements with the head nurse for her to be sent to join his daughters until her family could be located. If they ever would be. Sully hoped she'd be happy there.

He ought to be sleeping instead of letting his mind wander. This would be his first full night of rest in too long with nothing to fear. He asked for Elliot's help, and he knew he'd get it. Tonight no horrible dreams awaited him. No waking drenched in sweat with his pulse hammering. He could really rest.

Except where his thoughts and emotions incessantly returned kept him wide awake. He was remembering the way his heart pounded in the barn. Overwhelming longing ached in his chest. The massive mess of want and need he felt for Elliot twisting and twining with everything Elliot reflected right back at him. Elliot's hand on him, urgent and incredible.

Mine forever.

His stomach somersaulted, a giddy sensation coursed through him. The thrill of those words settled in his flesh and blood, and he wanted them to be true. Wanted to believe them.

Sully couldn't remember all the dreams they'd shared, but he recalled plenty. Enough to know for months he'd been dying to see Elliot again. Craved permission to touch him. Worried constantly if he gave in, Elliot might not ever come back. And here he was, lying in a bed, inches away from the man, and it felt like a yawning chasm between them. A chasm he himself was enforcing.

Why? Why when all I want is him? When he's right there and he said I could just ask him. Why can't I?

Flipping onto his back, Sully stared up at the ceiling. "Can't sleep," he mumbled, because it wasn't asking for anything. It was a statement. Maybe he could work up to asking.

"Do you want to talk?" Elliot shifted around until Sully sensed him watching his face.

"It's just..." Stretching his fingertips out and then clenching his palms to relieve the faint tingle in them, Sully made himself say something. Try. "It's just I don't know how to make sense of this. Whether I'll even remember what happens when you come into my dream."

"I could tell you we can't interact if you prefer," Elliot offered, voice light like he'd be fine with that. If Sully wanted to use him to sleep but keep him at arm's length. And the thing was, Sully could feel he meant it. "I'm sure you'd already know, if that's what you decide you want, but I could just be there."

Sully considered the proposal, gut twisting unhappily. He could remember how Elliot had slowly warmed up to casual touching in his dreams. The comfort he'd taken from a hand on his shoulder or an embrace on his worst days. He *liked* that. Coveted it even. How long had it been before Elliot when someone had comforted him through touch? How long since Sully had *let* someone? Had he ever?

"No," he said softly, tilting his head to meet Elliot's eyes, trying to see him clearly in the dark. "I want things like they were. It's just confusing me. I remember a lot. Not months' worth. There are gaps, but it's enough for me to remember how bad I wanted you then. And I know exactly how much I want you when I'm awake, and it's like it doubles the way I feel 'cause I never felt so strongly for anyone, any lover, in my life. It's so big." That last sentence came out barely above a whisper. His heart thumped in the silence that met his declaration.

Fingers slid across his cheek, until Elliot's palm was resting gently against it, his thumb smoothing back and forth in small soft sweeps. Felt nice. Sweet. "Neither have I. I won't lie and say I've never loved anyone else before, but this, with you, it's *more*."

Breath catching, Sully froze. The warm, enormous feeling inside him slotted into place. It was love. Of course it was. Different than he was used to, a new kind, reserved for Elliot, but it was unmistakably love. How could it be? How could he love someone this much? This fast? "I feel like I know so much about you, that I know you, but really, I only spent a night with you, and it's hard to wrap my head around."

"Maybe we haven't known each other very long out here, but that doesn't mean what happened in there," Elliot's fingers gently tapped Sully's head. "Was any less real. I've only ever told you the truth, even in dreams."

He let that sink in. Let the feelings Elliot gave off like content, glowing effervescence wash over him. It harmonized with the swelling in his chest, made him grin like a fool in the dark. Elliot loved him. *Loved* him. Had protected him. Cared about him enough to make sure he got the things he needed.

And Sully had treated him like shite for it. Hadn't let him explain. But Elliot wasn't asking for an apology either. Maybe because they'd both done things they weren't proud of. It could be different from now on. Couldn't it? They could be something special. Nothing good lasted, but Sully would take what he could get. Would take anything Elliot wanted to give him. "Okay. Maybe you're right. It doesn't feel pretend, all those months. It feels... yeah. Real. So what now?"

"For starters, you get some sleep. In your dreams I'll keep the same rules, which you may or may not recall."

"'No physical intimacy,'" Sully quoted, drawn down the rabbit hole of memory. Elliot bloody and mangled on the ground after dying in his arms, the way his heart broke until those soft thumbs brushed the tears from his eyes and made everything that hurt go away. Like being warm and toasty after years and years of ice and cold and misery.

Elliot's white teeth flashed in the moonlight. "Among others, but yes."

Sully smirked even if Elliot couldn't see him much. "Think that boat's sailed."

"Even so. It's muddled enough for you. I won't make it worse."

Rolling onto his side, Sully faced Elliot more fully. "What about here? Do we got to follow the rule out here?"

There was a slight pause, and then Elliot whispered, "Whatever you want."

Biting down on a grin, Sully gently pushed Elliot onto his back and pressed their lips together in a chaste kiss. "Like that?"

He felt the twitch of Elliot's grin a breath away from his own. "Mmm. Of course. Whenever you like. Within reason."

"Good." Sully kissed him again, deeper, slower. Then shifted to lie with his head on Elliot's chest, resting his arm heavily across Elliot's waist. "What about like this?"

Soft laughter tickled Sully's scalp. "That too. Are we finally going to sleep now? Because as much as I rather desperately want to explore this newfound playfulness, I'm not entirely sure how much longer I can keep my eyes open."

"Mmm. Not much could stop me from nodding off." Sully let himself enjoy the feeling of Elliot holding him close, so comfortable he could melt into him. For the first time since he'd been informed he was to report to training, given a train ticket and a date, and told the consequences of failure to comply, Sully felt safe.

THREE SHORT DAYS LATER, Sully once again found himself across the German line. He accompanied Bellona and Elliot, providing an illusion that kept them from watchful eyes as they crossed no man's land and traversed the trenches. When they landed precariously close to the edge of a trench above a group of German soldiers, he'd had to act fast as he scrambled for purchase. The dirt beneath his boot crumbled down onto a soldier who glanced up sharply.

Now they were safely holed up in an abandoned house outside of a city whose name Sully couldn't pronounce if he was held at gunpoint...again. The roof overhead was lined with dark wood beams, and the sturdy furniture was coated in a thin layer of dust.

The papers they'd recovered hadn't been fully translated. There were too many to sort through and not enough skilled soldiers or those with proper clearance who could read German. What they knew was a large-scale test would soon be performed. What that meant, none of them had a clue, but Sully grimly thought it was bad news for some unlucky bastards.

Some of the papers that had been translated mentioned the skilled German spearheading this initiative—Oberst Ulrich Brandt, an officer no one on their side seemed to have heard of. They needed more information. Desperately. Elliot had come up with a plan to infiltrate his dreams, discover what he could about the tests and the weapon.

The problem was, without a connection it was difficult for Elliot to find a particular person's dream. He said it was like finding a specific grain of sand on a beach—nearly impossible. Even a chance encounter could be enough to give him direction. "It's like sensing a vibration from them or a tune. When I'm searching for their dreams I simply listen and allow myself to be drawn to it," he'd explained.

So here they were, in Central controlled territory, about to risk their lives in a harebrained scheme to get him that connection. As far as their superiors knew, the mission they'd planned was to find any information they could lay hands on the traditional way. Elliot still wasn't willing to tell them about his dreamwalking, and Sully didn't blame him. Imagine if they didn't even let him rest at night because he could still be useful to them then too.

Sully grimaced at his reflection in a grimy mirror. He didn't look like himself. He was wearing a German officer's uniform, for one. The gray material was snug on his broad shoulders and biceps. The high collar fit but made him uncomfortable. He was scrubbed clean, shaven, hair elegantly styled away from his face and tucked up under an officer's cap with a black brim. A grotesque version of himself.

Just wearing this get up made him feel dirty. If it'd been an ordinary soldier's uniform he might not mind as much since he understood them more. They were following orders, awful orders, just like they were on the other side of the line. They might kill each other, but he had more in common with the average soldier across the barbed wire than he did with the officers in back on either side, than the Generals who ordered men about like toy soldiers to be sacrificed on a whim.

The door creaked open, and Sully glanced back at the noise. Elliot entered, dressed nearly identically. Somehow looking a thousand times better, then again, he always did. He tucked a shiny strand of blond hair back behind his ear. Gray suited him; Sully had thought that on the night they met. His pulse jumped as Elliot's eyes darted down to take him in.

"Ready?" Sully asked, the slightest hint of nerves betraying him.

Elliot sent him a sure smile. "Ready."

Brushing at lint that wasn't there on his sleeve, Sully asked, "And you're sure this is smart?"

Elliot's smile went crooked, his eyes bright. "No, not at all. It's risky and rash and slightly unhinged. However, as the only opportunity we have, we must take it. So long as you can hold up, we'll be fine."

"Piece of cake then. Long as no one asks me or Bell to talk. Not even sure how I'd go about convincing someone what I was saying is anything but gibberish." Sully frowned, thinking. "Hmm. Maybe I could convince them they heard the proper answer without saying anything at all."

Elliot reached out and gently squeezed Sully's shoulder, slim hands warm even in gloves. Or maybe that was just how his touch made Sully feel. "Yes, well, let's hope we won't have to test that hypothesis."

Distracting them both, Bell sauntered into the room. Her dark hair pinned up in an elegant style, wearing a lavender dress that must have been expensive. The bust glimmered, made from some kind of satiny material. Layered gauzy fabric draped from her hips to ankle length hem. Matching sleeves flowed loose and shimmery until they bunched around her wrists. A slim gold ribbon in a neat bow accented her waist. The color set off her blue eyes. She was as dainty as a fancy porcelain doll—and was that lipstick?

Her eyes narrowed. "I'm not interrupting, am I? Because you've both gone silent and you're looking at me oddly."

"No," Sully said, at a loss for words as his mind tried to reconcile this version of her with the tough woman in men's clothing he'd grown used to. "It's just…"

"I'm not quite sure I was prepared to see you in a dress," Elliot announced, theatrically placing a palm over his heart. "You might have stolen my affections." Bell squinted further, irritation spiking. If Sully were Elliot, he'd shut his mouth. Elliot, however, remained blissfully unaware he was heading for trouble. "In fact, I had no idea you cleaned up so nicel—" His breath whooshed out of him a second later when Bellona transported the distance of the room and jabbed him the gut hard enough to make him feel it.

Sully doubled over laughing, and she sent him a dirty glance too. He held his hand up defensively, still struggling to control his outburst. "At him, not you," he justified. God, it felt good to laugh though. To know Elliot was the kind of person who would take that punch with his own choked laugh. Delighted instead of spitting fire like most commanding officers Sully had known would be.

Bellona dusted her hands and rolled her eyes. "Now that that's sorted, we ought to be on our way, hadn't we?"

They arrived at the party late. Sully's illusion greased their way through security, and they walked inside a tall stone building. The room was extravagantly decorated and sweet-smelling with deliciously cooked food. No sign here of the deprivation they knew was choking the German people. Here it was glamor and polish and the thin veneer that existed only for the wealthy and powerful in hard times, giving them the self-fueled delusion they were untouchable.

It's people like this who order people like me to die so they can preserve their pride and lard their coffers. Wouldn't be surprised if some of these bastards have their hands in war businesses either.

In the background a band played a lively song, mingling with voices speaking a language Sully didn't understand. Emotions swirled around him, drifting and twining in the air. He focused on locating their target.

A photograph wasn't much to go on, and it took them half an hour milling among beautifully dressed, smiling, chattering people to spot their prey. Brandt was standing with a small group of officers each with a glass of wine in their hand and a beautiful woman on their arm. Sully bit down on the scorn that welled up in his chest at all these spoiled, arrogant, rich bastards holding this kind of party while the soldiers in their front lines practically withered away to nothing.

Making their way closer, all three of them effected a relaxed stroll in Brandt's general direction. The tension Sully picked up from Bell and Elliot was buried beneath a surface of calm enjoyment. They smiled politely and nodded at people they passed by as if they belonged. Sully ensured anyone they made gestures toward believed it was someone they recognized, so the gestures were returned.

As they closed in on their goal, Sully's heart rate picked up nervously. This was the moment it all came down to. Surrounded by hundreds of men who were no doubt armed, in enemy territory, and they weren't only trying to blend in and go unnoticed, but Elliot had to speak to their quarry. And Sully had to make it believable.

Closer now, almost there.

On cue, Bellona tripped over her heels and stumbled. Elliot caught her just as she bumped into Brandt. He faced them, black eyebrows raised over haughty piercing eyes. Elliot said something in rapid German, words flying fast and apologetic as Bellona hung heavily on his arm and giggled. If they survived this and either he or Elliot breathed a word of it, she'd kill them herself.

Brandt's gaze swept over Elliot and Bellona, then found Sully behind them. A chill swept up his back as cool eyes assessed him. The hairs on the back of his neck stood on end, and he almost panicked. Almost grabbed Bellona and told her to get them out of here, so strong was the sensation that Brandt saw right through him. As fast as it came on, the feeling evaporated.

Just nerves?

Brandt smiled briefly at Elliot, shook his hand, and said something in reply, his voice booming and jovial as he gestured at Bellona. Whatever it was made Elliot laugh and nod.

Had to be nerves. We'd be facing down Lugers now if he saw through me.

Elliot crooned something into Bellona's ear, and she pouted as though she understood him, though Sully knew she hadn't. Focusing intently on Brandt's emotional climate, Sully found it normal. He frowned, and Elliot cocked an eyebrow. Sully shook his head slightly, and with a final exchange between Brandt and Elliot, they slipped away.

Sully didn't exhale a sigh of relief until they made it back to the abandoned house they were squatting in. They changed into the normal civilian clothes they wore on missions in Central occupied land and regrouped in the kitchen.

"I can't say I quite expected that to go so smoothly," Elliot said, uncapping a metal canteen of water. Sully tried not to watch his throat work as he swallowed a mouthful.

"Try not to count all our eggs before they hatch, if you please," Bellona grumbled, unpinning her raven hair. "You've still got to get into the bastard's dream tonight and we've got to get back tomorrow. Plenty of time left to cock it up if we aren't careful."

Sully wholeheartedly agreed. Before his stint in the trenches, he wouldn't have called himself superstitious. It was there he'd learned to be. A man could only spend so much time around people convinced they were kept alive by the grace of their rituals or the lucky thing they carried into battle without absorbing the mentality. He'd had a letter from Anne and one from Edie folded into his chest pocket every single time he'd gone out. Like the power of their written words could keep him safe. He had them now, stuffed into the pocket of his pants.

"What did he say to you that made you laugh?" Sully asked, thoughts still on the odd exchange.

A grin twitched at the corners of Elliot's lips. "Oh. He told me I had excellent taste in women, but I needed to cut my hair."

"You do," Bellona agreed absently, still working at getting her own hair free. Jeez, how many pins did she have in there? "Need a haircut that is."

Elliot's eyes flicked to Sully, seeking his opinion. Sully pinched his lips together to keep from smiling and minutely shook his head in the negative. He liked Elliot's hair longer than regulation. Elliot's smile shifted into a smug smirk he hid by taking another sip from his canteen.

"Do you think he's gone to sleep yet?" Sully asked, pretending nothing had just happened. "Or is it still too early?"

Elliot inclined his head a fraction to the right. "It is early, but I don't want to miss the opportunity when it presents itself. It might take me some time to fall asleep after all the hubbub anyway. I'm still nervous as a hare."

"You hid it perfectly," Sully said, meaning it. "Both of you were impressive actually."

"Why thank you, Sullivan," Elliot said, beaming as he rose. "I did always love the dramatic arts. It could've been my calling if it weren't for my horrid stage fright."

"You?" Bellona asked, the last twist of pinned hair falling free to curl about her shoulder. "With looks like those, a fear of attention must be awfully inconvenient."

Sully smothered a choke of laughter with his hand as Elliot

grinned and left them to their watch, retreating up the stairs with one of the two lanterns that had lit the room.

Several quiet moments passed as Sully watched the flickering flame of the remaining lantern on the table. Orange and blue wavering together, chasing shadows.

"You two seem to be tolerating one another," Bellona said, keeping her voice quiet. Her lips curled upward in a knowing smile.

He hesitated a moment, then nodded. He wanted to trust her. Needed an ally here who wasn't Elliot. "We figured it out."

"Good, I'm glad. It's my firm belief that whatever happiness you can find in this godforsaken war, cling to it." She was sincere, and there was something lonely and sad in the way she felt.

Wanting to distract her, Sully cast about for a suitable question. "I've been wondering something, and it's really none of my business but...how did you end up here? Were you drafted too?"

"No," she said, pride seeping into her voice. "Not at all. I volunteered."

Sully blinked, attempting to process that. She'd come voluntarily. To join an army that would treat her with the lowest levels of respect because first and foremost she was a woman. It was bad enough for him, it must be doubly so for her. "You volunteered?"

A bittersweet smile crossed her face. "I did. I'm the oldest of my siblings, the only girl. My father was widowed and never remarried. For all intents and purposes, I raised my brothers, Edmund and Peter. They were always in trouble of one sort or another, fiercely independent. But they loved when I read them stories and tucked them in at night. And then they were sent away to school, Edmund first and a year later Peter. It left me bored to tears most of the year, but I found pursuits to entertain me where I could. And we all grew up. My father died. And then the war started."

"Are they…?" Sully didn't detect grief, but people could hide it well sometimes. It was often an instinctively protected sore spot, especially if it wasn't fresh.

"As far as I know, they're all right. They send me letters. Edmund was so eager to join the war effort that he joined the French Army because America wasn't planning on going over. He's cavalry now. He always loved horses, so there was no surprise there. It's a miracle he's survived, but he's had luck on his side for as long as I can remember. I have often wondered if it was a skill manifesting. If it is, he's shown no other sign. Peter followed him as soon as he was of age, and now he's a decorated pilot."

"Which leads us to you," Sully said, beginning to understand her feelings. "Two younger brothers in this war, worried at home I'm guessing."

"Going out of my mind with it," she confirmed, leaning an elbow on the table and propping her chin in her palm. The lantern light made her skin glow, the shadows of her lashes long. "I raised those boys and they were risking their lives for some silly European disagreement? They didn't even really understand what they were signing up for, nor do most of the boys dying by the thousands."

Bellona shifted back in her seat and crossed her arms, still defensive about this. "And there was nothing I could do to talk them out of it. Our youngest cousin, Johnny, had come to stay with me after his mother passed two years prior, he was thirteen when she died, fifteen this January. Taking care of him gave me something to do at least. Then a man from *our* army came looking for my brothers and found them gone. When none of his veiled threats about our family's magic would produce them, he wanted to speak to Johnny. He's still a child. And hardly skilled. He can manifest a wisp of fire. He can't even burn anything with it. So, I offered myself instead, showed him what I could do and told him I could help." She laughed, a bitter edge to it that Sully understood immediately. Once you saw the depth and scale of this war for yourself, the casualties and carnage up close, there was no room to believe any single person could make a real difference, no matter how skilled. "But at least I saved Johnny. At least he isn't here, and as long as I am, they won't touch him."

"You're brave," Sully said. "Braver than a lot of people to do that."

She shrugged. "Children don't belong anywhere near war. It shouldn't touch them."

No, it shouldn't. But too often it did. Destroying their homes, killing their loved ones, stealing their innocence. It wasn't fair.

"If you could've stayed home and saved him, would you?" he asked.

Would Sully have, if he'd been given the same reprieve?

Before Elliot had plucked him from heavy fighting, he would have answered that question with a resounding yes. But now? He didn't think he could give Elliot up in exchange for safety and home, even with the obligations he had there. Not after realizing how in love he was. Not when Sully needed him like his whole life he'd been struggling to get a lungful of air and the second those blue eyes focused on his, fresh oxygen flooded his system.

He'd seen so much death and despair, his mind was full of images he'd never be rid of, faces he'd never forget, but he wouldn't trade it.

Without missing a beat, Bellona shook her head. "Because I might not make a difference to the war or the Generals or most soldiers most of the time, but I *do* make a difference here. To my boys." The fierce protectiveness in her voice was matched by the warm possessive feeling she exuded. "I take it you didn't have a choice, though."

"No." Sully offered a wry grin. He raked his hand through his hair. "It wouldn't have been on my to do list. Got a cousin back home who relies on me. I'm all she's got. She puts on a brave face in the letters she writes, but I know how sensitive she is. She cried the night I left. Could barely stand the sight of me. I wouldn't have left her if it was up to me."

"I'd wager she's stronger than you think. But I understand how she must feel," Bellona said and they lapsed into silence for a while.

Once they grew bored, they searched the sitting room and discovered a pack of cards in a drawer. Time passed as they played, talking about whatever passing topic caught their attention. Sully told her about Edie and the agency and she excitedly inquired about the cases he'd worked. He didn't usually have the chance to talk about them with people, so he got caught up in telling her stories.

Sully wasn't sure how long it went on. The sun hadn't quite risen yet when Elliot finally stumbled downstairs, sleep lined face grim in a way that turned Sully's blood to ice before he even opened his mouth.

"The bad news: two towns have been targeted for simultaneous tests and we've only a few days to plan a counter mission. The good news: We can stop them from creating any more of the gas. Their whole production process is dependent on two skilled scientists, and I know where they'll be. If we put a stop to one of them, we end this experiment."

CHAPTER TWENTY-EIGHT

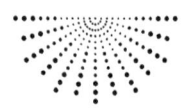

December 19, 1917
Fienvillers, France

THE STEADY BEATING OF Warren's heart beneath Elliot's ear should have been soothing. He ought to be enjoying the fact they were lying in their bed together, not a stitch of clothing between them—other than Warren's socks—Warren's chest hair tickling his cheek with every breath. They, like the others, had turned in early in anticipation of their mission, which would begin a few hours before dawn. They'd stripped down and crawled into bed, fallen into one another's arms, and held on. It was the kind of simple pleasure Elliot longed for. If only he could stop worrying quite so much.

Undoubtedly Warren could sense the mood Elliot was in, the fears that were playing on his mind. Moonlight filtered weakly through the window, touching everything with a blue-gray winter glow. Elliot watched Warren's large work-roughened hand trace up his forearm before sliding out of sight to smooth over his back.

"You ought to rest," Elliot finally whispered.

"Would if I could, but you got us both too keyed up. Didja want to tell me what's happening in that pretty head of yours?"

Inching closer, Elliot closed his eyes and exhaled. He rubbed his foot against Warren's sock in a self-soothing bid for time to think before speaking. "After Ollie died and I saw your folder in that pile, I thought it would be easier, safer if you were here, and I could watch over you. I thought it would ease my mind, and I knew you would excel with us, but it isn't easier at all. Before I worried you might be in danger. Now I know you are. Not only that, but I'm the one leading you into it."

Warren let out a slow sigh that dipped his chest. "I can take care of myself, Elliot. For what it's worth, this is a damn sight better than the trenches. There's a real bed for one. No one's sending me back out into the field on a few hours sleep every day. I could've died a thousand times over in the time I've been here. Might've died the night you came for me. Stuck behind the Germans advancing like that."

"And you might've died when I put you in the position of having to go on a mission without proper rest in days, when that bastard had his pistol pressed to your skull."

"And I could drop dead tomorrow of no apparent cause," Warren countered. "You can't stop it if my time's up, Elliot."

"The hell I can't," Elliot said hotly, pushing up onto one elbow and glaring down into Warren's face. He softened at the sweet lopsided grin Warren gave him. Instinctive anger melted into something less sharp, more aching.

"You can't. All you can do is make the most of the time we got. It's all anyone can do. And it's got to be enough even when it can't be."

A knot formed in Elliot's throat. He gave his head the slightest shake before capturing Warren's lips in a kiss that tore him to shreds. It started gentle, the soft pressure of lips meeting, tongues coaxing. Warren sighed, and Elliot pressed harder, needing to taste and touch until they were quietly gasping into one another's mouths.

Elliot tangled his fingers in Warren's hair. He tugged gently to angle him the way he wanted, trailing worshipful kisses down his neck, salty skin warm under his tongue. He paused over Warren's pulse and sucked, listening to his breath hitch, wishing he could do it harder and leave his mark. The thought made Elliot's cock throb and swell.

Lower, beneath the blankets, he scraped his teeth along Warren's hipbones, soothing with a flash of tongue. Bit kisses into his inner thighs. Warren's hand found his head, gently held him over the same spot. Elliot took the hint. Here he could leave a mark. Warren's legs trembled under his mouth and hands, necessity etched in the way he tensed as Elliot released the skin he was sucking in favor of shifting closer to Warren's jutting cock.

Consumed by the powerful desire to show Warren no matter how long they had together, it would never be enough, Elliot devoted his full attention to pleasuring him. He gripped the wide base of Warren's shaft. Pressed the softest kisses along the velvet underside, slowly inching toward the head, and when he got there, he delicately traced it along his open lips. Warren's soft whimper was music.

Elliot wished he'd thrown the blanket off so he could see Warren's face, but the room was cold. Besides, not seeing was arousing in its own way. He was utterly focused on the heady salt-bitter taste of the fluid he slicked his lips with, darting his tongue out to gather more.

"God, Elliot," Warren whispered, voice shaky with desire. "Please."

Breath stuttering, gusting over the damp tip, Warren's cock jumped in Elliot's grasp. How could he deny him anything? Closing his lips around the head, Elliot sucked him slowly, made him feel every inch of his mouth sinking down, holding his hips still with a firm grasp as Warren's cock pressed into his throat. Fingers curled in his hair, holding, not forcing. Elliot's own arousal begged for attention, but he focused on the slide of Warren against his lips, curling and pressing his tongue against the hot flesh filling his mouth. Every calculated movement he'd ever learned all turned to one purpose. *Christ,* he tasted good.

Tremors wracked Warren's body. His hips pressed up into Elliot's restraining hands on each downward stroke of his mouth. Under the blankets it was humid and musky with the scent of arousal. Elliot panted, the intense desire to make Warren spend for him overpowering. He needed this to be memorable, the best Warren ever had. So desperate, his eyes pricked with warmth.

And yet all it took was a quick, sharp tug on his hair to pull him up short, drag him away from the taste of imminent climax and back up to claim Warren's bitten-dark mouth with his own. Cool fresh air on his sweat damp skin and hair made him shiver.

Warren licked into his mouth with abandon, sucked on Elliot's tongue as if he couldn't get enough. A small whine escaped Elliot's throat. Keeping quiet was already claiming an inordinate amount of concentration and it was only going to get harder.

Christ, he wanted Warren so much it hurt, wanted him so much more than he could ever remember wanting anyone. Already loved him so fiercely it swelled in his chest with every frantic pulse of his heart. He wanted Warren in every manner imaginable and then multiplied in a thousand different ways. Most of all, right now, what he wanted was…

Elliot broke contact enough to whisper, "I want you to make love to me," against Warren's open mouth, need thick in his voice. Warren bit down on Elliot's bottom lip, muffling a soft moan. Pleasure surged hot in Elliot's groin, tingled in his balls. He stifled his own desperate sound, kissing Warren quiet. "Please," he murmured. "Please."

Warren nodded, still kissing him. Elliot was the one who had to tear his mouth away, casting his mind about for what they could possibly use to ease the way. He was about to ask for ideas when Warren beat him to the point.

"There's petroleum jelly in my pack," he said softly. "If that's what the inner struggle you're feeling is about."

Elliot couldn't help the laughter that burst out of him. "Of course you have some."

"Shut up. It's got all kinds of uses that aren't deviant, you sap. Chapped lips, prevention of trench f—" Elliot cut him off with a kiss, then scrambled to dig through the pack on Warren's side of the bed.

"Where, pray tell, might I expect to—oh, I've got it. Did you place it on top or was that a coincidence?" Warren's sudden silence was proof of the former and Elliot grinned, climbing back over him. He only got to enjoy the position for a moment before Warren rolled them over in a fast movement that left Elliot breathless, the bed creaking noisily. "Have to be mindful of that," he panted. "If we don't want to alert the entire house."

"Mmm," Warren agreed. "Or I could conceal the noise."

"Wasteful," Elliot retorted. "And besides, I'd rather retain your full concentration. I'm sure we can work around it."

After that they lapsed into silence broken by Elliot's gasps. It wasn't long before he was writhing under Warren's touch, thick fingers sliding into him, Warren's beautiful mouth hot on his throat, his tight nipples, wherever he could reach. Christ, he might go off prematurely if Warren kept rubbing that spot with his clever, strong fingers, sending bright sparks of sensation through him in jolting waves.

Too many feelings crowded into Elliot's chest. Warren had to be overwhelmed with them. He tucked his face into the curve of Elliot's neck and shoulder gasping as he withdrew his fingers.

"I need—" Warren's voice caught, and he fastened his mouth on Elliot's shoulder, breathing heavily. The prickle of his sharp incisors digging in shot shivery pleasure down Elliot's spine.

Smoothing his palms over the broad muscles of Warren's back, and lower to squeeze his arse, Elliot lifted his legs from the bed, angled himself, drawing Warren closer, silently asking for what he wanted.

The blunt tip of him pressed against Elliot, smooth and burning, and—and waiting there for something. *Permission?*

"Please," Elliot sighed into Warren's hair, not caring how he sounded. "Go on."

And then Warren was pushing into him, sinking inside slow and determined and everything that mattered while he held Elliot's thighs open with huge, wonderful hands. It was so, so much. The crushing, sweet, tender feeling in Elliot's heart. A fragile-strong, immense, clawing longing soared within him.

Above him in the moonlight, Warren was beautiful, his head bent, plump lip trapped between his teeth. Expression an exquisite cross between tortured and blissful. Warren's long black lashes fluttered open, his fierce eyes focused on Elliot's as he slowly rolled his hips in sinuous grinding motions that tingled to the tips of Elliot's toes and fingers. Warren was *inside* him. Connected so intimately, Elliot's entire body quivered.

Warren fucked him slowly, mindful of the noise, and the slow sweetness of it felt amazing. Deep thrusts as they kissed, made them both tremble. Damp skin gliding together, Warren's chest hair tickled Elliot's nipples. He combed his hands through Warren's thick hair, pulling gently as he sucked at Warren's lip, and echoed his quiet moan.

His heart swelled, and eyes pricked with unshed tears as he slipped a silent hand between them to stroke himself. He sucked on Warren's lip and tried desperately to keep quiet as they neared the inevitable release coiling tighter and tighter.

Elliot wanted to whisper all sorts of filthy, loving things to Warren but couldn't risk being overheard, so he kept them in. Instead, he felt them fervently somewhere deep in his chest as if Warren understood.

Christ he wanted it to never end.

But he knew better. He knew.

No matter how good or right or wonderful, love always had an end. One way or another. Always.

Later, when euphoric tremors had shifted to warm boneless satisfaction, after they cleaned off, the window cracked to air out the scent of sex, Elliot let Sully cradle him against his chest once more. They pretended neither of them could feel his sense of impending doom.

CHAPTER TWENTY-NINE

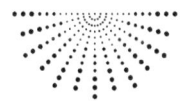

SPLITTING INTO THREE GROUPS was the right call, but Elliot didn't have to enjoy the prospect. When they parted, he held Warren's eyes a moment longer than necessary as the sun rose, a silent reminder that when they'd woken, Elliot had extracted a promise from him to be cautious, not to let his guard down again. He was being overbearing. Yet he couldn't rid himself of the feeling that without him, Warren might do something rash if it meant saving someone. Strike that, he knew in his heart Warren would absolutely sacrifice himself.

It wasn't that Elliot didn't care about saving innocents, he did, ardently. It was only that he cared about Warren so much more. Perhaps he truly was unforgivably selfish.

He wished he could kiss Warren, to remind him one more time what he needed to come back for, and hated that he couldn't. Hated more that even if he could, it might not be enough.

Charbonneau and Remonet were off to Béyonnes, a community of roughly five thousand before the Germans had captured it. Their intelligence indicated many of the residents had been driven off during the fighting, those that remained were turned to forced labor in factories or out in fields along with prisoners of war. It was there the Germans would be testing chlorine gas laced with necromantic magic. The outcome would be immediate gruesome death—choking on blood, gasping for air—and resurrection as a mindless tool of violent destruction.

Warren and Hoffman would be traveling to Toullanes, a smaller neighboring village where the magic was laced with phosgene. A colorless gas which could take as much as forty-eight hours for symptoms to occur and had the potential for so much more destruction. There would undoubtedly be those whose infection went undetected until it was too late. Coughing and shortness of breath could be mistaken for illness, and when they inevitably expired, the rampant chaos of unexpected attacks would be disastrous.

Elliot had manipulated enough information out of Oberst Brandt to know the gases would be stored inside of a factory in each town until it was meant to release shortly after lunch on the twentieth. Today, in a few hours.

The other thing Elliot learned was the focus of the mission he and Bellona would carry out. Hauptmann Eduard Richter was fusing Albrecht's corrupt magic to the gases which caused the dead to rise. Without her, not only would production of the weapon halt, her death might dissipate the magic animating any corpses.

That last bit was based on wishful thinking alone, though plenty of magic functioned as such. It depended on how strongly grafted Richter's fusion proved to be. If it could sustain a lack of connection to her power, the stores the Germans had built would continue to be of use. If not, they were in the clear.

Their objective was to remove the necromancer from the equation and get their hands on more gas to analyze. Grim determination to succeed motivated Elliot. Over the last few days, a debate had raged over who it was best to send. Hoffman and Bellona or she and Warren could have snuck in unobserved, but Elliot had the unshakable conviction it must be him. He struggled to articulate why, and in the end decided it came down to Charbonneau and Remonet working best as a team. It had been so for years and seemed unwise to break them up now.

Hoffman and Warren stood the best chance together of neutralizing the phosgene gas. They could easily get in and use the sigils Remonet enchanted for them to uncouple and disperse the magic in the gas. As long at the gas was still contained. Once it was loose, the sigil was useless. With more time and access to more information, Remonet might be able to come up with something better. For now it was all they had at their disposal.

Elliot loosened his strained grip on the handlebar of the motorcycle he was driving, once more clad in the gray uniform of German officers. If they crossed paths with anyone, hopefully they would pass muster.

The pistol at his waist weighed on him. Although he'd taken lives before, in the heat of battle during a mission, it never felt good. It wasn't something to be proud of. Objectively, it was no worse than a guard in the wrong place performing his duty or a young German soldier following his orders.

But those were split second decisions, live or die, in the moment.

This was an execution. An assassination. Even if he was sure she deserved it, could he do it?

Steeling his resolve, he adjusted himself in the seat and felt Bellona glance curiously up at him from the sidecar. Being a mind reader or empath was not necessary to understand that if he failed to take the shot, she would. Like him, it wouldn't be Bellona's first kill. Would it haunt her the way he was sure it would haunt him?

There was no time for softer feelings in war. You stuffed away most of your morality to examine at some later date when it was a luxury you could afford. Humanity and dignity were liabilities when you were fighting for your life. Elliot kept his in the sheaf of hastily scrawled poems in his breast pocket. Even here, he needed ways to safely let out the horror of the situation, the things he thought, and longed for, and loved.

Sometimes he wrote of home, sometimes what he saw. How glad he was none of this touched the people he missed. In the last few days, he had written an undue amount of shameless frippery concerning changeable hazel eyes and sweet wicked smiles.

Those thoughts would be a hindrance now and would only tear down his nerve when he needed to steam up his courage.

Bending his will to the mission at hand, Elliot went over the task in his mind. The task that had taken them, armed to the teeth, to the same compound they'd stolen the information from on Warren's first mission.

After the prior breach, it was bound to be more carefully guarded, but inside they would find the necromancer. Waiting for an easier opportunity hadn't been an option. The hazard of Brandt recognizing Elliot's dream manipulations for what they were would increase exponentially with every attempt. And they didn't want him to know Elliot could access his mind. Not while it could prove useful in the future.

Striking now was the correct choice. He reminded himself of that as they hid the motorcycle in the same thicket they'd hidden the cars. Bellona climbed out of the sidecar and straightened the black brimmed hat she was wearing with her hair tucked up inside. Her features were still feminine, but at a quick glance she could be mistaken for a pretty young man.

Elliot peered down at his own uniform, smoothing it. They might need the advantage of blending in without Warren or Hoffman to aid them. If they were spotted in this ruse, appearing the part might purchase enough time to complete their objective.

"Ready, Captain?" Bellona asked, reaching a gloved palm out for him to take. Apprehension wriggled in Elliot's gut and tingled up his spine. The last time they'd faced Albrecht, a member of his team hadn't made it home. They both knew it.

Elliot clasped her hand. "As I can be. Do be careful, yes?"

"Always. And you. We've got to get you back in one piece or I suspect I'll never hear the end of it," she teased, a playful sparkle in her eyes.

Elliot gave her a lopsided smile as her hand squeezed his in brief warning. Woods, road, road, field, field, woods, road. The scenery changed each time he blinked. If he hadn't long been used to the sensation, it might have been jarring or disorienting. As it was, when they came to a stop in the woods before the towering, barbed wire fence that surrounded the compound, Elliot was perfectly steady. He observed the grounds, and they waited as two patrols passed by.

It was early morning and broad daylight. They'd be expecting an attack in the dead of night if they expected their adversaries were imbecilic enough to attempt it again at all. Elliot suspected they would encounter more resistance inside than out. Timing and the element of surprise were crucial to their success.

After the third patrol strolled by, the soldiers conversing amicably, Elliot nodded to Bellona. A seamless transport took them all the way to the brick wall next to the laboratory window. The very same one he'd almost seen Warren die in. Bellona peered inside while Elliot watched for the patrol. She tapped his shoulder once, indicating she saw an opening to enter, and then gripped tight before the scene changed one last time, and they stood inside. Something uneasy crept into his chest, cold and unpleasant, coiling around his ribcage. Why? It was going perfectly. They infiltrated the building unseen. Now all that remained was to approach the office at the back of the lab where they expected to discover Albrecht ensconced with lists of the missing files she was tasked with replacing through memory.

Elliot retrieved his pistol. The sound would bring soldiers running, but he trusted Bellona to transport them quickly out of harm's way. With a little luck, they were nearly finished.

A nagging sense of unease multiplied as they crept toward the office. It was too straightforward. There were always complications on missions. Unexpected situations that required them to think on their feet.

He glanced to Bellona, and they shared a grim look that let him know she felt it too.

Fucking shitting hell-bent bootlicking shit.

The smart thing to do would be to call the mission a wash. Both of them well knew they might've entered a trap, but if it was a trap, they were already caught. Elliot's gaze flicked back to the window they'd entered through, the blue sky and brown grass.

It was the last thing he saw before a blast of energy knocked him off his feet, flinging him through the air. He crashed into a wall, the back of his head striking solid plaster with enough force to jar his teeth.

Beside him Bellona hissed in pain. Elliot fought off dizziness and sought her out, his vision swimming. Vicious sea green eyes came into focus. The abrupt pain of a fist crashing into his temple put a stop to his thoughts.

He regained awareness as he was divested of his weapons. Prying open his eyes, he searched the room for Bellona. Found her unconscious, strapped to a metal table, jacket removed. They were in the process of rolling up her sleeve. Elliot blinked; his tongue felt too thick. Perspiration broke out on his forehead. "Don't touch her!"

"Ah-ah," A woman's voice said, cold, and he knew as he struggled to move his head that those awful green eyes would greet him. She appeared precisely as she had in Brandt's dream. Slim and mean-faced, there was nothing particularly beautiful nor particularly ugly about her. She could be anyone he'd ever passed in his life without noticing. "You were going to kill me." She spoke German. Elliot struggled to gather enough wits to translate. "And your friend—we saw what she can do. It's best to keep her asleep for now. I feel that will ensure your compliance, yes?"

Elliot stared, trying to work out all the pieces of this, disoriented as he was. His breath came faster, chest tightening. "You knew I was coming."

"Yes, of course. The others as well." At something Elliot's face did, she laughed, cruel and amused. "Oh, little mouse, you thought you were so clever. Sneaking into Oberst's dream as though he does not have every imaginable defence protecting his mind. Besides, he knew to be on guard when your illusions failed to fool him at the party. He could have destroyed you then. Instead, he laid a larger trap to catch more mice. With one small difference from your situation."

Elliot gritted his teeth, pushing down on his instinctive panic. Was that why he felt it had to be him on this mission? Brandt had twisted things around in Elliot's head even as Elliot was attempting to do the same to him.

There had to be a way out of this. Had to. He needed to

determine a course of action. Bellona was dependent on him for rescue. If he was smart enough, fast enough, there might still be time to save the others. *Talk damn it.* "And what difference is that?"

"They will not survive the trap."

Elliot's blood turned to ice. His face froze, heart stopping. No. "What are you saying?" He shook his head, trying to clear it, and winced at the fresh wave of vertigo. "If that's true, why tell me? You've nothing to gain."

Her lips curled, a twinkle in her malevolent eyes. "Ah. Richter's suggestion. He believes you will fight us less if you have no hope to save your friends. And trust there is none. We did set two tests as you know. However, both tests have been already completed. Your friends will stroll into those factories and unleash a horde on themselves."

"No," Elliot spat, scowling. His denial ingrained. "My friends aren't that dense. They'll observe it's a trap. They won't fall for it." Would they though? Warren had promised to be cautious, but he knew what was at stake. Would he stop long enough to notice how much danger he was in? Would Hoffman? Neither was the type to be prudent regarding their own safety. Sick certainty washed through him. They wouldn't. They'd walk right into that trap and to their deaths. And afterward the Germans would have a new weapon that might change the tide of the war. What the hell was he supposed to do? There had to be something.

Albrecht glanced at the watch she wore. "Poor little mouse. Even if you managed to escape now, you'd leave her to us. And I promise you we won't be kind." She grinned sharply, her straight white teeth shining. "I want you to understand that I mean we have necro-phosgene gas on hand. I'll infect her and release her. So now you see your dilemma."

"Go to hell," Elliot bit out, hatred more intense than anything he'd known coursing through his veins like acid.

Her smile broadened as she stepped back. "Not yet. Perhaps one day. I have to win a war first." Elliot struggled against whatever invisible bond held him in place, alarmed distress finally catching up, forcing him to act. "Now that won't do. Vogel, some help?"

The pressure on Elliot increased, and his vision went spotty. Miniscule dark spots danced before his eyes, specks of light bursting in tiny white fireworks. He struggled for air, but drew none in.

This was the end. He failed his team. Failed Warren. Failed everyone. Led them into death. There was no hope left.

Hazel eyes.

Wicked smile.

Darkness.

CHAPTER THIRTY

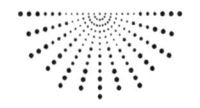

THE SIDECAR WAS STILL SULLY'S least favorite way to travel. Speeding along with no control over his fate would never be something he enjoyed. He was too busy trying to hold down the bread he'd had for breakfast to think much about what was waiting for them, or what the others faced. But he couldn't shake the strange way Elliot felt last night and this morning.

Or how Elliot looked at him when they separated, like he was committing Sully to memory. Like it was the last time he might see him. Did Elliot know something he hadn't shared? He knew Elliot's objective was probably the most difficult to accomplish. Did he suspect it was one way? Would he tell Sully if he did? Or would he keep it to himself so Sully wouldn't fight him on it?

His stomach twisted and rolled, compounding the nausea he was battling as bare trees and dead grass flew by in his peripheral vision.

As they approached Toullanes, Sully shifted some of his attention to an illusion muffling the sound of the motorcycle and hiding them from view. They left the motorcycle in a secluded alley, unsurprised to find the edges of the town quiet. Forced work probably kept most of the villagers in the factory during the day.

Pressing forward on foot, Sully remained at high alert, searching the cobblestone streets in front of them for danger. They were deserted. No sounds within the cream stone buildings. No footsteps echoing. An odd sensation swept Sully, a growing apprehension. Even accounting for forced labor, something was horribly wrong with this town.

Sully stopped Hoffman with a palm on his arm, a chill creeping up his spine, prickling at the base of his skull. "Hold on."

"What?"

Sully shot him an exasperated look. Hoffman raised an irate brow. Ignoring him, Sully focused on what caught his attention. The village was small, but it ought to feel bigger. It ought to feel chaotic with villagers and German soldiers maintaining order. There should be despair, wariness, probably bright bursts of happiness on occasion, even the oppressed found joy where they could.

Every drop of it was absent. *What is this?*

There was a singular sensation emanating from their intended destination. The hairs on Sully's arms rose as it washed over him. A gnawing violent emptiness cramped his stomach.

"We're too late," he murmured. The truth splashed him in icy waves. Other than Hoffman's confused trepidation, the only thing Sully felt was overwhelming hunger, brutal in its knife-edged need. Closing his eyes, Sully focused his magic, searching for anything beneath it. Anyone still alive. *Fuck.* "They're already dead."

Hoffman gaped at Sully. "All of them? You're sure?"

Sully looked away and waved his hand in the direction of the factory they were headed for. "Every last one. They're in there. It's..." He glanced sharply at Hoffman who cursed, the same realization flashing across his features. "Hell. It's a trap."

"They meant for us to walk in there and be torn to shreds. They knew we were coming." Hoffman tugged on the arm of Sully's olive coat, yanking him back toward the motorcycle. "You maintained the illusion?"

"Yeah," Sully huffed, thighs and calves propelling him as fast as he could go without turning an ankle on the cobblestones. "They probably got someone watching nearby, making sure whoever shows up dies, but they're not close enough for me to sense which means there's not a lot of them, or they'd be amplified. I wouldn't be able to miss it."

"Good, hopefully that means we can get out of here. We've got to get to Charbonneau and Remonet." Hoffman paused long enough to fill his lungs with air. "They have no idea what they're walking into. It'll be a slaughter."

"How many of those papers d'you think Remonet cooked up? And do they work if the magic's already in a body?"

"Not enough, and I have no damned idea. For their sake I hope so."

The two of them broke into a faster run, skidding around corners blindly and unobstructed until they reached the motorcycle. Sully clambered into the sidecar, barely settled in the seat before Hoffman kick started it and twisted the throttle. There were ten miles between Tullanes and Béyonnes, but the road connecting them was winding and poorly kept. Hoffman pushed the Twin's engine to the limits, jolting them dangerously. Sully didn't care; his thoughts were flickering wildly between whether they would arrive in time to make any difference and the fact Elliot had undoubtedly walked into a trap too.

Please let him be all right. Please don't let him be hurt. Don't let him be gone.

They needed to survive this because they were the only shot Elliot and Bellona had at a rescue.

If there's anything left to rescue.

His heartbeat faltered, chest seizing.

No, no, no. Elliot's fine. The two of them are resourceful. Hell, they'll probably be at the rendezvous point when we get there. He'll be waiting for me with that private little smile.

He tried to make himself believe it, but his gut twisted unhappily.

He will, damn it.

As they neared Béyonnes, he shut off his worries in favor of action. Old brickwork and white stone buildings sprawled below the hill they crested, cobbled streets cutting through them. It was postcard material if Sully couldn't feel the horrors lurking within.

He readied the two rifles tucked beside him, popped open two pockets on his cartridge belt and double-checked his coat pockets for the papers Remonet had given him. Right where they ought to be, not that he expected they would be much help. Sully had to be prepared anyway.

"How do we do this?" he shouted to Hoffman over the blat blat blat of the exhaust and the rushing wind.

"Will your illusions work on them?"

Now that was funny. "Fucking doubtful, they're dead. The only thought they've got is hunger. They'll see right through it."

"Wonderful." That was dry and caustic, and it made Sully crack a smile. "We're going to drive straight for Charbonneau and Remonet. Can you pinpoint them?"

Widening his senses, Sully searched the town, sifting through the hunger and writhing violence. There, on the northeast side, was hopelessness edged with fear and the determination to fight anyway.

"Yeah, I got them," he yelled. "Northeast. I can give better directions the closer we get. Bet that's where we'll find the infected too, so watch out."

Hoffman slowed slightly as they entered the village streets, enough to navigate the sharp corners. Doing his best to take them in the direction they needed to go when they didn't have a map. Dilapidated houses flashed by in a blur and Sully readied his rifle, bracing it on his shoulder. His gut lurched. "Left, turn left!"

Hoffman leaned into the turn, missing a lamp post by a hair. Sully's heart jumped into his throat. "Get ready to shoot! We'll draw them off. Make a few passes if we must."

The wheels screeched and the sidecar tilted dangerously. They should have a better plan than this. The building he could feel Charbonneau and Remonet taking refuge in came into view.

Fucking shite.

There had to be eighty or more gray and dirty people surrounding the house, clawing at doors, smashing through windows. They wouldn't be able to hold out long. Even if he fired perfect shots every time and one bullet did the trick, it would take too long. They'd be overrun.

No time to revise their plan now, Sully fired, the shot spattering the brains of a gaunt man climbing in one of the windows. He yanked the bolt back, ejecting the empty shell, and slammed it forward again, firing at the gray woman who took his place, then three more as fast as he could.

Suddenly, they had the crowd's attention. Every dead-eyed face paused to turn toward the motorcycle, bearing down on them. *Oh hell.*

"Don't stop whatever you do," Sully hollered, swapping one

rifle for the other. He braced it, lined it up and shot again as the stunned corpses began staggering in their direction, building up speed. Right as they would've impacted, Hoffman slowed enough to make a swift turn onto a narrow alley they hardly fit through, the metal on the sidecar scraping against brick.

Shite, shite, shite. Oh fuck.

Sully struggled around to check behind them. Some of the crowd were pursuing. Not enough. Reloading both rifles was a quick and practiced thing as they burst out onto a road parallel to the one they needed to return to.

"Coming around," Hoffman shouted, a devilish grin lighting up his usually somber features. "Let's really get their attention this time."

"How?" Sully demanded, sure he would hate the idea.

Hoffman's smile grew. Reckless courage and a wild excitement throbbing in the air. "I'm going to stop."

Sully straightened, bracing his rifle again. *"You're going to do what?"*

Hoffman didn't answer. He focused intensely, pulling them to a complete halt at a crossroads a few streets down from the roiling mass of corpses. Sully sighted a shot and fired. Beside him Hoffman must've retrieved his pistol, because retorts sounded between the ones Sully made.

This might work. This could work. We just need—

"Hey!" Hoffman yelled, waving his arms over his head in a wide gesture. "We're right here. Come and get us!"

"Shite," Sully muttered, switching weapons as the corpses began staggering toward them. A quick glance back showed the ones who'd pursued them gaining.

There were still far too many. A roar of outraged, mad hunger bounced off the walls as they started running, ringing in his ears, spiking his pulse. Sully shoved the bolt forward and fired at the front runner, hitting him in the shoulder, knocking him off balance.

He jerked the bolt back, pushed it forward, sighted a woman in a bedraggled dress who was leading the pack now. He fired. "Hoffman! They're getting awful fucking close." Three more shots before he had to reload.

This isn't going to work. This is a terrible fucking plan.

"Get the ones pounding on the door. It's almost clear," Hoffman ordered.

Sully followed his line of sight to three by the door. *Three corpses, three bullets.* He heard Hoffman returning his pistol to its holster. Sully aimed his rifle, and picked them off one by one. His fingers and shoulder aching as the last shot rang out.

Sully focused a burst of illusion: a flare to warn Charbonneau and Remonet the coast was clear as it was likely to get.

Hoffman twisted the throttle on the left handlebar. They bounced forward, corpses in close pursuit. Sully wrenched around in his seat to watch behind them as his fingers fumbled more ammunition, catching it at the last second and loading the weapon without looking. He could hear shots being fired as Charbonneau and Remonet made their escape. Felt the pulsing beat of their hope rising as they ran in the opposite direction. "Slow down a bit! We've got to keep them on our trail!"

Sully divided his attention between picking off infected corpses and monitoring Charbonneau and Remonet's wellbeing. It was impossible to tell if his shots were having any effect. The hunger pursuing them didn't dampen. At best, he was only slowing the bastards.

Once he felt a rush of relief and triumph, he knew

Charbonneau and Remonet had gotten to their motorcycle. "Head out, they're clear!"

He sent up a signal to let them know they ought to head for the rendezvous point. Hoffman picked up speed. They rounded a corner and drove straight into a group of corpses who'd cut them off, perhaps not quite as brainless as Sully pegged them for. He fired and missed as Hoffman veered left, another left, then a right. "D'you actually know where you're going?"

Hoffman's grin bordered on manic. "The general direction!"

Sully swore, focusing more intensely on where Charbonneau and Remonet were headed. He shouted swift instructions to Hoffman and when they sped out of the village, he really opened up and took off. They rapidly lost their pursuers.

Hoffman was still buzzing as Sully sagged back against his seat, muscles weak with relief. *We made it. We saved them. Shite that was close.*

Finally, they caught up to Charbonneau and Remonet who let out a whoop of relief and saluted them gratefully. There was no choice but to leave the infected corpses behind and pray they didn't wreak havoc for the time being. They had nowhere close to enough ammunition to kill them all. Sully was already running dangerously low on bullets. It didn't rankle any less. Those poor people deserved to be put out of their misery. He hoped they weren't aware of what they'd become. Hoped they truly were mindless.

Now that he was out of immediate danger, Sully's thoughts turned to Elliot. And the terror he'd been pushing down finally rose to crush in on him.

Be all right. Just...hell, Elliot. Be alive. I need you.

CHAPTER THIRTY-ONE

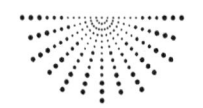

THE THROBBING PAIN IN Elliot's skull wouldn't let up. He squeezed his eyelids tighter to block out the bothersome light and suppressed a miserable groan. Elliot's sluggish mind scrambled to take in his situation, but his thoughts were still fracturing too easily. He was strapped to a hospital cot, helpless. Panic surged in his blood.

After a few seconds of nausea, he focused on what he could hear around him. Someone was moving nearby, metal instruments shifted on a metal tray.

Oh, that cannot possibly be good.

He cracked his eyes the slightest bit. A tall, slim man with graying blond hair in a lab coat was fiddling with a large needle. Inside a clear fluid through which deep blue swirled like smoke. The needle alone was concerning, but the blue liquid sent a chill down his spine and goosebumps prickling over his skin. Whatever it was, Elliot could sense evil emanating from it, the kind of evil that evoked an instinctual ancient fear.

Oh, this is very fucking bad.

He must not have quite smothered his gasp, because an emotionless gaze met his. "Pity you woke for this; it will hurt." The man spoke in thickly accented English, German. Right. Captured. In shit up to his eyeballs. He needed to think. *Stall?*

"What are you doing?" Elliot asked, tongue clumsy, mouth dry.

A faint smile graced the man's face. "Testing something new. Albrecht has only now finished it. She's talented you know, it's a wonder the things she has been able to do for us. If this is as successful as we hope, the possibilities will be limitless."

Elliot fought the fruitless urge to struggle with the leather bindings. *It won't help. Focus, Stone. Put on a show. Everything is all right.* "Richter, I presume?"

"Mmm. Hold still for this would you?" Richter said, reaching out to pat Elliot's hand in mock reassurance, and *there,* that was his chance.

As soon as Richter's fingers made contact with the back of Elliot's palm, he shoved every ounce of magic he could summon into an immense burst of horror, flooded everything he had into Richter. He'd never let it loose in such an uncontrolled, uncoordinated rush before. It felt like frozen sludge surging through Elliot's veins, making his fingers tremble with cold and effort.

Richter's face instantly drained of color, his mouth forming a silent 'O' of surprise. The muscles in his face spasmed twice and he stared at Elliot in complete terror, body frozen stiff and unable to move. Silent tears streaked over his chalk-white cheeks.

"Try to pull away from me, and I'll flood you with more than your mind can handle before you so much as twitch. You'll never recover," Elliot bluffed. "I'm going to ease the flow slightly. Undo that restraint with your free hand and it all stops."

Richter shuddered, mouth working, like he was trying to scream for help, but the only thing that came out was a wheezing choke. His fingers scrambled with the belt mechanism on Elliot's left wrist. The second he was free, Elliot sent a renewed spate of horror through the connection, intending to render Richter unconscious. Richter dropped to the floor, twitching. His chest seemed to struggle for long minutes in the unsuccessful attempt to breathe. And then it stilled. Elliot blinked down at him, his own lips parted in shock. Richter was dead. Elliot had killed him.

Richter hadn't been their target but eliminating one part of the equation was nearly as good as the other. There would be time later to puzzle out his feelings on the entire situation. Now he needed to focus. No telling how long he had before someone returned to check on them.

Elliot worked his right wrist free of the restraints, then his ankles. He pushed to his feet and staggered toward the door, wishing he had Hoffman or—no, he could not think of Warren right now. If he did, he would crumple to the ground and let the German bastards take him.

He was halfway across the room when he remembered the needle. His stomach rebelled, but he couldn't leave it there. Who knew what it was? If Albrecht had cooked up something new, it needed to be investigated. There might be more of it somewhere. With a shudder, he stumbled back to the silver tray it sat on, nestled in a syringe case. He snapped the metal lid shut and jammed the case in his pocket.

Elliot cautiously approached the door again. He peered out the window and glimpsed a soldier walking his way. Reaching into his pocket, he located a slip of paper Remonet had given him ages ago, he'd hidden it among the poems he always kept with him. When he was divested of weapons it must have gone unnoticed.

As the soldier closed in, Elliot opened the door and launched himself forward. Sucking in a breath, the German prepared to call out as the paper landed on his chest with a muffled smack of Elliot's palm, and in the nick of time Elliot whispered, "Sassafras."

The soldier's face and posture went slack, his mouth closed, eyes glazed. It didn't sound nearly as funny now as it had when Remonet first told him, not when it'd just saved his arse. Glancing around to ensure no one else was in the corridor, Elliot used a guiding hand to propel the soldier into the room he had exited, shutting the door firmly behind them.

This particular spell rendered the target suggestible, suspending their ability to exert independent cognitive function. It would last a half-hour at best, in Elliot's experience, and he intended to use that time wisely.

Speaking in German he asked, "The other American, do you know where she's being held?"

The soldier's vacant expression didn't alter. "Yes."

"Right," Elliot wanted to ask how she was, if she had been hurt, what they had been doing to her. But he wasn't sure he could hold his temper if this young man gave him the wrong answers. "I want you to listen closely. You will take me to her. You will hold onto my arm and…" Elliot pulled the pistol from the German's holster, emptied it of ammunition and handed it to him. "Hold this on me. Be convincing. If anyone asks what you're doing, you're to say Richter ordered you to take me…oh I don't know… tell them you're taking me outside to shoot me."

That seemed like a plausible enough lie. What use was he to them after all?

Complying, the German took hold of Elliot and did as instructed. Dragging him roughly through corridors. They garnered a few curious looks, but no one outright questioned them. Elliot wondered how common the scenario he had proposed was. Then he thought of Emilienne and her missing family with a pang.

It wasn't long before they approached the room where Bellona must be held. Two soldiers flanked the door, expressions uneasy as they approached.

"What do you think you are doing?" The one on the right asked, burly and dark haired.

The one on the left squared his slim shoulders. Blond eyebrows raising over apprehensive blue eyes as they approached. "We've orders not to let anyone pass."

"Don't stop," Elliot said under his breath.

"Hey! I'm talking to you."

The two soldiers were reaching for their weapons when Elliot broke free of the hold his 'captor' had on him. He smacked his hands to their faces and jolted horror through them, more careful this time to hold back enough. They collapsed instantly. Elliot stepped past and peered through the window, relieved to find Bellona inside alone. Less relieved to find she remained unconscious.

"You there," Elliot said to the soldier still under his sway. "Take that one, bring him inside. Then get the other."

Entering first, Elliot watched the soldier gather his fallen comrades, then closed the door once all three of them were inside. He retrieved the empty pistol, reloaded it, and tucked it in his jacket. He confiscated the other soldiers' weapons for good measure. No sense leaving them armed to shoot him in the back.

With hurried clumsiness, he unstrapped Bellona's arms and legs. She didn't appear to have been harmed further. Whatever drug she'd been injected with earlier had kept her sedated. He wished he knew how long they had been unconscious for, or when it was due to wear off. "It would be a lot easier on both of us, if you'd been the one to devise this escape you know," he muttered, considering her.

She made no response. Elliot searched the room for something that could wake her, as if he knew what any of the various jars labelled in German were for. It wasn't as though they would label it 'wake up time' was it? During his search he made certain to devote partial attention to his unalert but still awake captive lest the spell wear off.

"Christ, what am I going to do. If I carry you out of here, we'll both be shot escaping, and before you say it, I won't leave you," he told her as if she was in any state to argue. Giving up on his search he returned to the bed and shook her shoulders gently. "Bellona, you've got to wake up. Bell, I'm afraid I must insist. *Winifred.*"

Precious minutes stretched uncomfortably long as he stared down at her, willing her to wake. When that didn't work he raked his hands through his hair in anxious frustration. Time was ticking.

"I don't know what to do Bellona," he admitted, holding one of her cool hands in his. "I haven't a clue this time. I need to save you because I couldn't..." His throat hurt. "I think he's already dead and seeing you out of this jam is the only thing preventing me from cracking up completely."

Two explosions outside shook the building, windowpanes rattling against the bars that lined them.

What on earth?

Whatever it was, it didn't sound good. Footsteps pounded past their door. Elliot thanked his lucky stars none of them had the sense to notice the missing guards. Bellona's hand weakly squeezed his. Relief pounded through Elliot like a beating drum alongside his staggering pulse as his gaze met Bellona's hazy blues.

VANORA LAWLESS

"Wha's...?"

"Oh, thank Christ. Can you get up? I'll explain it all later, but we've got to get you out of here."

"Nnn," Bellona grunted as she struggled to sit. Elliot quickly helped her out of the bed. She leaned heavily on him for support. Even then, she was wobbly.

"Can you transport yet?" He asked as he walked her to the corner of the room where her jacket had been tossed. Elliot leaned her against the wall as he retrieved it and quickly slid it onto her, fingers flying over the buttons as her brow furrowed with concentration.

"No'yet. Hard. Focus." She shook her head in negation, eyes rolling up slightly as if she was about to lose consciousness again.

"No, no. None of that," he told her firmly. She blinked hard and her blue eyes fixated on his once more. "Right. There's a bit of a crisis out there it appears." He took a pistol from his pocket and placed it in Bellona's. "The bastards are distracted—this is our chance."

Elliot darted a glance out into the corridor and found it deserted, he tucked Bellona against his side and helped her along. The hallway they were in was familiar enough from their first breach of this facility that Elliot was confident he was leading them to the exit, except once there, they'd be exposed. Could they slip away in the chaos? He doubted it. There would be soldiers guarding the entrance at the very least. Perhaps a window closer to the entrance wouldn't be barred? If he could make better sense of the layout in his mind, he was certain he could find one, but every second that ticked by risked discovery.

"Listen to me," he said to Bellona. "Can you escape? Just you? Can you get at least enough power for that?"

She glowered at him. "M'not leaving you, Captain."

"You damned well are if I say you are," he snapped. His chest felt raw, and his head ached. Warren was probably dead. The rest of the team too. What was the point of him surviving this? Why would he want to?

"Take this." Elliot once more leaned Bellona against a wall. He reached into his pocket and withdrew the syringe case. "It's extremely important you get this to HQ, do you hear me?"

Bellona scowled up at him, her ocean eyes glittering. "Don't make me."

"They're all dead. It was...it was a trap. The whole thing. That bastard fed me misinformation, and I got them all killed." Elliot forced away thoughts that wanted to drown him. He could get one thing right. He could still get this *one* thing right. "I won't get you killed to save myself. It's...Winifred, it's better this way. I'll draw their attention, you'll escape. Is that understood?"

"Captain..." Elliot watched the protest forming on her features. She was steaming up to an argument.

He cut her off before she made one. "That's an order, Bell."

Her eyes hardened, and she forced herself to stand, her mouth flattening into a line to keep whatever she wanted to really say from spilling out. "Understood."

"Excellent. And you are not to blame yourself for this, do you hear me? I wanted it this way. Warren and the others...It was my fault. You didn't leave me behind, you understand? I ordered you to go. Remember that for me."

Wetness gathered in her eyes, and Elliot swallowed down on the despair suddenly choking him. "At least let me try—"

"We're not dead, you sapskulls!" Warren's disembodied voice called out. Elliot whipped his head around, heart slamming against his ribs, throat blocked off with roaring emotion as Warren appeared out of thin air running toward them. "Snap out of it!" He skidded to a halt in front of them, boots squeaking against the floor, gaze skipping between Bellona propped against the wall, and Elliot frozen, gaping at him. "For fuck's sake! Hoffman, a little help!"

"Right here." Elliot blinked as Hoffman rounded the corner, took in the scene and guessed. "She can't transport?"

"Not more than one," Bellona said shakily. "Can't quite walk either."

"Right," Hoffman said, glancing between Elliot and Warren. "I've got her, you get the captain?"

"Yes," Warren instantly agreed.

Vaguely, Elliot realized he ought to be the one giving orders, but he was still in shock and couldn't take his eyes off Warren's handsome, glorious, animated face. In his peripheral vision, he saw Hoffman scoop Bellona up, almost laughing at the squeal of surprise she let out and knew he would pay dearly if he allowed that bubble of joy to escape. "You...you're..."

"Alive," Warren said tone flat, eyes furious. *Why is he angry?* "Yes, and we're going to talk about all of that—" he waved his hand around indicating what had just happened "—later. Right now, we're getting the hell out of here."

Warren reached out and grasped Elliot's hand. Elliot clutched at him, grip too tight. Something in Warren's face softened. Elliot took in a deep lungful of air. The crushing sensation in his chest lessened. He wanted to kiss Warren rather desperately, but now was not the time..

Instead, he allowed Warren to pull him into a mad-dash, and they made their escape.

CHAPTER THIRTY-TWO

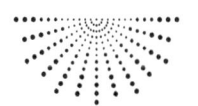

BACK IN FIENVILLERS ONCE MORE, no sooner had everyone gone up to their rooms by silent agreement to collapse and deal with the fallout of their mission the next day, than Sully backed Elliot up against their bedroom door. He was emotionally exhausted. Still scared. Fucking relieved they'd gotten there in time to save him, but what if they hadn't? What if Bell had left Elliot there? What if he'd done offered himself up as a diversion for her escape and what if he was gone? *What if he was gone?*

Sully was frantic for Elliot's mouth on his. The same desire poured off Elliot, saturating the air around them until Sully could hardly breathe for how much he wanted. How much he needed. One moment he was staring at dark shades of blue flickering in the pre-dawn glow, the next they were kissing as if it was their last chance, their only chance.

They grabbed at one another, pressing close, fingers digging into shoulders and backs, hips instinctively flexing, grinding. Every bit as desperate as they had been in the barn. More than, because every part of Sully was reaching out for Elliot. From his heart and soul to his body, all of it. He could've lost him. He could've...

Sully couldn't stop touching Elliot. He dragged his hands through soft fine hair, down his neck, over his strong shoulders and arms, sucking in Elliot's plush bottom lip, biting down and tugging gently as he pulled away. He dropped to his knees on the hard floor right there in front of him.

Elliot let out a quiet wounded sound at the sight, and Sully spared enough thought to hide any noises they made from being overheard. He was determined to draw more sounds from Elliot. Needed to hear them.

Pressing his face to the front of Elliot's gray pants, Sully inhaled the musky scent of him and savored the shudder he drew from Elliot with hardly a touch. Their eyes locked, and Sully slid firm hands up Elliot's thighs, rubbed his palm over the straining ridge of his cock beneath wool, watching from close up as Elliot pushed into his caress, head dropping back against the wood, exposing the beautiful line of his throat.

He was torn between wanting to take his time and needing this to be fast, punishing. He couldn't forget coming upon them in the hallway, seeing Elliot so defeated because of him. He wanted to push it out of his mind, too upset to think about it, so he fumbled open Elliot's belt and pants. Jerked them down his thighs along with his underwear, watching the long sway of hard, flushed cock bob in front of his face, mouth flooding.

Elliot's hand settled in Sully's hair, brushing it back from his forehead. The fingers of his other hand reverently traced Sully's cheekbone. The mix of tenderness and the raging passion Sully felt beneath the surface were dizzying, too much, too little. He wet his lips and went to work. The heavy, hot drag of Elliot's cock in his mouth filled Sully's senses and narrowed everything to lips and tongue and salty arousal. He took Elliot in as far as he could, swallowing around him. Rubbed his tongue along the underside as he pulled off. Flicked and played over the head, again and again, building a methodical rhythm that had Elliot's hips twitching with barely restrained thrusts.

Sully moaned, a sound Elliot mirrored, filthy slick noises echoing in the room. Cupping Elliot's balls with one hand, Sully worked his own belt and buttons open, desperate to relieve the pressure of his rigid cock constrained too tightly.

He focused on the velvet feel of Elliot's stiff shaft sliding past his sensitive lips, pushing into his throat, making him shiver with sensation. The pulsing, mad, fierce rush of pleasure like a thundering heartbeat reverberating between them.

Sully couldn't hold back. He stroked himself fast and hard, groaning around his mouthful. So desperately close already and he knew Elliot was too, could taste it, could feel his orgasm rising like a massive wave ready to crash on the shore. Lifting his lashes, Sully gazed up at Elliot, skin glowing in the pink of dawn, shining with sweat, staring down at him with those blue, blue eyes full of wonder and lust. Love expanded in Sully's chest, wrapped around him like a warm blanket.

"Warren," Elliot panted, fingers reflexively tightening in Sully's hair, prickling along Sully's scalp. Another layer of delight mingling with the trembling sensations already hollowing him.

He sped up, sucked the slightest bit harder and Elliot's hands clenched, fingernails scratching in a way that sent violent spasms of pleasure igniting through Sully's blood as warm release flooded his mouth. Sully swallowed it down, possessive pride swelling in his gut.

Elliot whispered his name, broken open and unpolished and

that was all it took to send Sully tumbling after him, shaking and crashing into such intense euphoria that for long moments he didn't even breathe.

When he managed to draw back and gasp in a ragged lungful of air, Elliot collapsed to his knees, practically on top of him. Instantly captured Sully's bruised mouth in a clinging, urgent press. Elliot's tongue slipped into his mouth, claiming, brutal. Sully kissed him back, fierce and urgent. Kept him close with his arms around Elliot's shoulders.

"I thought," Elliot gasped against his lips, then kissed him again. Whatever he thought lost to Sully's plundering mouth.

"I made you a promise," Sully mumbled, tugging on Elliot's hair, resting their foreheads together, breathing heavily. "I was careful. You should know by now I keep my promises, Elliot."

"Yes, well I thought…" Elliot squeezed his eyes shut, the pain on his face overwhelming. "They said…"

Sully rubbed his nose against the side of Elliot's. "I know. I heard you. And I'm fine, but Elliot, we got to talk. Let's just…can we get in bed?"

He felt Elliot nod before he shakily stood, offering Sully a hand up. They undressed. Neither of them rushing. By the worried sadness Elliot was trying to hide, it was clear he knew Sully had something serious on his mind. And maybe that was Sully's fault. Maybe he was looking at Elliot the way Elliot had looked at him when they parted for their mission, like he was memorizing everything about him and the way it felt to be together because things might not ever be the same again.

Swallowing, Sully crawled beneath the quilts as Elliot crossed the room in the grayish pink light. He seemed fragile, tired, so much younger than either of them really was, and something barbed stabbed and contorted in Sully's heart.

Elliot settled with his head on Sully's chest, and they held on to one another, pulses slowing. Gently pressing his lips to Elliot's soft blond hair, Sully breathed out heavily.

"Tell me," Elliot said, not moving.

"You tell me," Sully countered. "Why you were about to give up like that and send Bell off by herself."

"She couldn't transport us both."

"I got that. But to me, it seemed like you gave up so fast. You were just going to stay behind. Tell me why."

There was hesitation in the emotions swirling through Elliot. "She needed to bring back the new formula. You didn't see it, Warren. It feels evil. One of us had to get it out of there. She was more likely to survive the escape if she left me. We couldn't risk waiting."

Maybe that was true. But it wasn't all. Sully sensed him holding something back. And the idea of what it might be squirmed unhappily in his stomach. He couldn't be responsible for Elliot giving up like that. No matter what, he wanted Elliot to keep fighting. To survive this war. To get the chance to publish those poems he talked about on the first night they met. The ones he'd recited for Sully in dreams when he thought they would be forgotten. He wanted Elliot to live and if what they had put that at risk…

"And what else? I can feel what you're not saying," Sully prompted.

Elliot was quiet for a while, and when he spoke it was whisper quiet. "And you were dead. You were all dead. It was my fault—I sent you into a trap I should have seen coming and it got you killed. Just as I got Swift killed. I'm not cut out for this. I should never have been put in charge. I'm selfish and make terrible choices and I could see where it had gotten everyone. Of course

Bell needed to get out of there and I had to stay behind. She was the only one I was still able to save. Christ, Warren. I thought I'd lost you."

Sully's heart broke. How could Elliot think he was selfish? He constantly made choices to protect the people around him. To protect Sully. Wasn't a good leader? That was news too, because the way it felt to Sully was like Elliot was the best damn commanding officer he'd ever had. He cared about his people. And not just about what they could achieve for him, but *about* them.

Stroking his fingers through Elliot's soft hair, Sully struggled to find the right words. "War is dangerous, Elliot. We all know we could die at any time. I've made peace with the fact I might not get home. Watched everyone around me cut down day after day, blown to bits or shot or trapped in barbed wire. What I can't live with is you thinking you owe it to me or any of us to die too if something goes wrong." Sully took an unsteady breath, chest twisting painfully tight. "You're not selfish—No, shut up, I'm not done. You're not. I've seen how much you care about everyone on this team. I've seen you willing to sacrifice. Hell, you were about to sacrifice yourself for Bell. And I understand that, I do. If it was just about the mission, then fine, I could accept that's what needed to happen."

Elliot still didn't move. "I make bad—"

"You got duped. That doesn't mean you make bad decisions. It means you had faulty intelligence and there was no way to know that. If I die on a mission you sent me on, that's not your fucking fault. That's being a soldier. You didn't ask to be here any more than I did, but you know what? I'm glad it's you. Because I know time after time, you're gonna do everything you can to give us a fighting chance. I need you to understand it's not your fault. If something happens to me, to any of us, you've got to forgive yourself." Sully couldn't make heads or tails of Elliot's feelings. Too jumbled, too confused. "And Elliot, look at me."

Elliot lifted his head and stared at him, the depth of emotion in his wet eyes increased tenfold by what Sully could feel beating against his senses. A dangerous mix of despair and longing and a massive warm feeling Sully barely had a name for. He didn't say anything, but his breathing was ragged.

"I need you to live. Even if I don't." Some people might think their lover dying for them was romantic. Sully didn't. Living for him was. "I don't want to be responsible for your death, not in any way. I care about you way too damn much. I need to know you're not going to give up because of me."

Silence rang out at those words, almost as loud as it would've for the ones Sully had really wanted to say.

"Simply don't die then," Elliot said, tone light despite the dampness nearly overflowing in his eyes.

Sully chuckled wetly, thumbing away tears Elliot hadn't quite spilled. "You know I can't promise you that, Elliot. Even if it wasn't hell on earth, I couldn't promise that."

Elliot blinked away the residual wetness, his pale blue eyes almost colorless in the dim morning. Sully could feel him thinking, the weight of his roiling emotions crashing over them. "All right." Clearing the thickness from his throat Elliot gave a soft nod. "If you promise me the same."

"Promise."

Elliot nodded. "Right. Excellent. And I know you don't break those, so I suppose I can't either."

The corners of Sully's mouth twitched into a lopsided smile. "Suppose not."

Elliot bit his lip, then offered a tentative smile that felt warm as the summer sun, made warmer by the rush of delight he sensed from Elliot. And for now...For now, those promises were enough. This moment, the two of them together...it was enough. Had to be. It's what they had.

    Sully tilted his chin up and Elliot met him with a soft kiss that felt like one more promise.

CHAPTER THIRTY-THREE

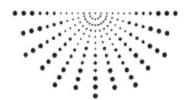

December 24, 1917
Fienvillers, France

THE SOUND OF MERRIMENT filtered out into the quiet night as Elliot slipped into the dark backyard. It was nearly eleven and he'd left Warren playing cards with Hoffman. Remonet was playing the piano he'd spent the morning tuning in the parlor while he and Bellona sang Christmas carols, his voice deep and rich, hers light and slightly off-key.

They were full of good food, half-corked on decent wine, and celebrating a few well-deserved days off.

Elliot approached a faint glowing red ember. Charbonneau didn't glance over at his footsteps. Withdrawing his own cigarette and a match from the metal tin in his pocket, Elliot stopped nearby and lit it, drawing the smoke into his lungs.

"I miss him," Charbonneau admitted after a few moments of companionable silence, voice aching.

"I know. So do I." He ought to add more. What else was there to say?

Through the darkness, Charbonneau nodded. Elliot struggled with whether to prompt him for more or leave him be. He didn't know which would be kinder.

Eventually, Charbonneau tossed the stub of remaining cigarette into the snow and crushed it beneath his boot. "In the mail yesterday, my sister sent letters from my girls."

Elliot went along with the change in subject, though he wished he'd thought of a way to talk more about Swift. "How are they?"

"Well." There was a smile blossoming in Charbonneau's voice. "They miss me, of course, especially this time of year, but Justine and Anaïs are very brave. They write how they are helping my sister with the animals and how Emilienne is growing more at ease with them. They like her a great deal, which is a relief."

That was a relief. "I'm glad she's adjusting. It was kind of you to take her in."

Charbonneau waved a dismissive hand. "Bah, what was I supposed to do? Leave her with no one? The girl needed a home and we have the room. It was right. That is all."

"You're a good man," Elliot said, meaning it. A cold gust of wind whistled around them, blowing icy air down the collar of his jacket. Elliot tossed the last of his cigarette onto the ground and watched the ember gutter out. "Should we head in? Or are you planning to freeze us both to death?"

Charbonneau chuckled. "All right. Come."

When they went inside, they found Bellona and Warren had both gone up to bed, Hoffman and Remonet invited them to play cards. Elliot declined, feigning exhaustion, Charbonneau accepted. Remonet gave Elliot a subtle nod as Charbonneau took his seat. Whether or not Remonet knew what he was going through, he seemed to understand Charbonneau was still troubled and would look after him.

Upstairs in their room, Elliot smiled when he caught sight of Warren in the flickering lamplight, sitting with his back to the wall, the blankets pulled up to his chest, tucked beneath his arms. Knees up, using his thighs as a writing surface. He glanced up at Elliot's entrance and smiled briefly before returning to his task. Shutting the door behind himself, Elliot wandered over and sat on his side of the bed, unlacing his boots.

"Writing to Anne again? Or is it Edie this time?" he asked.

"Hmm? Oh. No. A friend. Back at Havrincourt." Warren fell silent, concentrating on the letter as Elliot undressed. By the time Elliot settled next to him beneath the covers with a plain brown paper wrapped parcel, Warren was stuffing the letter and pencil into his rucksack. He glanced curiously at the package Elliot deposited on his lap. "What's this?"

Elliot's grin was only a little sarcastic. "A gift. I thought that was rather obvious. It is nearly Christmas after all."

Warren's face went pink and adorable as he ran a thumb along the edge. "How didja even have time? I didn't know we were—"

"Don't. It's something I've had for months. And I hadn't meant it to be a gift until recently. I expect absolutely nothing in return so do stop panicking."

"I'm not panicking." At Elliot's raised eyebrow he let out a chuckle. "I'm not. I just wish I had something to give you too. You're…You mean a lot to me."

Elliot's chest warmed. "Mmm. You might have mentioned caring about me *too damn much*."

"Don't know what you're talking about." Warren's eyes sparkled, his mouth curving in a slow smile he was trying to hold back. "I'd never be so sappy."

"Oh really? I'm fairly certain—"

"Didn't." Warren held out a moment longer, then laughed. Elliot echoed him. "Fine, I care about you. A lot. All right?"

"Better. Now open the gift, Warren."

"Okay, okay, I'm opening it, jeez." He tore into the paper and revealed the dark blue cloth cover of a book. The title lettered in gilt read, THE WANDERINGS OF OISIN AND OTHER POEMS. Warren's fingers grazed the gold lettering, his eyes wide, mouth soft and parted. "Elliot...you..."

"I had my sisters send me a copy. After the hotel, I wanted to read it again. Is that odd to admit? It might be odd."

"No—it's—Elliot." The way Warren was staring at him, all wonder and brilliance made Elliot's chest warm further and expand.

"I told you I was fascinated with you. Possibly more than I admitted to myself at the time. And I've wanted to give this to you from the moment I laid eyes on you again, only it would've felt like too much until recently and—"

Warren cut him off with a kiss full of sweetness and joy. Elliot surrendered to the press of his mouth and the silken slide of his tongue. When Warren finally pulled away they were both breathless and pink-cheeked. Elliot's delight was irrepressible.

"You like it then?"

Warren laughed again, a bright bubble of a sound. "Yes, I like it. I like it a lot." He tilted his head a little, a calculating expression on his face. "I'll like it even more if you read it to me."

"Oh, would you?" Elliot asked, as if he didn't love the idea, as if he hadn't imagined exactly this scenario. In bed with Warren, reading him poetry. He thought about the sheaf of paper in his uniform pocket, the ones he'd penned with Warren in mind. Maybe someday he'd read him those too. For now, he picked up

Yeats and leaned back, smiling softly as Warren tucked himself close to listen.

Outside, the wind shivered cold air over the barren fields and through the trees. War was at a temporary standstill. If they had only a short time to enjoy this peace, Elliot couldn't think of a better way to spend it. He pressed a kiss to the top of Warren's head, wavy brown hair tickling his nose, and started to read.

THANK YOU SO MUCH FOR READING!

If you enjoyed Imperfect Illusions, please consider writing a review. Even brief reviews on Amazon or Goodreads help new readers discover indie authors.

Want an exclusive peek at emotional concept art of Sully and Elliot? Subscribe to my newsletter.

Want to see what happened the first time Elliot showed back up in Sully's dreams? Check out the bonus scene in my Facebook Group: Vanora Lawless Flawless Readers.

ACKNOWLEDGMENTS

My deepest gratitude and appreciation to:

Andria Henry for the amazing line edits that truly helped this story and the characters shine. Any remaining errors are my own, she did brilliant work!

Klayr for the beautiful cover art. I'm still every bit in love as I was the first time I saw it.

Skye, who kept me going when I wanted to give up so, so, so many times, who beta read more than once, and without whom I would never have gotten this far.

Allie for the wonderful cheerleading, commiseration, advice, and gentle encouragement.

Every single beta reader who helped to polish and refine this story into something I'm proud of.

All of my friends who shouted about this book from concept to finish line. Especially Charity, who always takes the time to lovingly yell at me. Kitty, who keeps me laughing, and Maureen who read along and encouraged me each step of the way here.

Everyone who was in in the Author Burnout Crew. Your kind words and advice meant more than you know.

The readers who took a chance on this book, the reviewers and bloggers who work so hard to share their love of books, and anyone reading these words.

From the bottom of my heart, thank you!

ABOUT THE AUTHOR

Vanora Lawless is a bisexual genderfluid Canadian with ADHD and a passion for telling love stories set in magical or niche historical worlds. A graduate of Saint Mary's University, Vanora has a B.A, majoring in psychology. As a Nova Scotian, loving long walks on the beach is practically a law, so Vanora takes every possible opportunity to explore the best sandy shores. In spare time between crafting new worlds and stories, Vanora can be found behind the lens of a camera or in a blanket burrito with a good book.